DESIRE TO WALK IN LONG ROBES

A Mystery and Transformational Love Story

Written by: LAWRENCE D. YAKLIN

DISCLAIMER

This is a work of fiction. Names, characters, businesses, places, events, locales, and incidents are either the products of the author's imagination or used in a fictitious manner. Any resemblance to actual persons, living or dead, or actual events is purely coincidental. Certain long-standing institutions—including religious institutions, agencies, organizations, public offices and their descriptions, properties and references to their names and/or relics associated with them that may exist or be like others that may exist are referenced in this story in a fictitious manner. Any characters involved or descriptions presented in the book narrative regarding those institutions or institutional actions taken by an organization, their philosophy or doctrine are wholly imaginary. Actual book titles, mentions of their contents in the story narrative are either purely coincidental, used in a fictitious manner or the books are in the Public Domain. Quotes from the Christian Bible are taken from the King James Version (KJV) and the American Standard Version (ASV)—both of which are in the Public Domain.

DEDICATION

To my Mother, Grandmothers and Aunts. Your lives have provided many of the elements of this story.

PREMISE

It was beautifully handwritten by fountain pen on manila card stock in a graceful calligraphy-style—likely by a woman named Chloe Stevens. It is a verse from Christian Scripture taken from the then newly published translation of the Bible—the American Revision of 1901, now known as the American Standard Version. The card was included as the cover page and was undoubtedly the inspiration for an essay written by Chloe's granddaughter, Helen Laurinda Wilcox.

"And in his teaching he said, Beware of the scribes, who desire to walk in long robes, and to have salutations in the marketplaces, and chief seats in the synagogues, and chief places at feasts: they that devour widows' houses, and for a pretence make long prayers; these shall receive greater

condemnation."

Mark 12:38-40 - American Revision of 1901

INTRODUCTION

My name is Michael Jacobs. Roughly forty years ago, I inherited a set of cookbooks from my maternal Grandmother, Helen Laurinda Wilcox-Phillips. After her passing, they sat untouched and largely forgotten in a stored box of family memorabilia. However, those cookbooks were recently rediscovered by me while unpacking boxes after I moved to a new home after my divorce. Opening them for the first time since my Grandmother had decades earlier, I was surprised to find dozens of what appeared to be personal diary entries and a nearly complete handwritten essay written by her. That composition was bundled together with a pink ribbon.

Family lore recounts that decades earlier Helen had inherited those same cookbooks from her maternal Grandmother, the previously mentioned Chloe Stevens. The revealing set of *dated* compositions found within them were penned in the 20th century— with most of them falling between the years 1910, when Helen would have been around ten years of age, up to the late 1960's. There are some additional sporadic entries which date into the mid to late 1970's.

Additionally, many *undated* written entries found in

the cookbooks are thought to be much older. Based on known historical events, family genealogical facts and penmanship comparisons, I have determined that those were most likely written by my Great-Great Grandma Stevens—which would date them as far back as the mid to late 1800's.

It is important to note that two of the three *cookbooks* were not traditional cookbooks at all. They were repurposed old books. These actual publications; The Eleventh Annual Report of the Secretary of the State Horticultural Society of Michigan – 1881 and The Great Galveston Disaster by Paul Lester, Library of Congress, 1900, had apparently outlived their usefulness as reference material or entertainment value to the original owners and were being used by my relatives as repositories for their recipes—many of which were hand scribbled in the page margins, on the flyleaf pages and inside the front and back covers.

The third book—which *was* an actual cookbook, is much older and in extensive disrepair. It is missing most of its cover, binding, and large portions of several pages at the front of the book, which made its author a challenge to identify. But from the few fragments that remain, the running headers on the interior pages, and with the help of online research, I am confident that it is an exceedingly rare copy of: The Compleat Housewife, or, Accomplish'd Gentlewoman's Companion by Eliza Smith. Originally published in England, I believe my version is most likely from the 5th edition published in Williamsburg, Virginia in 1742.

All three of these books housed loose recipe cards, other scraps of paper containing favorite recipes clipped from magazines and grocery shopping lists for meals long ago consumed.

Also stored in the volumes, other random materials included; sales receipts for purchased linens, a manual for a new electric hand mixer manufactured in the 1930's, one for the original cast iron coal furnace in Grandma Helen's home, which was built in 1912. There were also several U. S. two-dollar bills, various articles and serialized short stories by anonymous authors which were cut from newspapers that were published in the 19th Century.

Still other writings in the collection included several examples of exceptional anonymous poetry and selected verses of Scripture from the Christian Bible. Those verses were cut from the pages of another much older publication of the Bible—a King James version, and were uniquely and lovingly attached to the pages of the cookbooks with things like straight pins or even embroidered onto the pages with needle and thread—as one would in the creation of a linen sampler, or as some do in today's modern scrapbooking. By archiving them in this manner, it shows that someone must have considered the literature interesting, inspirational, and worth saving.

Many times, personal notes on a variety of topics— written by *both* Grandmothers, were often added to the backs of their recipe cards or squeezed into the blank page margins or any available spaces in the books. Quite often, Helen's and Chloe's additional annotations appear juxtaposed to the printed Biblical verses and certain saved articles. They seemed to have an opinion on almost everything they stored in the books. As a practical matter, by including so much additional content throughout their cookbooks, it gave them something to read and to contemplate while they waited for their bread doughs to proof, their ovens to pre-heat or their egg timers to *ping*.

Some of the most endearing non-food related items I recovered from the cookbooks were several personal letters written to Helen's mother—my Great-Grandmother, Alma Stevens, when she was an adolescent. They were sent to her by her female friend—most likely a cousin named Mary. In one, it describes how a young woman could flirt with a male admirer in a mailed correspondence to him. It details instructions on how to express her attraction to him based on how she placed the postage stamp on the envelope of the letter. From what I can ascertain, the instructions in this correspondence were not just general in nature—the stuff of chatty teenage girls. They were intended to be utilized in letters to an unnamed boy who was serving in the United States Military. That would have been around the time of the Spanish-American war. At some point, I hope to discover who he was and if there are any saved love letters from Alma to the boy by any of his family's descendants—should they be able to be identified. I am in the process of making that story a compelling prequel to this story. Mostly though, I am curious to see how the postage stamps were placed on the envelopes.

Besides the books used as a place to store recipes—some of which I have tried and are unique, usually made with simple ingredients and nostalgically delicious, also served as a woman's diary without a lock. They ingeniously provided a private storage space for my two Grandmother's personal collections of thoughts on relationships between the sexes, religious practices, politics, and others. In those times, it was a safe bet that no man's prying eyes would ever be interested enough to crack open this type of book—one that was stored in a drawer in a room they rarely entered. Thus, their most intimate thoughts, criticisms, and several stories expressing their deepest love and devotion for their friends and members of their family, were safe from ever being exposed.

There appears to be nothing in the records personally written by my Great-Grandmother, Alma.

Overall, the frugal nature of this kind of book recycling and storage—some might say *hoarding*, was a familiar trait of my ancestors and it makes the collection even more unique and treasured.

As mentioned, most of the dated diary entries from the 20th Century and most of the longer essay materials in the cookbooks are attributed to Helen. The ones with more prolific phrases and developed themes are generally thought to be hers considering that she was the first in her family to graduate high school at a time when that was rare in the working class. They are professionally written, colorful and many—as you will read, are controversial. She also displays a propensity for organization with her consistent habit of applying the European style of day, month, and year notation to almost all entries. A few of the earlier entries attributed to Chloe Stevens were dated in the same manner, which would have been expected from a 19th Century immigrant of Great Britain with Dutch heritage. Helen must have learned that same style from her Grandma and continued the tradition.

Also, family legends recount that some of Helen's other writings of poetry and concerning local society events—the uncontroversial ones, were thought worthy of circulation and published with her byline in a local newspaper, affirming her proficiency in literature and language arts. It is important to note that none of the *provocative* feelings and pronouncements expressed by Helen in her cookbook essays and diary were ever put on public display to my knowledge. The controversial ones had always remained hidden—that is, until now. Moreover, I found that substances of the more volatile compositions were in sharp contrast to the life I saw her live.

Another dominant theme throughout several of Helen's compositions are random thoughts and brief diary entries against the norms of her society as dictated by men, which were ingrained in the religious institutions that she encountered and from those by which she felt ostracized. They are stark observation of the roles and restrictions that suppress women by limiting their roles in the church hierarchy by the male leadership who point to archaic texts in the Bible as justification. She outlines with clarity, rails against their centuries old established practices and summarizes her frustrations with the words, *'treats the entirety of womanhood as but a second-class citizen.'* That succinct passage, and possibly my favorite from the entire collection of her works, appears a few times in separate entries. Her other frequent themes in the writings highlight the general abuses of men in the domestic setting.

In all, the expression of Helen's thoughts and her many pronouncements are obviously not the kinds of things a young woman would openly publish or even announce in her polite circles of the early and mid-20th Century. And there is no evidence she ever spoke out about them or even passively advocated for them at any time in her life in order to modify the norms of her society—as seemed to be her goal expressed within them.

Not completely explained, her zeal somehow faded abruptly when she chose to fall into a more conventional role of marriage, children, responsibilities, and household routine, which lasted the remainder of her life. Perhaps that happens as an unavoidable loss when youthful ideals pass on to adult concerns. Perhaps they become less important when one finds a more enjoyable focus. I can understand that. Then again, perhaps her zeal was thwarted by the very forces she criticized.

No matter the facts, I do not believe she ever completely abandoned her beliefs. And I am sure she never wanted her depictions of them destroyed. Her only further action was to continue to accumulate them while keeping them hidden in the pages of those cookbooks—just as her Grandmother had, from anyone who might destroy them and most certainly would work to dispel their truths.

Observationally, as Helen's years progressed, instead of the lofty ideals expressed in her earlier commentary, she began to concern herself with the more personal slights, joys, and remarks regarding family life. Over the span of her life, the contents evolved into more of a personal journal which documented expressions of love, rather than a manifesto for change. The *why* of that is a subject for another book. The only thing I can be sure of is that the words she penned were important to her and were silently obscured for a long time in a set of cookbooks, in a drawer, in a kitchen. Fortunately, they were not lost to antiquity and have offered immeasurable guidance for me and I think serve as a lesson to us all.

In a broad comparison, my discovery of what I call the *Cookbook Diaries* and their truths are like the discovery of the Gnostic Gospels unearthed at Nag Hamadi, Egypt in 1945. Those Gnostic texts and codices were hidden from purges by the early Church with their sustained efforts to discredit differing viewpoints on Christianity. Those efforts successfully suppressed dissent and preserved the all-male hierarchy in leadership. There are historical accounts that the Gnostics had a more progressive attitude toward women and allowed them to participate in church rituals much to the dismay of the established

Church. So, to a lesser extent, the hiding of and recent reemergence of Helen's works parallels a similar scenario to those of the Gnostics and serves as fresh criticism on some of those same ancient, untenable ideas and efforts of the orthodoxy. However, to me, Helen's ideas on the subject are far more personally relevant.

You may ask yourself, why am I mentioning any of this? Why are Helen's and Chloe's writings important in the telling of this story? Let's unpack some of that.

The significance of the *Cookbook Diaries*, is that time and again, so much of what has happened to me over the last few months had already been experienced, documented and commented upon by previous generations of my family going back a hundred and fifty years. I find it uncanny that what I have lived through recently and even in my childhood, has a direct correlation to so much of what was expressed generations earlier by my ancestors.

Ironically, the same underlying troubling themes referenced by both Helen and Chloe and the subject matter of the Bible verse from the Gospel of Mark in our Premise, are all cyclical themes in my story. It's almost as if they were penned as a prophesy to offer invaluable direction for me for the same kinds of challenges, choices, and decisions I would have to make, as the Grandmas did in their times. Moreover, the compilation of writings will continue to shed additional light onto Helen's and Chloe's legacies while ultimately achieving their desired purposes to insist for continued independence of thought, to redirect our respect to those who truly deserve it and compel us to share the kind of transformational love for others for which they advocate. They do so in the same manner as we are charged to do by our pledge to Christianity.

Additionally, the reader should also note this confession. Helen's preserved verbiages—her poetic phrasings—both the old-timey ones and the ones filled with high-brow eloquence, have been included verbatim in some instances or weaved into the narrative of the following story. I have tried to credit her when possible, but most are not because I have passed them off as my own.

To explain, unwittingly, Helen's colorful descriptions—some of which I know originated from her Grandmother Chloe, had already been absorbed into my own vocabulary years before. When I heard her utter them in person, I knew they made an impact on me and became ingrained in my lexicon of thought and expression. So, I apologize for allowing the reader to think that they are my original thoughts. But I think the Grandmas would forgive me for plagiarism, as I consider it to be a part of my inheritance.

As I begin to document this story, I realize the complete set of compositions from the cookbooks deserve their own separate publication to do them justice. Only that would provide a comprehensive insight into their chronological order and significance. So, they will not appear here in their entirety. For this story, the inclusion of a few of their selected comments, notes, and stand-alone quick stories from my two Grandmother's cache of literature and some of the more relevant highlighted verses from Scripture found within, will appear at the Chapter heads. When they do it is because I was reminded of them and the impact they had when certain recent events in my life unfolded. I've included them to draw parallels to or provide distinctions—either emphatically supporting themes in the story at those points or serve as critiques. It all depends on the situations and events. Thus, they will weave their way throughout to offer prescience to my account.

At this point of the Introduction, you've probably absorbed enough of the details of the backstory to skip ahead to Chapter 1. For those of you who refuse to do that, because you prefer a complete and exhaustive preface to get your money's worth, in order to tell this story completely, it might also be helpful to discuss the significance of the above Premise of this story—that being the verse taken from the Gospel of Mark in the Christian Bible.

So, we continue.

The writer of that Gospel thought Jesus' words regarding those *who desire to walk in long robes* significant enough to include in his manuscript. The verse tells us to be wary of the *scribes*—those who are in the positions of leadership. He details what they seek, what they devour—specifically regarding *widows*, how they want to be treated and how they have the attitude that they are filled with self-importance as evidenced by their pretentious long prayers. From the verse, it is clear that Jesus was not impressed with their behaviors and cautions us that those who perform as the *scribes* do are disingenuous. It is also clear, that He reserves a higher level of condemnation for those that conduct themselves in this manner.

So, the *scribes* and *we* have been given His counsel on the matter. But *where do we find ourselves today*? From the time the quote from Mark's Gospel was authored—some twenty centuries ago, just a few decades after it was first proclaimed as a quote from Jesus, to today, there have been many factors that have influenced or have been ignored in how we have responded to the admonitions outlined in that verse. Those factors have blended over time to perpetuate conditions that are fertile for the sustained development of a succession of *scribes* and their behaviors. From my recent experiences, I now know that firsthand.

However, in addition to my recollections on the issue, which you will read, I believe those factors are best explained in detail in Helen's most consequential composition—the earlier mentioned nearly complete essay on the topic—the one tied with a pink ribbon. The outspoken observations in it are frank and inciteful passages expressing a young woman's frustrations regarding not only her place in the world but also those of her female contemporaries.

Based on the style in which it was written—with contemporaneous notes penciled in the margins, that essay appears to be crafted as a speech to a ladies' social activist group—like a meeting of the Suffragettes. Or, it may have been intended for publication in an organization's newsletter. It reads that way to me. The date of its authorship falls in a timeline consistent with that era. So, my best guess is that it was authored, circa 1920. It is also possible that it was assembled as an early draft of a manuscript for publication—perhaps the basis of a short story or novel. In a way, after nearly a century, it has been here. The essay is titled: Where Do We Find Ourselves Today?

The following are a few of the important opening paragraphs of the manuscript which should provide additional insights.

Where do we find ourselves today? I would like to start with a verse from Scripture from the fairly recent translation of the Bible—the American Revision of 1901. It is from Mark, Chapter 12, verses 38 to 40.

'And in his teaching he said, Beware of the scribes, who desire to walk in long robes, and to have salutations in the marketplaces, and chief seats in the synagogues, and chief places at feasts: they that devour widows' houses, and for a pretence make long prayers; these shall receive greater condemnation.'

How many of us knows somebody that fits that description? No one needs to raise their hand. It is a rhetorical question.

First and foremost, in our present western society—a Christian society of now the 20th Century, we continue to exist in the evolving aftermath of a single, celebrated life—the one who uttered the warnings in the verse in year 1 of the Christian era. We believe that life was historically remarkable and ended tragically on this earth on a cross. Most of our society believes that the celebrated life, and most critically, the death of that individual on a cross, to be an unparalleled act of love—which was intended for His contemporaries and the society in which he lived and for every future generation including ours.

According to our Christian beliefs, that act of love was freely offered to transform humankind by providing forgiveness for its sinfulness that had developed from the time of our beginnings by the choices of our free will—along with the aid of Satan. Although I personally believe he may have made the seven deadly sins more available to us, we should not pass all the blame onto him. I'm of a mind that we should hold claim to the lions-share of our own bad behaviors.

None the less, the prevalent belief in our Christian Faith also encompasses the conviction, that with the completion of that act of love, it would provide a way for us to rejoin our God upon death. In the interim, the act of love was to inspire us to live a transformative life of love and to share it with everyone. Sadly, for far too many, this has seldom been the outcome as most have ignored its simple directive and a few have used it to gain power and benefit themselves—mostly at the expense of women.

The essay goes on for many more handwritten pages expounding on the subject matter. The full essay— minus some pages that were either removed or missing from the end or stained—causing the ink to fade and be illegible, is included in its remaining entirety at the end of this story in the Epilogue.

Taking all the above family historical material into consideration, the following contemporary story is a continuing chronicle of the struggle for fairness between men and woman and the inequities the latter must deal with. It is a struggle that has been a constant in humanity since our beginnings, with religion playing a critical role. In this narrative I offer the stories I have collected from my family as additional anecdotal evidences which point to logical and universal truth about all the above and all that will follow.

In doing so, this story will underscore the risks of being an outcast from *inclusion* by those who control the *inclusion processes* under religion's conventional wisdom and practices. This account also occurs during a significant time as the emergence of modern sciences open new possibilities for us. Those possibilities touched upon, may someday offer tantalizing prospects toward shedding light on one of the deepest mysteries of Christianity itself. But here, like it will be for the foreseeable future, those prospects come with the ever-present potential for some to exploit. However, adding Science to the *scribes'* traditional efforts to control, gain prestige and profit from the inclusion processes, does not alter the all too familiar tactic of those who *desire to walk in long robes.*

That is the complete—and admittedly lengthy, multi-layered family backstory. Then again, most complex family stories usually are. Taking a cleansing breath, now here is the story.

Chapter 1.

Assumed to be archived by Chloe Stevens, circa 1900. It was clipped from a Bible and sewn, with needle and black thread, onto page 89 of the oldest cookbook without a cover— The Compleat Housewife, or, Accomplish'd Gentlewoman's Companion. That page began the chapter: All Sorts of PUDDINGS.

"We are troubled on every side, yet not distressed; we are perplexed, but not in despair; Persecuted, but not forsaken; cast down, but not destroyed."

2 Corinthians 4:8-9 - King James Version

The alarm sounded. Was it Wednesday or Thursday?

I bolted upright in bed and instinctively swung my feet to the floor. I know it was a workday, otherwise I would not have set an alarm. I tapped the off button on the top of the squawking box and stared at its LED numbers in the dark room. 4:30 am. The house was silent until a few seconds later when the coffee pot set last evening for a delayed start began its gurgle of brewing.

Mr. Caffeine—my only friend at this dreadful hour, I thought. Every day—at least every workday lately seemed indistinguishable from another. Life had fallen into a predictable rut of restless sleep, hit alarm, shower, coffee, dress, drive the annoying 45 minutes to work, punch in, perform menial tasks and watch the clock till the workday ended. Then I had to make the return trip to the claustrophobic, partially remodeled, minimalist, two-bedroom house and wait for the cycle to begin again.

My domestic refuge consisted of an old cottage in the middle of the woods. It was a place of solitude but also somewhat of a prison, where it seemed I must make amends for my many failings. It was there that I must serve out my time for the crime of saying exactly what I felt without a filter.

Most verbally law-abiding persons usually employed what I call a *vocal filter* to keep them out of the kinds of troubles that had significant repercussions on their livelihood. On the other hand, I always spoke first without weighing the consequences of what my honest, but ill-conceived words might bring. Those consequences most often resulted in regret, loss of money and self-created difficult situations that could have easily been avoided if not for my big mouth. The difference between me and pragmatic people who bite their tongues at appropriate times, is that they realize they should hold their contentious ideas in, whereas, I blurt them out. So, I found myself at this juncture. I had put my life in this present condition and for now had to deal with it. The only bright spots in this self-inflicted penance was that both the job and house were close enough to my ex-wife to maintain a shared custody of my two daughters. Those two little girls were the only things that kept me from falling into deep depression.

Continuing to stare at the clock, I began my morning ritual. I whispered my mantra: *For my two girls. For my two girls.* It somehow always seemed to give me the strength required to reconcile myself to facing another day in this monotonous, five-days a week routine. At this moment every morning, I bolstered my endurance by telling myself that I was lucky to have this job—despite it not having much of a paycheck or any prestige. My mantra gave me the endurance to survive the drudgery of the work and the demeaning atmosphere of the company for which I worked—right down to the requirement of having to punch in and out to account for my work hours.

For someone like me, who had always worked in a salaried position, recording work hours was a new and unnecessary requirement as far as I was concerned. There were no time clocks in my previous employment. There was always a flexible work schedule. You accepted that whatever number of hours was required to complete the task, and you were willing to put in the time without supervisory oversight. The employer trusted you to do that, and you had enough pride in yourself to follow through. It also helped that you were interested enough in the work to do it with your best efforts.

By contrast, my current employment had no elements of trust. It was not a position for anyone who had ambition, or a streak of independence like me. It was just a job where you accepted your subservient role, stayed quiet and went along with their program in order to fit in and to survive. Those parameters fell right in line with the same kinds of requirements that have been historically expected in most employer-employee and/or master-slave relationships. My ancestors and unknown previous generations followed the same set of rules, for the same reasons. Now it was my turn—at least for the foreseeable future, to do the same. Even though I hated every aspect of this arrangement, I told myself I could make it through one more day.

So, I worked hard at the Genome 23 History company to complete my workload. Though, I worked even harder not to reveal *anything* to *anyone* about how I really felt about *anything* in their workspace—which would let them get a glimpse of the kind of person I really was. My mantra: *For my two girls,* silently accompanied each audible "clunk" of my timecard as it was inserted into their employee time clock at the start of each workday. However, reflecting on what led up to my employment here, I am surprised I was able to acquire any type of job at all.

Chapter 2.

Written on the back of a 4 by 6-inch recipe card with instructions for canning Chili Sauce. Discovered tucked between the pages of the book: The Great Galveston Disaster.

4 February 1922

It is a perpetual wrong and I wish to impress it upon them by weaving in a phrase from the Gospel for my own translation of the Truth. Their ways are backed up by antiquated scriptural references of two thousand years ago that are not to be questioned, go to establish the dominance of men at the head of their churches, and other structured organizations, and are coupled with the impressed subservience of women in those groups. The conventional traditions we have today in all walks of life, only live on because they were, and are, solely nourished by women, for the exclusive misguided benefit of men who desire to walk in long robes. My pointing this out is nothing new.

Helen Laurinda Wilcox

I can still see the look on the government employee's

face when she scoffed at my resume' and stated, "We don't got *nothin'* like that round here—I don't think. We do have some temp openings packing boxes at a water testing company. Do you have reliable transportation and capable of standing on your feet 8 hours a day? You got your *papers*? If you don't have your *papers* all here, you need to get your *papers* and come back in another appointment."

"Yes, thank you for those questions. Yes, I am quite physically fit with no back problems whatsoever. My vehicle has recently had maintenance and is quite reliable. I have always abstained from drugs of any kind and I am unfamiliar with strong spirits. And yes, I believe all my *papers* are here compiled for your review. Thank you."

That's what I should have said. Unfortunately, it didn't quite come out that way. During her condescending instructions to me, I could feel my internal *voice filter* in the process of initiating in what would turn out to be a futile attempt to reshape my impulsive response into something far more polite than what I was really thinking. I tried, but the filter failed to engage in time.

"All my *papers* are in front of you." I pointed out emphatically. "It might benefit *both* of us and expedite this...*thing*, if you perhaps—I don't know, take a peek at them! Stand 8 hours a day? Yes, of course *I* can stand 8 hours a day." I inadvertently emphasized the word *I*. "And I can pass any drug test." I ended my rudeness to her with an unintended quick glance down at her more than ample secretary's spread. That, she clearly noticed. She took it as my effort to *throw down the gauntlet* to her in this interview—challenging her ability to either stand or clear a substance abuse screening. It was a supremely bad move on my part.

Honestly, I truly didn't intend it, but my big mouth had started something—again! I'm sure she was thinking the exact same thing. However, it was clear that *she* was going to be the one who ended it. Turning abruptly in her swivel chair and peering down over her bi-focal reading glasses—which were pressing down over her rapidly flushing cheeks, she launched into a rant about every man my age coming in here thinking she didn't know so and so, and how she had to put up with it every day and so on. It was a rambling indictment against all men and seemingly was going to have no end without some sort of intervention. No other staff personnel in the office made any moves to do that and so she railed on.

In her position, she was fortunate. She could get away with this kind of venting because of the power she held over every unemployed client groveling before her—with their incomplete papers, a medical condition that only allowed them to stand 7 hours a day, or was a sure candidate to pee on a test strip for illegal drugs and turn it blue. After all, she had a job to do with specific requirements for each applicant to meet. It also helped that she was in a tenured government job with union backing and there would be no repercussions for her if she let off a little steam now and then on that kind of clientele. Most likely, many did deserve her tongue lashing. Even though I didn't think I qualified as one, I was a bit ashamed that I was moderately rude to her and would be lumped into that group by her too.

I tried to interject. "Ho! Hold on there. I don't want to get in any argument with you, Mam. I apologize for the way that remark seemed to question your ability to stand up for 8 hours or pass a drug test or your thoroughness in the way you perform your job." If I thought that this would diffuse the confrontation, my words only threw gasoline on the fire.

She escalated her diatribe about *my kind,* and although I tried to tune out her lecture to me, I think I detected an insult toward my *"Momma"* and how she raised me. Normally, those would be fightin' words if someone insulted my Mother. If she were a man, I might have even launched into a brawl right there in the building. But in this moment, the prudent course of action was to try to take the blossoming conflict down a notch with another more heartfelt apology.

That was going to be difficult with the frustration about my whole job situation still pulsing within me. What I *so* wanted to say was, "Can *you* stand for eight hours on two legs—not four? Your meat hooks would seem to indicate your knuckles drag the ground when you walk and I'm surprised with your lack of opposable thumbs that you can operate a QWERTY keyboard with any level of proficiency for filling out your all-important *papers!*" But I didn't say any of that. I simply and meekly stated, "I'm not here for an argument, Mam. Everything is right in front of you. What else do I need to do?" With that, I had succumbed to the State Unemployment Bureau's requirements for applicant subservience. The confrontation then resolved itself as I was directed to another waiting area for a follow-up interview with someone else. While in the waiting area, I made a mental note to get the on-switch for my vocal filter checked first thing in the morning.

Another 30 minutes passed in the waiting area. Knowing my chances for securing a paying gig from *Ms. Papers*—I had already forgotten her name, or through this employment system was toast, I got up, walked out the door, got into my truck with a self-assuring, "I don't need this kind of B. S!" I started the vehicle and drove away, squealing the tires with a wave of the middle finger of my left hand out the window toward the Unemployment Office's store front window. While doing so, I marveled that *my* left hand *did* have a fully functioning opposable thumb. I tried to convince myself I really didn't need the $112. weekly unemployment benefits anyway. I happen to like Rahman noodles. So, the joke would be on her when she would be required to add to her workload by wasting valuable time processing my *papers*. Of course, those *papers,* might just as likely be in the "circular file" next to her desk by now. As it turned out, Ms. Papers didn't see any of my parting wave. She was nowhere to be seen. I must assume she was off somewhere on her hourly, 45-minute break.

My anger quickly turned to worry. With each mile of the 26-mile trip back to my little cottage/prison in the woods, there was a steadily growing sinking feeling in the pit of my stomach. It became increasingly clear that I probably shouldn't have boldly blurted out anything in the way I did to that woman. She was just doing her job—albeit somewhat unprofessionally in my estimation. Her tedious job each day was for her to go through all those *papers* of umpteen numbers of illiterate, lazy, uncaring clients—most of them men, who were out of work and seeking some way to survive in the shrinking labor force of a recession. And, it was all up to this woman to provide that for them. Admittedly, it was all highly unfair to her, and she had a right to be moderately surly, but that's the way it was. And from what I knew of history, that's the way it had been for a long time.

A few more miles passed on the drive home and I did some self-analysis. Yes, men can be jerks—at least some of them. Some can make life for Ms. Papers and others like her miserable in the job environment and elsewhere. To be honest, she probably had more responsibilities and education than any of them. She was the one trying to get them employment without much of an effort on their part. I would like to believe that I was an outlier in the flood of men she had to put up with. Though, in my recent interaction with her, I was not. I admonished myself for not distinguishing myself from the unwashed masses and I vowed in the future to be more mindful to avoid the traditional behaviors of my brethren.

I believe I more easily came to this epiphany because I had recently read about the same kinds of conflicts in the lives of someone whom I respected and admired and another whom I had heard many stories about. The subject was addressed in detail in the rediscovered cookbooks of my Grandmother and Great-Great Grandmother.

After moving out of the family home during the divorce, while unpacking boxes in my new digs, I came across the books in a box of memorabilia. I nostalgically leafed through them and read some of the revealing diary entries and essay thoughts that both women had stored in them. It made me fondly remember my Grandmother and painfully relive some memories I experienced as a child. The bittersweet reflections made an impact on me amid all the current upheaval in my life. Unfortunately, the written lessons taught in them, and ones I had heard in lecture form in person from Grandma and my own Mother, had momentarily eluded me in the Unemployment Office.

In hindsight, this Ms. Papers, was dealing with the same kinds of frustrations as had my previous generations of female relatives. Briefly, I had also slipped into the category of boorish men who exercise the same pattern of bad behavior that so many men do. I fell in line with their credo: *'I believe the sun shines out my ass. Womenfolk should wear a high SPF sunscreen or expect to get burned.'* I'm paraphrasing, of course.

Well, I now recognized the discrepancy in how I had just acted, versus what I should have known better to do. If only I had paused to think first—something I always struggle with, I might have handled the situation better. Now I deeply regretted helping to prove Ms. Paper's negative attitudes about men were correct. Maybe I'll send her a fruit basket or something to make up for it, I thought. Nah, probably never cross her path again. Can't afford that anyway. Don't have a job. It was a safe bet my performance toward her would not result in any job referrals.

My shame then quickly turned to envy. At least *she* had a guaranteed government job and a paycheck. Right now, I had neither. But that would soon change, and I would be reminded of a lecture my Mother had often recited to us. Surely it was one passed down through the generations. *Things happen when you least expect them and in ways one cannot imagine.*

Chapter 3.

An excerpt from Helen's essay: Where Do We Find Ourselves Today?

"Over the span of two millennia, much of the above orthodoxy of the Christian belief—which has been continually cultivated and re-enforced in our religious institutions, tended to perpetuate a blind adherence to it, while offering no way for Christian culture to question, modify or refute any of it—that is, if they had a mind to continue to be fully a part of the Faith. To question, modify or refute would find you on the outside looking in through the stained-glass windows."

A note penciled in the margin of page 78 of the book: The Eleventh Annual Report of the Secretary of the State Horticultural Society of Michigan – 1881

Undated

Griping about something is not the same thing or achieves the same results as Praying about it. While both may address the problem, the former will never lead to solving it.

      Helen Laurinda Wilcox

Before turning into the driveway, I rolled down the window of the truck to check the mailbox. There were many envelopes stuffed in it. Among them the usual: a card inviting me to a steak dinner with all the trimmings if I would sit through a presentation about an incredible opportunity to secure my retirement future. Bills, bills, bills, and on the bottom of the stack what looked to be another job rejection letter. Should I even open it? I had memorized the text of what the form letter would probably read:

      Dear Mr. Jacobs,

      Thank you for submitting your resume to our recent opening for a: phlebotomist/drywall finisher/CEO of our marketing firm—fill in the blank. However, we have pursued another candidate that more suits our list of qualifications. Good luck in your future endeavors.

Sincerely,

Bla, Bla, Bla.

There was no reason to open it, but I did so out of habit. To my surprise, this was not a form rejection letter, it was an offer to interview.

Please call us at your earliest convenience to set up an appointment, it read. My earliest convenience happened to be right then!

Not even bothering to pull into the driveway, I rolled up the window on the truck and frantically punched in the numbers on my cell. A very business-like voice on the other end answered.

"Good morning, Genome 23 History. How may I direct your call?"

"Appointment! I blurted out. Um, received a letter! About the job—a job at your, um…" I then realized I didn't even take the time to find out the name of the company after ripping open their letter, and I couldn't remember what she just said to repeat it back to her.

The voice on the other end of the line was patient. "Are you calling about the entry-level opening in our Prep Lab?"

Scrambling to find the letter in the stack on my lap, I was able to retrieve it and open it one-handed to confirm that the job was for a Prep Lab position at uh, what she said.

"Tomorrow? Let me see. Yes! I have an opening in my schedule at 10am. I'll see you then at Genome 23 um, History." I read from the torn envelope. "Thank you for your assistance Ms...?"

"My name is Julie, I'm fill-in Executive Secretary for Mr. Orrin. He's our company owner. We'll schedule you tomorrow morning at 10. Please bring your driver's license and Social Security card with you. Do you have any questions?" This woman was very professional and efficient.

"No, thank you again, Julie. See you tomorrow."

"You'll actually be interviewing with our Hiring Manager, Mr. Welch. Please ask for him."

"Oh, ok, that's fine. I look forward to it." I ended the call. I had no idea what this company did, and the woman had said this was an entry-level job. That was discouraging but at least it was something to generate income until I could find a more career-type position. I prayed that this Julie had not perceived any of my disappointment.

In the job interview, I applied the hard lesson I had learned the day before. I needed to adhere to strict politeness, deference to their authority over my financial security, and to dumb myself down a bit by trying to knock five points off my I.Q. I had learned from previous pre-screening job interviews that no employer for this type of low-end work wanted anyone with advanced education or career ambitions. In too many businesses, this one among them, what the employer really wanted was to limit turnover and blunt a go-getter's ambitions. They preferred an applicant to just go along with the company program, while they crush any thoughts that the job seeker may hold of rising to a management position. They only wanted a warm body that would complete the work while not causing trouble. Their ideal candidate would refrain from calling in sick too often, meet their deadlines and quotas and just stay invisible for large stretches of the day.

Knowing that, I completed the extensive employment application, an aptitude test and put my signature or initials on every piece of paper they gave me—including blank pages and on forms I never even read. I just wanted to make sure I got it all submitted before they changed their mind on me and brought in someone else.

So, I got the job and that was almost three months ago. This was a significant milestone in any employment. Ninety days on the job and I could qualify for unemployment benefits should there be a reduction in force, and I was to be one of the unfortunate ones laid off. There was a lot of that going around after the recession hit. If I *were* laid off, there would still be a safety net of *some* income. But to receive it, I would also have to again face Ms. Papers at the U.C. office to apply for it. Hopefully, that would not happen, and I would not be forced to purchase that fruit basket for her.

I pushed the memory of what had transpired prior to this point out of my mind and tried to focus on the menial work. That was almost impossible, and I found my thoughts continually drifting to the payoff when this day was over. It was going to be my custody weekend with my daughters once I got out of here at 5 o'clock.

Chapter 4.

Written on letter stationary. For some unknown reason, it was stapled onto page 109 of the cookbook: The Compleat Housewife, or, Accomplish'd Gentlewoman's Companion. That page was the start of the chapter: All Sorts of PASTRY.

2 September 1954

From the drawer, I picked up what was left of the old family Bible from Grandma Stevens. I recognize by the printing, that many of its pages that have been cut out are the ones stitched into my cookbooks. Not sure why she would've done that—except to perhaps separate the wheat from the chaff. But I'm quite sure I had read a quote about this state of affairs before. Maybe it's one of the verses that was cut out and already in one of my cookbooks, but I can't find it amongst all the other clutter in them that has accumulated over the years. I'm sure I wrote something or other about it too one time, but I can't seem to find that either. Who's been in my kitchen drawer? I wish they'd ask before just taking. It leaves such a disarray for me to sort out.

None the less, the question is, why has no one followed the words? I find it contradictory that the Preachers make a spectacle of public prayers and enforce homage and tithings be paid to them while they continue their centuries old practices of consuming more than their shares of precious tangible resources. I remember the phrase. Something to the effect of, drawn from the "widow's houses" and others on the lower rungs of existence. They do this while many also abandon responsibilities attached to their positions of power and wealth while only embracing those of a ceremonial nature. They are the worst examples of talking the talk but not walking the walk.

They demand to be the head gardener and be first to dine on the bountiful harvest while seated at the head of the table. Yet, they abstain from the dirty work of tending to the weeds, but they insist the hired help use outdate implements to perform the prerequisite tasks.

Helen Laurinda Wilcox-Phillips

Written on a loose piece of letter stationary. It was included in book: The Great Galveston Disaster.

15 August 1941

Some people can work all day in a bushel basket. It's hard to see if much of anything in particular ever gets done by them.

Helen Laurinda Wilcox

A funny thing about this company. Genome 23 History was run like something out of 1940's Corporate America. It was an old-fashioned environment with what I would call antique office supplies. There was nothing modern in our Prep Lab except the cubicle walls and swivel chairs and most of them were refurbished. From inside our closed space of the Prep Lab environment, there was no way to communicate with the outside world other than by our own cell phones—the use of which was prohibited during work hours outside of break times and lunch. We rarely had much of any cell signal in the enclosed office space anyway. There were no outside business land lines as there was no need for us to interact with customers. It was strictly order processing for me and the half-dozen others in the lab.

In addition, there was not a computer in our sight in the building—although we suspected that there had to be ones along with advanced scientific equipment used in the Final Lab. That was off limits to everyone except three shadowy employees who never interacted with any of us for the entire time of my employment.

Even our paltry weekly paychecks—which also reflected amounts more suitable for the 1940's cost of living, were printed with typewriter and hand signed by the boss, Mr. Orrin. There was no such thing as an electronic direct deposit with this operation.

All this was odd since the overall job of what we were doing at Genome 23 History was a 21st Century emerging technology. Mapping genetic profiles for individuals was a recent scientific innovation. The technical stuff required to complete the orders is what went on behind the doors of the Final Lab. We underlings in the Prep Lab were just the initial clearing house and subsequent shipping clerks of the operation. Thus, there was no need for Genome 23's management to invest in upgraded equipment to do *our* chores. The outmoded ways were labor intensive but more cost effective.

For example, we addressed the boxes for return shipment on old lick-em style labels using a typewriter. The one on my desk was a heavy model that I'm guessing was manufactured around the turn of the century. To be clear, I'm not speaking of the turn of the last century when 1999 rolled over to 2000, I mean the turn of the 20th Century—that being 1899 to 1900! No kidding!

Some of my braver fellow employees used their own saliva to moisten the dry, past-their-shelf-life labels to get them to stick to the boxes. I was not one of them. I wetted my allotment of the typed labels with a dampened paper towel. It proved to be slower than the lickers' tongue-on method but I would be the one who managed to avoid paper cuts and the residual taste in my mouth of old horses who had met their demise at the glue factory decades earlier.

I likened the efforts of the *lickers* as being a swap of their anonymous saliva DNA sample with the customer. They send one to us. We send one to them. However, we sent their sample back to them too in the return box of results—with exception of a very few the company chose to keep for some unknown reason. I was glad the bulk of them left the building. If we had warehoused them, I'm sure the penny-wise, Mr. Orrin would make us inventory them each year for tax deduction purposes.

In short, this was not suitcoat and tie work. Rather, I would have been more suitable in this environment had I worn bib overalls. But because buying overalls would require me to spend funds that I did not have, I wore a suitcoat and tie every day—although it was covered in a grungy lab coat that they provided employees. Those filthy company properties were never washed by Management and we were never allowed to leave the building with them so we could take them home to wash.

Though there was only a slim chance of it, I hoped my unique choice of wearing professional apparel among my peers would be noticed and provide an opportunity for advancement in this company. That was despite the atmosphere around here that suppressed that kind of optimism.

Taking a deep sigh, I began unpacking the latest incoming shipment of boxes. Each would have a completed customer order form in it and a small capped, plastic tube that we had shipped to the customer when they placed their order. The plastic tube is what held the sample of the customer's saliva. Also enclosed was the all-important customer check for $99. made out to the company.

The procedure in the Prep Lab was first assign a unique sequential number to the order onto old, green pages, which were cut from vintage ledger books. Those became the company's Master Ledger. By the way, this was not done by typewriter. Per Management, this had to be filled out by hand. I suspected that our individual handwriting was an extra layer of quality control to trace who had prepared the sample. Also, onto the Master Ledger, we would record information gleaned from each order form—the name of the individual, their address and whether they were male or female next to the sequential number. Then we had to create a separate individual job ticket for each order. This was a duplication of the information on the Master Ledger, and in my estimation, was superfluous. With every order I processed, I thought, if we just had a simple computer spread sheet program around here, this could be so much more efficient.

After the initial paperwork of cataloging, we were then required to write the same sequential number on the customer's plastic tube sample with a permanent marker. We then opened the container, added a small piece of a solid chemical reagent to it along with a few drops of saline solution. We closed the lid and shook it vigorously for an uncomfortable amount of time to make sure the reagent and saliva was infused completely in order to stabilize it. In every professional scientific lab—apart from ours, a shaking procedure like this was performed by a machine. However, at Genome 23 History, each of the workers in the Prep Lab could look forward to being future candidates for carpal tunnel syndrome and a wrist brace.

Not done yet, we would then reopen each tube, swab some of the sample onto a hand numbered microscope slide—the number matching the one we assigned to it on the Master ledger.

The anal nature of this whole computer-less operation continued with a rubber stamp of red ink placed next to each name on the ledger to indicate completion of our first stage of the process. There was a required hand punch on the created job ticket to indicate that too. Then the slide and resealed tube along with the job ticket and completed ledgers were placed on large stackable trays and parked outside our Prep Lab where they would eventually be sent to our Final Lab for analysis by the three Shadow Brothers—as we nicknamed them. The Brothers undoubtedly used far more sophisticated equipment to complete their jobs than our paper, permanent markers, and elbow grease. That would be a requirement if they were to map DNA from the samples to reveal percentages of ethnicities and world region of origin of the individual. There had to be some sort of advanced computer system in the Final Lab for them to create results that could compare genetic markers of similarity between individuals in our growing data base. It would be essential to tell a customer, in layman's terms, who your distant cousins were and if you shared DNA with anyone famous.

As the old green ledgers, job tickets and stacks of sample trays grew, a frail, silent woman—devoid of any discernable personality—rumored to be the permanent Executive Secretary, descended the stairs from a room adjacent to Mr. Orrin's 2nd floor office to retrieve them from outside the Prep Lab. This routine occurred four times a day.

The Ancient One, as we called her, made her rounds once each during our morning and afternoon break when the Prep Lab was empty of employees. She swept through again during our midday lunch period and one last trip after 5 o'clock when the workday was done. Before our prep work continued onto the Final Lab, she would carry the loaded trays up to Mr. Orrin's office. This required several trips up and down the stairs for her octogenarian legs. It was said that Orrin would review our work with the head Shadow Brother, and then the timeworn woman would have to make several more trips on the flight of stairs to carry the trays down to the Final Lab for analysis. The remainder of the Ancient One's day was devoted to reshuffling that day's job tickets and microscope slide samples in numeric order and then collate them into the Genome 23 History vault—which was under lock and key in the Final Lab. The vault contained every job ticket and slide the company had ever processed. And I thought my job was mind numbing.

Upon completion of the technical work on the

samples in the Final Lab, the Shadow Brothers would place a second red stamp upon the green ledgers next to each name indicating completion of that part of the process. The lot was then returned to us just outside the Prep Lab during the final hour of the day where the Prep Lab personnel were transformed into a Shipping Department for the job of address labeling, boxing brochures of the customer's lab results, along with their original sample bottle of spit to be returned to the customer—except for those certain ones the company chose to save. I must admit, sometimes the thought of handling processed saliva by the hundreds, made me nauseous and was another reason my own tongue never encountered the dried-out shipping labels we used.

Finally, to complete the job cycle, we would shrink wrap the return boxes onto palettes for pickup by the shipping carrier. A third red stamp was then imprinted next to each customer's line on the green Master Ledgers by us to indicate they were out of our custody. At day's end, those too would be gathered for filing in Mr. O's office by the ancient, silent woman.

This woman, whom I only discovered after a month on the job, was *Mrs.* Orrin. She wore the uniform of the subservient—somberly attired in faded housedresses with opaque support hose. Her plain, black, lace up shoes with crepe soles, made no sound which might draw attention to her while she made her periodic rounds. Her long gray hair was piled on top of her head in a pentecostal, church-lady style. The thick lensed, cat glasses she wore were something right out of every black and white family reunion picture taken in the 1950's.

Just an observation here. Occasionally, I noticed on their return trip from the Final Lab to us, there was also a rare and curious additional yellow stamp—a star, in an unmarked column next to certain individuals' names on the green ledgers—maybe one in a couple thousand orders. This column had no heading and offered no explanation for the stamp. I'm not sure if the stamps were placed on the ledger in the Final Lab or by Mr. Orrin, but I seriously doubt it was *Mrs.* Orrin as it seemed she was not allowed to get involved in anything beyond her marginal responsibilities. She seemed confined to the "pack-mule" aspects of the operation only. Additionally, those outgoing customer orders with a yellow star happen to also be the ones that the company chose to hold back their saliva samples.

Keeping my thoughts to myself, I never questioned the overall redundancy of this daily process-engineering routine to anyone. If that's the way they wanted it done, lowly Prep Lab "rats"—as we called ourselves, would go along with the program. It wasn't worth my effort to complain or suggest improvements. Privately though, I determined that this disjointed and inefficient operation could only have been developed by an anal, tightwad, control freak. That was the inside skinny on the owner and founder, Mr. Wendell Francis Orrin.

Surprisingly though, despite every inconsequential and inefficient exercise in our workforce, Genome 23

History was a growing and profitable enterprise in this relatively new industry. Businesses like ours— and there were a few other competitors in this emerging field, received a lot of media attention of late. Those publicly traded were doing quite well. None of that really mattered to me though. My attitude: Did *anything* even matter?

Chapter 5.

Archived by Chloe Stevens. Circa 1900. Attached with a straight pin to a page of the book: The Eleventh Annual Report of the Secretary of the State Horticultural Society of Michigan – 1881.

"In everything give thanks: for this is the will of God in Christ Jesus concerning you."

1 Thessalonians 5:18 - King James Version

In exceedingly small, cramped penmanship, written on the inside back cover of the book: The Great Galveston Disaster.

15 January 1926

It is not enough for the preachers to be filled with

wonder regarding the transformational event that God has unfolded in front of us and leave it at that to be revered, respected, and followed. No, with no real ability to understand God's knowledge with their limited human intelligence, they none the less feel it is upon them to be the arbiters of something infinitely complex and in fact beyond their simple knowledge. After all, they only know what they've been taught and led to believe is enough. They never study beyond that and venture into the volumes of additional information available which would give them the perspective that they don't really know everything on the subject.

Most egregious is that they then fraudulently enforce their testament, it in even less intelligent thought, to their even less intelligent followers, in order to justify and bolster their high positions in their created institutions—which stand as a monument to their limited knowledge. The circular logic of it all is a spiraling downward one.

Helen Laurinda Wilcox

I was jolted back to reality. Oh, wait, it was Friday! *That* did matter! I reminded myself that this Friday was one of the every-other weekends of custody where I could relish Dad-time with my girls, Elizabeth, and Mary. Today was also payday.

At the very last few minutes of every payday, after all the day's orders were shipped, we in the Prep Lab waited like patient puppies expecting a treat. We then marveled at the paper document we received—which we knew were handwritten and signed by Mr. Orrin himself, as if it were Manna from Heaven. I imagined, from what was rumored about him, that he held onto the checks to the very last minute before distribution, as it likely pained him to part with a cent of his money. Each paycheck was sealed in an individual envelope. Could they have been sealed by our fearless leader—by Mr. Orrin's own saliva? No, I bet it was the Ancient One's unpleasant task to lick each envelope closed. Maybe that's why she never spoke. Her mouth was glued shut.

I had heard from other employees in the Prep Lab that on a frequent basis each envelope also contained a handwritten note on a scrap piece of paper penned by Mr. Orrin. The notes could be reprimands for excessive absences or sloppy work, but mostly they were quotes from the Bible which also served as not so subtle hints and admonishments for what can best be described as "sins of the flesh." The notes regarded drink, gluttony, carousing, or anything that might be construed as fun. Funny thing, the paycheck envelopes with notes always seemed to be received by the employees who *did* engage in the seven deadly sins. I wondered how Orrin knew that. I had never received one in my paycheck envelope to date, so I figured the suitcoat and tie must be working.

His old-school style of management mirrored certain titans of industry and their business practices of the early 20th Century. I had read histories of how one early auto industry pioneer had his management team scour the neighborhoods of his factory employees to monitor their living conditions and lifestyles and then issue them warnings. Without a doubt, it was an intrusion into their civil and worker's rights which would never be tolerated today. But no one at Genome 23 History ever raised the issue with management about the notes in their paycheck envelopes, lest they lose their job. This was a right-to-work State and labor laws did not favor us bottom-of-the-barrel ilk.

Another thing in this work environment—which should also be deemed illegal, was all of the overtly puritanical quotes taken from the writings of prominent preachers from the 1800's that were mysteriously scribbled onto several whiteboards around the facility. We all decided the religious graffiti most likely occurred after hours for employees to discover anew each day. They were in the unmistakable hand of the boss as they matched his signature on our paychecks. No one besides me seemed to pay any attention to them. None of us ever said a word about it to anyone in authority, but it made me wonder about the world in which Mr. Orrin's mind lived.

All this ultra-conservative Bible thumping should have made any sane, free thinker bolt for the exits of this arguably hostile workplace. I thought of doing this daily, but I constantly reminded myself that I desperately needed this job at this critical time—*for my two girls*. I told myself, I had to be thankful.

Chapter 6.

An excerpt from Helen's essay: Where Do We Find
Ourselves Today?

*"With little or no checks on the leadership scribes
and their institutions, and with human nature being
what it is to get over on folks for their own benefit,
there arose documented examples of prideful and
sometimes dishonest interpretations—what you might
call add-ons to their preaching of the Gospel and its
original tenets. The subsequent applications of those
misguided views by the leadership have always fell on
each of us in discouraging ways."*

Written on the back of an owner's manual for a Star-
Right Magic Maid Electric Stand Mixer. It was
purchased in 1930 per included sales receipt. The
manual was included in the pages of the cookbook
The Compleat Housewife, or, Accomplish'd
Gentlewoman's Companion.

28 January 1959

*Sometimes a person forgets what they are doing as
their mind is filled with worry. This morning, I sat
with my morning cup of tea waiting for it to cool so it
would not scald. As I looked out the window, I noticed
a thread hanging from my sheer curtains above the
bureau. It bothered me to no end that they are*

starting to fray from the last time I washed them. So, I cut off the errant thread with my sewing shears.

For some reason, I held the thread in my hand, balled it up and then dropped it into the cup of tea as if I were placing a lump of sugar in it. Now why did I do that? I don't even use sugar in my tea.

The deed done; I wonder what the greater value is. The embarrassment of telling the kids about it or the amusement they'll get from hearing about Grandmas silliness.

A good story is a good story. So, I don't mind telling them and having them laugh at my expense. It will lighten the mood of the current troubles of our family.

Helen Laurinda Wilcox-Phillips

Oh, God! There was still two more hours of work. Anxiety rose in my throat. How much longer can this suffering go on? I wanted to get up and bolt for the door—never to return. But I knew I couldn't. Again, I tried to push away the rudimentary aspects of this job and focus on the bigger picture. Hang in there!

In my mind I rattled off all the positive aspects of this job. The list was short. Let's see, this job was within driving distance of the Ex for exchange of the girls on the custody swap weekends. This job allowed the girls to remain in the same school and daycare. I reasoned that their lives had been disrupted enough with the divorce and they didn't need additional change to add to their anxieties or mine. It was paramount to insulate them from all the changes taking place and to maintain a proximity to them. Daddy didn't need more uncertainty in his income right now either, so it was best to stay put in this job.

If I could stick this out, I could show my children—emotionally and financially, that I was still the same devoted parent they knew before the divorce. That meant there could be no upheavals or radical changes in my life. I would show them I was always going to be the reliable father they knew and expected—even though it was now only every other weekend. My girls were not going to be victims of the fallout from my divorce or used as a tool of my vindictiveness toward the Ex, as they were sometimes being used in that manner toward me.

Well, all that internal justification and pep talk only chewed up five minutes on the clock. Enough of the past for now. I needed to turn my thoughts to time with my children. I could find some solace in those. So, I began to plan what the girls and I would do this weekend.

Our weekends together usually fell into the same routine. Every Friday night we would have dinner—their choice of restaurants or take-out—usually pizza. There would be a shopping trip to the mall—mostly to look, then rent a movie. Saturday plans would be up in the air. They could sleep in, we could take in a movie at the theatre, spend the afternoon at a park or whatever. They never asked to have any school friends over, although that would have been just fine with me. However, they never inquired about it, and frankly, I don't think they wanted to share their limited Dad-time with anyone else. Sundays followed the same course. It would be that way until 6pm Sunday evening when all three of us would shed tears before the exchange back to their Mother in the parking lot of the local burger joint.

The clock finally advanced. On this Friday, the team finished the shipping duties a little early and our paychecks had been distributed to us, but company policy was that we were not allowed to fritter away the remaining few minutes left on the clock before the end of the workday. So, I returned to my workstation and began a new ledger, dating it for Monday, and returned to thoughts of the coming weekend and activities with my daughters. Even with only less than a half-hour left of this workday, I found I still needed a *"daydream sedative"* for the constant anxiety in me about this job and everything in flux in my life. Looking forward to time with my children for a few more minutes was the only way to forget the drudgery of processing yet another customer order.

Deep in the thought of them, I assigned a sequential number to the next order, writing it on the first line of the ledger, #17-80043. However, when I opened the box, I was snapped out of my trance. The specimen that dropped out onto my lab table was not our usual small plastic vial with a snapped-on lid that was provided to the customer when they ordered. It was old, made of glass—like an early version of a test tube with a stopper. The stopper looked to be made of cork, but possibly wood. It had a wax sealed string attached, which secured the stopper. Inside the scratched, occluded glass, there appeared to be a small, dark brown, stained fragment of cloth. There was no order form in the box. I turned it over to read that the return address was a P. O. Box in Bruges, Belgium. I wrote that on the ledger.

Getting submissions to our company from other countries was nothing unusual. There had been an increase in orders coming from mostly English-speaking countries over the last few months—which indicated company growth. Lots of the submissions were from Europe—especially France. There was also a substantial number arriving from the Middle East, too. Genetic research was a growing worldwide phenomenon.

I stopped to ponder this unusual submission—when at that moment, another co-worker in the Prep Lab yelled out, "5 o'clock! I am outta here!" That was followed by a great rustle of voices, desk chairs moving and the activity of gathering coats and other personal belongings. Then doors slammed, and I found myself alone in the quickly evacuated office. "Don't let the door hit you in the ass." I said sarcastically out loud to no one.

I penciled the sample number of the corked bottle onto my calendar desk blotter with a note to myself to question Management about its unusual nature first thing Monday morning. I could then resume prepping and cataloging it—at least that was my plan.

Before that, I was to meet their Mother to exchange custody of the girls per the court ordered agreement.

Minus the barrage of verbal snipes that would be hurled at me, it would be the first thing in this grueling day that I was joyfully anticipating.

Chapter 7.

Archived by Chloe Stevens. Circa 1900. Attached to a page of one of the cookbooks with what appears to be a mixture of flour and water. Family genealogical records show that Chloe had a niece named Mary. She would have been a first cousin to her daughter, Alma. She is also most likely the same friend and cousin who wrote to Alma about how to flirt with postage stamps on a letter. They were near the same age, and after long lives, both were buried within a few plots of each other in the same Village cemetery.

"But one thing is needful: and Mary hath chosen that good part, which shall not be taken away from her."

Luke 10:42 - King James Version

This weekend would prove to be incredibly beneficial to both the girls and me. We reconnected as we did every weekend, but this one even more so. We instinctively knew that these weekends were a limited commodity. Our lives were evolving. Nothing would stay the same forever, so we held tightly onto what we had in the present. I suspected their lives at their Mother's house was also changing, but I refrained from quizzing them about her. I was on guard for the emotional turmoil that would alter my time with the girls should my Ex decide to move, get married or whatever. I put all those thoughts out of my head so it wouldn't interfere with our plans this weekend. I also buried the recurring thought that someday, when my daughters became teenagers, they would prefer to spend their weekends with friends and not dear old Dad. So, we would cherish this needed time together while we had it.

We entered the Mall entrance for our Friday night excursion of mostly looking but not buying. However, coming to the first endcap of merchandise, just inside the entrance of an anchor store, there was a display of rolled up, inexpensive, fleece snuggle blankets. The girls wanted one and of course and I obliged. After rummaging through the display and each child picking out their favorite pattern, we took a few more steps into the store with each girl holding one of my hands and their opposing arm tightly wrapped around their new blanket. A few more paces and my youngest announced, "Do we need to go shopping? I really just wanna go home and try my blanket." The oldest jumped in, "Yeah, we can just get a pizza and rent a movie and watch it all cuddled up on the couch. I'd really like to try my blanket out too." The brief shopping trip was over.

This is the way things usually went every weekend

with the girls. My wanting to be the best Dad possible, coupled with my fear of losing them to their Mother completely was so great, I over-planned and over-expected what they might want to do with their limited time with me. Turns out, they *only* needed *time*—the time spent in the space of something familiar. That, and a pair of $2.50 blankets was more than enough. Simply to be physically close to each other was the correct therapy for our shared anxieties.

With one stop for a $5.00 takeout pizza and another stop at the video rental store, we headed to the security and familiar, calm surroundings of my little cottage in the woods. There, per regular routine, after pizza, we all fell asleep on the couch before the end of the animated movie.

I woke during the end credits of the kids flick with a stiff neck and one child leaning her head against my right shoulder—both her arms wrapped tightly around my bicep. She was out like a light. The other was draped across my lap sleeping the unburdened sleep of the innocent. When I looked down upon them during these moments, I wondered what each of them might be dreaming. From the looks on both of their perfect faces, they were peaceful, happy thoughts. There were no worries intruding in *their* dreams. I wished I could attain their level of deep and restful sleep. I couldn't remember the last time I did that.

Even though the awkward posture was killing my back and my foot had fallen asleep, I dared not move. I remained motionless so as not to wake them. Listening to their rhythmic breathing and occasional light snoring always brought peace and a sense of fatherly pride to me during these moments. I had been a part of their creation. I was there from their beginnings—first to hold each of them after their birth. I remember changing their first diapers and happily volunteering to take the 2 am feedings after their Mother stopped breast feeding. Those quiet and nurturing times in the middle of the night with them were not just a reflection of pleasant memories, they also fulfilled a kind of fatherly role and provided the benefits for my children that I had been denied in receiving for much of my own childhood. To me, these early mornings of providing protection, comfort, and infinite love to them, was a *pay-it-forward* obligation.

After another 30 minutes or so of absorbing this tender scene, I managed to slip out from under them and let them gently flop to each side of the hand-me-down couch. It was big enough for both. Each child's head was pointed in opposite directions toward the armrests. Their little legs intermingled. That would be no problem while they slept, but in the morning, there would usually be a skirmish between them accompanied by considerable kicking until I broke it up. As a Father, my role as arbiter would also make me smile.

I gently covered each with their newly purchased blankets, then crossed the darkened room and eased into the rocking chair on the opposite side, just a few feet away. This rocker was the only stick of furniture I was allowed to take from the marital home. I think the only reason my Ex parted with it was that I insisted it was an inherited family heirloom from my Great-Grandmother. It was not. I think my Mother got it in a yard sale for twenty-five bucks in the late 70's, but the story worked. She begrudgingly allowed me this one item out of a sense of momentary compassion. Lanie once had plenty of it, but it was in short supply over the last few years of our marriage.

Turning off the TV, the only light in the house now came from the small light over the kitchen stove. It cast a faint beam into the living room which illuminated the outlines of the girls on the couch.

So, there I sat, watching over my girls. It was always the same routine every Friday evening into Saturday morning. I would spend the remainder of the night thinking of what I could have done differently to salvage my marriage and our family. There was never a resolution of that. Intermittently—with my ever-present anxiety, and to the tempo of their breathing, I would resolve to keep going *for my two girls*. Eventually, I too would fall into a fitful, shallow slumber in the couple hours left before the breaking dawn. Once the girls were up, they would have all the youthful energy you might expect. I would have to match it.

Sleeping in a chair was never restful for me. Despite the obvious discomfort, during these times, quite often and abruptly, I would lift my head off my chest with an immediate panic upon waking. Over the last several months, my sleep ended this way more frequently. I imagined it to be the same experience for people who had sleep apnea. Maybe I did too. The feeling is a brief panic and helplessness when reaching the bottom of an exhale and suddenly realizing that the inhale of fresh air expected next—as it had a billion times before, might not be forthcoming. It had to be the same panic that a fully conscious person felt as the life ebbed from their body at the moment of an accidental death. For them, knowing that this was their last breath, I imagined they could either feel peace, comfort and completeness of their life, or terror and despair for what was next to come. During my many anxious moments at the bottom of an exhale, I think I leaned toward terror and despair.

Although these moments of panic seemed like an eternity when they occurred, only a split second would actually pass. When that next inhale did finally come for me, I would regain my composure, and to keep from waking the girls, I would slowly rise from the chair in order to minimize the creaking of its ancient wooden frame. From there, I would silently shuffle into the tight galley kitchen, make coffee, and blankly watch each strong, brown drip fall into the carafe, pour myself a cup and then re-enter the living room. Often, I would nestle myself onto the edge of the couch, cup in one hand, and sometimes reach out to gently pat each of the girls on their hips or backs with the other. It was never enough of a pat to wake them, but enough to let them know I was there, and that things were safe for them. This early morning habit started the first weekend they spent with me. I did this so that I would be the first thing they saw when they awakened in the new and strange surroundings. I had continued the habit as much for my benefit as theirs.

Predictably, this would turn out to be like every other weekend with the girls. It was uneventful. I suppose I should be thankful for that, based on what had happened prior to all this—which again, was caused by my big mouth.

Chapter 8.

Handwritten—most likely by Chloe Stevens on the back of a 3 by 5-inch recipe card. It was undated and found in the pages of the cookbook, The Compleat Housewife, or, Accomplish'd Gentlewoman's Companion. It is an independent translation of what seems to be the verse taken from Ecclesiastes 6:11.

Many words create a foolish vanity. That should not profit a man, but it has.

Also found in the same cookbook, it was written on the margin of page 81 next to the recipe: To pickle small Onions.

23 August 1933

Know your onions before you cut them, lest they

bring tears.

    Helen Laurinda Wilcox

The following was written in margins of a copy of a very brittle, so-called 'Suffrage Paper' titled: The Woman's Journal, published in Boston, Chicago, and St. Louis. The edition was printed in July 1872. It was discovered in the book: The Eleventh Annual Report of the Secretary of the State Horticultural Society of Michigan – 1881

16 May 1919

By my arithmetic, it was 47 years ago they were talking about it in this paper and it hasn't changed. Not in this home.

'So, how was the Ladies Auxiliary Meeting with the other hens?' Papa jokingly asked today. I laughed. 'It was mostly like all the others.' I tell him. Which was a fib as we had a special speaker advocating about the Suffrage movement. She was so inspiring. I want to travel on a speaker's circuit someday.

'I could never set and listen to all that. What was the meeting about this time?' He asked.

'Oh, you know how women can be. This and that— gossip and such.' I replied. I hoped that my flippant answer was enough to allay Papa' suspicions. If he only knew, his ears should be burning from the

content we discussed.

So not to make it sound too frivolous and then he would not allow me to go anymore, I added. 'We chatted about how to make our local society better.'

'Society?' He shot back.

That was a poor choice of words on my part. It was a trigger to him.

'Now you shouldn't be filling your head with all that.' Papa stated. 'You're starting to sound like that Roosevelt bunch back east. And we don't need that kind of rebel rousin' round here. Next thing you'll be demanding the vote.'

I responded under my breath so he would not hear. 'If I have anything to do about it.'

    Helen Laurinda Wilcox

As mentioned, my big mouth's bad habit of speaking without first thinking everything through fully had always gotten me into trouble. The most recent example being the confrontation at the Unemployment Office. At 50 plus years old, I should know better. I wished I had the foresight to put my thoughts in writing and them bury them in a cookbook as my Grandmothers had. The environment I always seemed to find myself in—when the urge to blurt something out came upon me, was never the sanctuary that a book, in a drawer, in their kitchen was to them. My habit of, *shoot-from-the-lip and let the words fall where they may,* would emerge during another far more consequential confrontation that landed me and my girls in the space we occupy now.

I had made the king-of-all mistakes by letting an honest, but ill-conceived expression of disgust—and some might say a threat, escape from my mouth during the final breakpoint with Lanie. As I stood there in the driveway of my now former home, with what few clothes I could gather in my arms to toss in the truck upon my exit, she screamed at me from the front porch, "I hope you die!" That was hardly an appropriate response to my leaving for good since she was the one caught cheating. But then again, since she was supremely unhappy with me and self-medicating a well know mood-enhancer with known side effects of emotional outbursts, I guess I should have expected her to overreact at my departure. It was just like the time, a few months back, when I cursed the *F-word* during an argument about her undermining my authority with the kids. She responded by taking both of her balled-up fists and launching a punch into my chest with all her might. That was unlike her, uncalled for and probably a side-effect of her meds.

I have never retaliated to any woman in the physical sense, and I did not this time either. But without the governing filter for my vocal cords, I replied forcefully in the heat of the moment, "Then I hope you die too!" I should have stopped there. but I didn't. I added the words, "And I hope to start making plans for that soon! Watch your back!" I was bluffing of course, but it was my bad!

Little did I know the Ex's new BF had been cowardly hiding in the basement when I gathered my belongings, and he was now behind the front door inside the house, in order to stay out of the altercation brewing between Lanie and me in the drive. He was listening to everything though and would later recount my threat in an affidavit submitted during divorce proceedings. This gave the Judge in our civil case all the justification she needed to limit my custody of the girls to an every-other weekend arrangement, and hit me with the maximum child support—plus a little more to cover trumped-up, unpaid medical expenses for the girls the court claimed was in arrears. They were not. I had already paid those, and I had the receipts, but the court simply ignored that fact and piled on by levying the extra amount onto my support payments. I am convinced the Family Court system is filled with a staff without the basic skills of being able to add or subtract.

Money! My thoughts then shifted to money worries. How was I going to make this month's rent payment and juggle my checkbook to account for the five bucks I had spent on snuggle blankets last night? The dollars were that tight.

In the dark, on the edge of the couch, sipping my coffee, I began to daydream about other possibilities to meet budget. I supposed I could go to a cheaper brand of caffeine rather than the more expensive premium roast. I calculated the savings. Maybe it would yield a couple dollars a month. I should also start using coffee creamer rather than real half and half. That would save tens and twelves of cents right there. Hmm, I doubted that my backyard soil was of the right kind to grow my *own* coffee. Now, that *would* save big bucks if it were, but I knew it had to be volcanic soil and the climate here above the 45th parallel was all wrong. So, I put the whole enterprise out of my mind, but did take smaller sips to make the remaining coffee in the pot last till the next morning. I would reheat the stale brew then to save the cost of making another full pot. I reasoned, in just a few months of frugality, I would forget what the taste of good coffee was like, so it would be worth the sacrifice. Would I ever again be able to afford a $3.50 store-bought mochaccino latte again? Doubtful. This is what my thought processes had been reduced to under all the recent financial stresses on me. I was sure it was going to be my initial steps toward dementia if something didn't change soon.

Amid the moment of my lament on how my life had been reduced to a pathetic caffeine miser, Elizabeth rolled over, opened her sleepy eyes, and said, "I'm hungry." That woke Mary. "Me too!" She said. And so, our day together began.

Rather than the mess of trying to make them breakfast here, especially since the choices we had in the refrigerator were few—not even milk, we decided to go out to a local pancake cafe' nearby. It was their favorite restaurant and it was just down the street past my work building. I checked my wallet to make sure I had enough cash to leave our waitress a tip. The rest of the expense would have to go on "the card" which was steadily reaching its credit limit.

Chapter 9.

Attached to page 255 of the book, The Compleat Housewife, or, Accomplish'd Gentlewoman's Companion with needle and black thread. That page had the recipe: To make Necklaces for Children in cutting Teeth. Archived by Chloe Stevens, circa 1900.

"Servants, be subject to your masters with all fear; not only to the good and gentle, but also to the froward."

> *1 Peter 2:18 - King James Version.*

Written on letter stationary and found folded between the pages of the book: The Great Galveston Disaster.

12 September 1946

I had to laugh. Then I had to sigh. Then I had to paddle a behind, after I made the youngest set to the kitchen table till supper to practice his times tables. I didn't want that chore, but he offered me no choice when he angrily blurted out, 'You're not the boss of me!' No, I'm often not the boss of me either.

> *Helen Laurinda Wilcox-Phillips*

A light snow had fallen overnight, trying its best cover the grittiness of the industrial park where Genome 23 History was located. The strings of blinking holiday lights on office windows and plastic reindeer on the lawns of most of the little, low-rent, metal office buildings and small factories did little to create a Christmas atmosphere. As I passed my workplace, I noticed a car in the lot. I recognized it as Mr. Orrin's. I thought it odd that he was in the building on a Saturday. His entire weekends, per gossip in the building, revolved around his church where he sat on the Church Counsel. Word was he spent almost every hour there every Saturday and Sunday.

I observed that there were no other vehicles in the parking lot and no other tire tracks left in the snow. His car was a well-worn, faded black relic—no longer in production. I forget the model. It's the one that had been out of production since the early 1960's. It was legendarily unsafe—especially in winter weather, due to its heavy weight in the back of the rear engine vehicle, which could cause the front to lose traction and direction on slippery roads. It was a miserly choice of transportation for anyone today but seemed appropriate for Orrin.

Adding to Orrin's cheap persona, each day he wore the same outfit to work. He probably had more than one, but they were all the same. Each was a faded, out of style, black suit with a frayed white dress shirt, thin black tie, and well-word black wing-tip shoes. The ensemble matched his car. The rumors of his legendary parsimonious practices also included saving all the envelopes of any incoming mail. He would then tear them open and use the inside of the envelopes as recycled notepads. I'm guessing this saved him tens of twelves of cents each month. Coincidentally, it was the same amount I hoped to reap in savings from my backyard coffee plantation— should it ever come to fruition. I'm sure Mr. Orrin would approve of my frugality.

The sight of Orrin's vehicle and pondering his lone-wolf behavior reminded me of the only encounter I ever had with him to date. Early on in my employment, I was summoned to the old man's office. It was accessed via a back stairway to the second floor of the facility. A few days into my employment I was told by the hiring manager, Mr. Welch, it was required for each new employee to introduce themselves to the owner. I was to knock on the door of his office, in his words, "gently so as not to startle Mr. Orrin." Upon entering, I would introduce myself to him then allow him to share the *Company Mission* with me and ask questions of me. Under no circumstances should I stay in his office for more than five minutes. On my exit from the office, I should make a point to emphasized that I was a diligent worker and happy to do whatever I could to achieve whatever business goals he imparted upon me during the interview. Any superfluous chatter, views expressed, or errant attitude displayed by me, might be enough for Mr. Orrin to terminate my employment in short order. I was warned by Welch. "He is a strict disciplinarian on the conduct of his employees and within his workforce." I was glad for the warning based on my tendency to, let's say, elaborate.

I had accepted the work rules but questioned them to myself. Had I entered a job in an industrial setting, or had I somehow been enlisted in the Marines, stationed at Paris Island for boot camp—where I would be broken down, humiliated and expected to lose my individual identity for the strength of the team? Maybe this was an authoritarian cult and I was being groomed into a secret society with all this decorum, I mused. I admit I was a bit reluctant to attend the required meeting, but I would make every effort to comply with the company's expectations. It was Orrin's business and he could run it the way he wanted. I knew if I ran afoul of the rules or said something stupid or without filter, I could find myself walking the pavement—back in front of Ms. Papers at the Unemployment Office.

Although I did not realize it at the time, and despite my attempt to keep myself to the point, my performance, and the few words I expressed to Mr. Orrin during the meeting, I would later regret. They would unwittingly get me into a verbal contract of sorts with him. It would be yet another unfortunate result of the plague that seemed to follow me of saying too much to the wrong person at the wrong time. Whatever it was that I said in that initial meeting, I think it led Mr. Orrin to expect far more from our employer-employee relationship than I was aware of at the time. That meeting would launch intrusions into my personal life and involve my family in events that would go far beyond what I was ever willing to offer or accept.

The girls and I wheeled into the parking lot of the local breakfast restaurant. They began discussing what type of pancakes they were going to order, but my mind was still on that first encounter with Orrin.

In keeping with the established protocol, I tapped lightly on the office door as instructed. After several long seconds, a faint, "*Come*" from inside could be heard. Entering I found Mr. Orrin seated behind an old, oversized executive desk at the far end of the room. It reminded me of the Resolute Desk in the White House. To his back was a bank of three uninsulated windows steamed over with moisture. Those windows were the only source of light in the room, which put him in a slight silhouette. He was a smallish man dwarfed by the desk and clutter on top of it. The desktop was covered in manila folders and various papers stapled together. Some were stuffed into binders. I recognized some of them as the same Master Ledgers I compiled daily at my workstation in the Prep Lab for our thousands of worldwide customers. There were also some of our customer order forms, a few sample vials and enough other unidentified papers and folders on his desk to make me wonder how Orrin or anyone could accomplish anything in this mess.

The overall ambiance of the office was musty and of a recycled nature. The green and blue shag carpet covering the floor was accented with what appeared to be bits of dry dog food and an almost equal number of dog droppings. I was glad for my sharp eyesight and was able to navigate them without stepping in any on my way toward his desk.

There in his lap was the culprit who had laid the minefield of excrement. It was a matted, white Maltese I later found out was named, Zephaniah. The animal only added to the annoyance factor of the interview by repeatedly smacking its lips. Moving closer, I could see that amongst the disorder of the desk, Mr. Orrin had sprinkled in a few dog treats for the pet. Next to his desk was a potted fern that had obviously not been watered in quite some time. It only had a few green fronds left on it. Much of its desiccated and brown foliage was scattered on the carpet below its wire plant stand. The office was an unkempt hellhole and Orrin seemed oblivious to it.

The only thing that *was* organized in the office was a tall pile of personal checks from our customers made out to Genome 23 History. They were neatly stacked on the right side of his desk, holding a place of honor in the hoarder's nest. Each one was made out for $99.

"Mr. Orrin, It's a pleasure to meet you," I firmly stated.

His response eerily came after a pause of three or four seconds. "You start today?"

"This Monday." I kept it brief as I was instructed.

"8:30 am sharp. Thirty minutes lunch." He flatly stated.

I didn't know how to respond other than offering a

confused, "Ah, yes."

Pausing again, he finally asked, "You married?"

An odd question I thought. "No, divorced." Was my sheepish, contrite reply.

"Lots of people getting married. Then getting divorced." He perked up in a following series of statements. "Having too many children. Damn Catholics. Further diluting the genetic pool. Makes our Missions harder. Might better stay single. Serve the Lord makes our Missions easier. Clearer. My church Mission."

Ok, now I didn't know how to decipher this drivel he was uttering. I wondered if what he was saying even amounted to a question. Did it even require a response from me? I had no idea. I understood now why the HR manager, Mr. Welch, had to prep me for this interview. From his coaching I was prepared to expect something between a witness taking the stand in a murder trial to being summoned to appear before the Inquisition. I thought, what a disjointed jumble of strange things to say. What was that about his *church's* Mission? I thought I was here for his *company's* Mission. How did church come up in the interview? What church? The slam on Catholics did not go unnoticed, but I pretended to not be offended by that or show any facial sign of displeasure for his bigotry. In the past, that kind of reaction by me always got me into trouble. I wrote off his ramblings as symptoms of early-onset dementia.

I couldn't formulate a response, so I waited for him to

make the next move in this uncomfortable conversation, but he didn't. He just kept staring at me—no, more like through me. His thoughts had obviously drifted off to something else. His ruminations on marriage, mission and/or missions and the genetic pool was a pool too deep for me to wade through. I simply wanted to get through this brutal exercise and get back to work.

After an uncomfortably long period, I decided now was the time to make my exit before another awkward exchange. Besides, I was sure my five minutes of interview time was up.

"Well, I better get back to the hiring manager and continue training. Nice to meet you." I stated. "I look forward to applying my expertise and hard work toward your Mission—Missions," I clarified. "The goals that you have outlined—thank you for that—them." As I backed away trying to retrace my steps to avoid the landmines of dog defecation, I opened the door and took one quick glance back, offering a bit of a bow at the waist as a sign of deference. He slowly refocused his gaze upon my retreat and although he said nothing, I think I noticed a small smile creep across his haggard face—although he remained transfixed on his own last words.

I closed the door gently, not wanting to wake the old man from his trance. I whispered, "I *think* I nailed it! Whew!" My old skills as a PR man had come to good use and I beat a hasty retreat down the stairs. I then realized I was sweating profusely—my collar wringing wet. I swiped away beads of perspiration which had formed on my upper lip with my sleeve. "Holy Crap! That was bizarre." I muttered. I hoped that would be the last interaction with Mr. Orrin for the duration of my employment. That turned out to be wishful thinking.

Chapter 10.

Written in the margins, blank pages, and the inside back cover of a Holland Furnace Co. owner's manual, manufactured in 1948. It was saved along with its warranty card in the pages of the book: The Great Galveston Disaster.

28 May 1956

I tell the grandkids that you always must do what is right, even if there are some whom you are trying to help that do not approve of it or you. That is the Christian way—even though it seems you are being treated poorly. You must keep a Faith that right will always win out over wrong—eventually.

That was the way when your grandfather was first courting me. His mother was not so keen on me. He was still living at home and had a good job in the Auto Factory and would always give his Mother some money from his paycheck every week. She thought that she would lose out on his help if he married me. In those days, there was no old age pension yet, so the dollars he brought home was all she had.

He never denied her anything and I wouldn't have allowed it either. But she was cold to me for a time. I never said anything to her that would cause us to fall away from each other—though it hurt that I was not accepted at first.

When she became frail, I took care of her as I would my own Mother. And at the end, on her deathbed she said that she was glad that I was her daughter. I was glad I was able to hear that. So, you see, you always need to do what is right, even though some might not want you too. Your reward will come.

Helen Laurinda Wilcox-Phillips

My mind refocused on the drive to the restaurant with the girls this Saturday morning. I'm not sure how much if any nutritional value there was in their ordered breakfasts outside of the glass of milk. But true to my pattern of overindulgences on their behalf, in the attempt to prove I was the greatest Dad, they had free range of the kiddie menu. It was chocolate pancakes with blueberry syrup for Mary. She devoured it with delight based on the crumbs sticking to her little cheeks. "Use a napkin, hon." I urged but didn't enforce. What's the use? Napkins would only interfere with her enjoyment.

Elizabeth ordered Belgian waffles with strawberries and whipped cream but was only completely satisfied with her choice after the waitress brought additional sprinkles to top her waffles on her second trip to the table. A third trip was also required when Mary too needed sprinkles for *her* pancakes. I promised our waitress I'd make sure she got a good tip for her extra attentive service. A fourth trip to the table by the waitress was a coffee refill for me. I savored the full-strength brew while I could, as I knew it would soon be cut from the budget in a cost-saving measure in my own kitchen.

As mentioned, the rest of the weekend proved to be uneventful, but that was fine with us. Our enjoyment was special because we were again a family—of sorts, with lots of hugs and a generous amount of, *I love you's*. Hopefully, I provided enough of those to last them for the next two weeks. As the hours passed, I silently dreaded the eventual exchange of the girls back to their Mother. 6 pm Sunday evening always arrived too quickly.

The dread of that upcoming exchange was made worse for me as we were now in the buildup to Christmas. I was missing out on Mary's and Elizabeth's excitement about the coming visit from Santa. I only had a small, table-top Christmas tree up in my house for them and no presents under it yet. It seemed pathetic compared to the boxes of holiday decorations I would put up in the house weeks ahead of time for Lanie and the girls when we were a family. I wondered if their Mother even had any for the girls this year.

When the time came for the custody exchange, the girls clung to me for just one more hug and kiss. They were then strapped into the seatbelts of the Ex's car and their little faces faded away as she sped off. I drove straight back to the cottage, my eyes filled with tears. Sunday evenings, every two weeks was always an early night for me. I went straight to bed to forget the sadness that fell upon me each time they left. I hoped to drop to sleep as soon as possible to get away from the thoughts about the way our family had fallen apart. Before drifting off to another troubling sleep, I muttered, over and over, "God, please give me a *direction* to fix this. Please!" Monday morning would be here soon enough, and the grind would begin anew.

Chapter 11.

Written on the inside of a water stained, folded open, brown paper envelope. The envelope was from the Consumer's Power Co. Muskegon, MI. It was refolded with its bill for 96 cents enclosed. Paid, September 1932. It was found in the cookbook, The Compleat Housewife, or, Accomplish'd Gentlewoman's Companion.

Undated

I was reluctant to go, but Erma insisted that I attend the square dance at the Oddfellows hall. I'm not much of a dancer and prefer not to be the focus of attention and usually sit with the other spinsters, but on occasion I will square dance.

I couldn't take my eyes off the caller this night. He had a gravelly baritone voice and a hearty laugh at times on the call and he had a warm smile. No one would call him dashing or overly handsome but of good solid stock. Erma said he was from the Vassar area. We kept making eye contact until later in the night and someone suggested we all do a polka. They put an old record on the Victrola. I knew that was my cue to take a seat but halfway to my seat, I felt a strong hand grab mine and pull me onto the dance floor.

The gentleman who had been calling the square dance grabbed me at the waist and started twirling and hopping to: Roll out the Barrel. He was a wonderful dancer and made up for my awkwardness. After playing the other polka on the B side of the record, I was so winded and dizzy. Thankfully, he said he needed to go back to the calling but asked if I might be back in two weeks as he was scheduled to call again. I thanked him for the dances and told him I most likely would. I didn't want to seem too forward.

That's how I met your Father. You see, it happens when you least expect it.

Helen Laurinda Wilcox-Phillips

I waited right up to the last minute before I had to exit

my truck to enter the building. Dutifully crossing the parking lot, I dragged my feet toward what I knew was to be another seemingly endless day of work. It was dreary and drizzling outside and it set the mood for what the next eight hours would hold for me. Without a thought, I grabbed my timecard from the metal rack that held it. Inserting it into the 1950's style timecard machine located next to the rack, I waited for the distinctive sound of the time stamp which signified that I was now held in work "incarceration" until 5pm.

I bobbed my head in a courtesy nod to a few of my other fellow work zombies who had already donned their white lab coats and the required full-face shields, which were tilted in an upright position on their heads. Some were stretching on their sterile nitrile blue gloves for the day's tasks. The incoming shipment of pallets loaded with boxes of customer orders was exceptionally large this Monday morning. Over the last few weeks, the amount of work had steadily increased for us in the Prep Lab, and as we were already understaffed, we were pressed to complete the orders by day's end. The volume of work could either make the day go quicker by keeping us incredibly busy, or it could add to the overwhelming depression and anxiety presented by this mountain of menial drudgery.

One of the other lab zombies, a diminutive woman, whom I guessed was in her mid-40's, had never spoken to me before—despite being stationed just a few cubicles down the row from me in the Prep Lab. She appeared to be a silent wallflower-type. No one, to my knowledge, ever interacted with. She was unremarkable in almost every way but for the distinctive and overt amount of curly red hair she possessed. It stuck out from under the headband of her face shield nearly out past her shoulders. It was an impressive, yet comical amount of hair. After she punched in at the time clock, just before I did, I was caught off guard as she paused, turned, and addressed me in addition to the customary employee morning nod.

"Have a good weekend?" She asked in a manner as if she had fallen overboard and was asking for someone to throw her a life preserver.

Startled that anyone would speak words in a complete sentence at this early hour—let alone any of them to me, I faltered, trying to manage a coherent response to her sandy, almost sultry, lower octave posed question. I thought to myself, not only is her hair distinctive but also her voice. It was also somehow recognizable. As it turned out, *she* was the *Julie* I spoke with on the phone to set up my initial job interview with the company. I later found out Julie Douglas frequently filled in as executive secretary for Mr. Orrin, when the permanent one—his wife Mrs. Orrin, was absent to attend one her many doctor appointments for diverticulitis, arthritis or some other *itis* that afflicted her.

I choked on my response to her. "Uh, yeah it was fine, you?" not actually interested in anything meaningful she might reply.

"It could have been better!" she stated firmly after a

big gulp to hold back her tears. "Broke up with my boyfriend this morning. I finally had enough of being his backup. I'm no one's second choice. He wants her? Ok, he's got the trophy girlfriend he always wanted, but I'm not gonna be backup insurance."

This woman was obviously still simmering in the aftermath of her recent turmoil. I knew what that felt like, but I didn't know how to respond.

She continued to vent. "I'm not holding down the fort while he's got someone else. I'm not good enough to be in public with him at his social events?" She posed the question to me. I did not respond. Geez, I thought. I hoped that was a rhetorical one, because I was not about to engage her in a discussion on this topic—especially not right now. After a few seconds, she answered her own question. "Well, he can have *her* for his arm candy at his corporate events now!"

I looked around wondering if she meant this unloading of her weekend drama for someone else. There was no one else within earshot. I quickly tried to get past the subject.

"Oh, sorry. Been there. Well, it's time to start work."

"Been there?" She persisted in the conversation. I almost ran to the door of the Prep Lab to put some separation between us.

"Uh, yeah, say let's continue this at break time?" I offered in a question form, so it had some modicum of empathy and not to sound as if I were shutting her down. I didn't want to appear rude, but I wasn't overly interested in getting involved. I was still taken aback that she chose me with which to share her story, but the others in the Prep Lab—all male, surly types would not have been good targets for her rant. They were untalkative in general and uncaring about the kinds of family or relationship things that might require thoughtfulness and a response in a chit-chatty conversation.

"We're gonna be late for start time. You know how they are around here. Besides, it'll give *you* a chance to relax a bit." I added with a smile as a subtle hint that she was coming in a little hot.

She perceptively got it. "Oh, I'm sorry, it just happened, and I guess I needed someone to unload on. Unfortunately, you were in the line of fire. Really sorry."

"No problem. Check with you at the break."

She nodded with acceptance of the proposition along with a little embarrassment about her loss of self-control. With that, we began the retreat to our lab-coated, face-shielded, workstation cubicle anonymity. But before we did, I could see under her plastic face shield, that she gave me the kind of radiating smile one gets when you meet an old friend. It was one I would see more of over the coming weeks.

I began my work, but my thoughts dwelled on Julie.

Julie Douglas was about 5 foot 2, petite and fit—I assumed. It was hard to really tell for sure. She always wore a lab coat about two sizes too big for her. That unruly crop of her shoulder length, curly hair bushing out from her headband reminded me of those iconic pictures of Hendrix taken at Woodstock. But hers had a lot more volume and was bright Irish red! In all, she had an *emerald lass* kind of look to her—complete with wire rimmed glasses framing a pale skinned, cherubic face. If you took the time to look closely—past the face shield and past the glasses, she had pretty and intensive green eyes. As mentioned, her voice was unusually low for what you would expect of someone who looked like her and did not match her persona. She would have been better matched with a lilting traditional Irish brogue.

Overall, I would describe Julie as unusually interesting and not bad looking—if one took the time to really contemplate it. I would not describe her as being *my type,* although I wasn't quite sure what my type was anymore after being married for so long. Julie looked nothing like the Ex. And to hear her tell it, Julie's ex-boyfriend did not appreciate her subtle qualities either. I'm guessing he chose a classic, glossy bimbo look over hers for public exhibition.

Ahh, on to the work. Maybe the promised 10 o'clock coffee break chat with Julie would offer some distraction for this mundane Monday.

Settling into my workstation, I reacclimated to the surroundings. Ok, where did I leave off last Friday at quitting time? Right. It was the unusual sample with the glass vial. Where was it?

I remembered I had jotted down the number of the sample on my desk blotter, #17-80043. Hmm, where is the *sample* for order #43? No customer order form for #43 either. I tried to retrace my count looking for the previous samples 39, 40, 41 and 42. No, those had all been completed, placed in the tray with all their accompanying paperwork and I assumed had been gathered by Mrs. Orrin. Let me do a quick check of the new green Master Ledger I had started. Wait! That was missing too. However, orders 44, 45, 46 and so on were all waiting to be processed. Huh? I shuffled through everything on the desktop. Nothing! Had it fallen to the floor? No, it was nowhere to be found. It was as if #43 never existed. But it *did* exist. I had already written that number on the ledger, but now the sample and it was gone. That would be proof that I had lost it and worse, cause to get fired. What should I do? Tell someone? Who would that be? "There is no way I'm gonna knock on the old man's door and tell him!" I muttered. So, I chose the cowardly way and did nothing. Then I remembered I had seen his lone vehicle in the parking lot on Saturday morning as the girls and I drove by to breakfast. Is it possible that he took the order and ledger from my workstation? Why would he do that?

Well, I thought, I would wait for my fate. Somebody probably knows that #43 exists and is now missing. I'll just start a new ledger and begin it with the next sample in order, #44. I'll have to deal with my discrepancy later if the missing one turns up. I hoped it would, but then I would have to explain how it turned up missing in the first place. This was bad. Maybe this might be the one time they let something slip past them. Then again, based on the meticulous record keeping here, I doubt they would let it slide and my error would end up costing me this crappy job.

I was sure that would be my fate, because a few weeks back, a now former employee dropped a huge stack of specimen trays—which took the entire team in the Prep Lab the rest of the afternoon to reassemble the correct paperwork with the right specimens and then re-do every preparation. A few could not be salvaged and that cost the company money by having to issue a refund to those customers. The next day that employee's workstation cubicle was empty. The day after that it was filled with a different new-hire lab coated clone.

I had also witnessed another employee who got their numbers and samples out of sequence—which caused another grinding halt to the testing and analysis, and that lab "rat" was immediately let go too. He was marched out of the building after getting dressed down by Management. He relinquished his lab coat and face shield to the higher-ups just outside the Prep Lab window. The scene was akin to an old-west movie, where someone was being drummed out of the Cavalry by having his epilates ripped off. I'm sure the performance was intended as a warning to the remaining personnel lest *they* screw up something. They even made him strip off the company's disposable blue nitrile gloves and surrender them to the Shadow Brothers from the Final Lab. I'm not sure what value they would find in those.

The entire Prep Lab staff had paused from our work to observe the spectacle. But we all quickly redirected our focus to our cubicles when Management's exit interview team caught us looking. Ugh, we were such a woeful lot. We acted like pathetic children in a nineteenth century sweat shop forced to go back to work under the watchful gaze of the overseer. It was best to just keep plowing forward and not make the same or similar mistake. I prayed my missing sample would turn up without incident.

Chapter 12.

Found between pages in the book: The Eleventh Annual Report of the Secretary of the State Horticultural Society of Michigan – 1881. It had torn away from the deteriorated black thread which had held it to the page. Fragments of the thread were still stitched through the page. Archived by Chloe Stevens, circa 1900.

"But I trust I shall shortly see thee, and we shall speak face to face. Peace be to thee. Our friends salute thee. Greet the friends by name."
        3 John 1:14 – King James Version.

Written on a piece of blank newsprint and affixed with flour and water glue to a page of the book: Great Galveston Disaster. It is almost anti Zen-like in its thought.

All the children tell me I am always worrying too much. Such a worry-wort they say. But I say, all the worrying I've done about a thing, and that thing never happened. So, maybe the worrying did some good. I'm sure worrying is just another way of praying on it.

Helen Laurinda Wilcox-Phillips

Worry about the lost sample now constantly nagged me. The next two hours dragged on till the 10 am break. At least then there would be fifteen minutes of relief along with the satisfaction of knowing that only three more, two-hour periods of this torture remained for this day. I filled my coffee thermos cup with the acrid brown liquid the company passed off as coffee. This was the quality of brew I would have to subject myself to for the foreseeable future to make rent. Julie interrupted my thought with a cheery "Hi! Again, really, really sorry about blowing off steam on you this morning. I assure you, I'm much better now." She ended with a slight giggle.

"No problem. Say, let's chat with a stroll around the warehouse—ya know, for privacy. Just the three of us."

She stopped walking as I continued. "Three of us?" She asked.

I turned to look over my shoulder to her but maintained my pace. "Yeah, you, me and this *coffee* which could probably stand up and walk under its own strength."

She smiled, followed it with a quick burst of amused laughter, then picked up her pace to catch up with me. "Yeah, it is pretty awful, but full of needed caffeine." She mused.

The Genome 23 History front offices, Prep Lab and Final Lab were each housed in separate prefab buildings within a much larger metal industrial structure. It had previously been used as a materials warehouse distribution center for some company that went out of business with the last recession. The Genome 23 operation only used a small amount of the cavernous interior and the rest was filled with row after row of tall metal shelves—all of them empty. It was a good place for private conversation and to stretch one's legs on break.

"So, where were we? Your boyfriend, huh?" I began.

"That jack..." She paused to correct her vocabulary before completing the vulgar insult. "Jack-donkey!" I had to suppress my laugh at her replacement of the word, while admiring her ability to employ *her* voice filter in a timely manner when she thought it was needed. She continued, but her light demeanor quickly reverted to where we left off at punch-in time, and her volume and anger increased. "I suspected it. Tried to make myself believe his lies were true but deep down inside I knew better."

"Well, stuff happens." I vaguely summarized attempting to bring the volume of the conversation back down to a normal level. I was still not sure I wanted to engage her in this topic, but I continued and tried to change the subject. "How'd you end up working here?"

"It was close by." Her normal volume resumed. "Literally was the first job ad I saw after I realized I needed one."

"You didn't need a job?" I set up for a punchline. "I sure wish I was independently wealthy too!"

"Ha, nothing like that." She breezed past my attempt at humor. "I had never faced the prospects of having to seek out a career, pay for anything or have to actually provide for myself. I never really wanted to either—guess I was lazy. There was never a serious effort by me to have to be responsible for myself or anything. When it's all paid for, you get kind of complacent and lose perspective of what real people have to deal with." She waved to the empty warehouse. "A place like this."

She continued. "He paid for everything. I got what you might call a *stipend*—like a kid with an unlimited allowance. Any money he gave me was just play money for me—spas, shopping trips. Jason handled all the serious expenditures. He's the Ex." I figured that was the case and let it pass.

She continued describing the situation. "He controlled it all and that included me. I guess you could say I was his "trophy" girlfriend, although I don't think I ever fit the description of it. I mean, look at me! I'm not blond, tall, or leggy. No big boob-job." She indicated with her hands toward her chest. Then her face turned beet red realizing she was directing my gaze toward her breasts. She pulled her lab coat tighter at the lapels to compensate for her perceived immodesty. I made a conscious effort not to look down.

Her voice changed from one of anger to regret. "A while back he said I should look for a job—you know, give me something to do during the day. He was worried that I might be getting bored all day just waiting for him to get home. Huh, what a narcissist. I didn't want to, but I did it for him. Can you imagine that screwed up logic? I went to work for *him*. He just wanted me out of the house for his *nooners,* as he called them. You know, he had a woman over."

"Yeaahh, I've heard the term." I drawled.

She continued ignoring my sarcasm. "I think, now in retrospect, I had to work awfully hard at compromising myself just to stay in his good graces. I did everything for him—for years, with no prospects of ever getting married. I was always too reluctant to ever bring up the subject with him—afraid he would permanently end any discussion of it and then there would be no hope for it. So, I never did. Turns out I was more of a maid and *concubine* to him when nothing better was available. I eventually found out there *were* several others available that he worked into his schedule." She paused to what I assumed was a reminiscence of those times. "I could always tell the mechanical aspects of his love making was not a true feeling for me." "I should've known I was fighting a losing battle and could never fix things after..." She didn't finish the sentence.

Ok, I thought, now we were getting close to the *red line* of TMI—*too much info* about her personal love life. I was not going to cross it.

She continued to ramble—an outpouring of hurt spilled from her. I cringed as I took this as a sign that she was growing more comfortable with me. "He tossed a few dollars at me as payment. I started to feel like it was a payment for my *services*. All those things I did for him—*everything."* She emphasized the last word.

"Nuff said!" I blurted. "I get the picture." She could stop anytime now.

She failed to get the hint and continued. "It was in retrospect, a degrading form of transactional prostitution, although I always tried to convince myself he really *did* care for me—beyond what was convenient. Turns out he didn't. Was probably happy when..." She didn't finish that sentence either.

Suddenly, realizing she was amid the same running diatribe again and had crossed into uncomfortable territory for her audience, she stopped abruptly, "Oh, sorry. There I go again. I apologize. You must think I'm crazy?"

"Well," I wryly said, "Its a lot to unpack."

Thankfully, our walk was headed back in the direction of the Prep Lab. This 15-minute break would soon be over. I realized I did not have the time or desire to assist in unpacking someone else's box of drama on this coffee break or at any time soon. I hadn't even unpacked my own yet. The coffee break had drawn to a close. If Julie and I did this again, I'd make sure we'd talk about something else.

Chapter 13.

An excerpt from Helen's essay: Where Do We Find Ourselves Today?

"It is an inescapable characteristic of humanity for most to be vulnerable to exploitation by the few who seek leadership, power, money and prestige. For them, this enduring ugly attribute of humankind is used as a tool in their arsenal to control the inclusion processes at the expense of the weaker/followers."

The next two days at work passed with nothing significant happening. That was good news in part, as no one brought up the issue of the lost sample, but I was still on guard for the other shoe to drop on it. Wednesday at the 10 am break, I felt a light tap on my shoulder. I turned in my swivel chair to see Julie behind me.

"Wanna take a walk? They made new coffee a couple

minutes ago! Better get it while its fresh."

"Is that why we didn't go on a walk yesterday—old coffee? I questioned.

"No, I had my meeting with the owner." She said. "Mandatory after hire. But we can take a *walk-n-talk* break today." She added hopefully.

Pausing a moment, I said, "Sure beats all this!" As I pointed at the clutter on my desk.

We stepped out of the lab into the warehouse and she began." You have yours yet?"

"Meeting with the boss? Yeah, right after I was hired. You've been here longer than me and you're just now getting around to the big boss interview?"

"Typical." She said with acceptance. "They interview the men first. Women are afterthoughts—here *and at home.*" She stated under her breath. "The women aren't taken seriously as a contributor to the business. We're just window dressing and assigned menial jobs, but somehow, I'm good enough to be Mr. Orrin's Executive Secretary from time to time—when Mrs. Orrin is out or overwhelmed, but I still have no prospects of advancement. I'd like for him to try to find something in his rats-nest of a filing system." She continued venting. "It's a man's world." She ended with a perfunctory, "Huh!"

"Sounds like you have a case. Ever think of saying something?" I cautiously asked.

"Oh, no. I could never do that." She confessed. "I'm

not one to stir the pot."

"Well, that's certainly not the way I would handle it." I said. "But to each his—or *her* own." Then I suddenly felt very guilty. Here this woman does the same work as me—plus, fills in as Executive Secretary—which should warrant some combat pay for having to work with the strange Mr. Orrin. But only now, after months on the job, does she finally get the Business Mission lecture? I didn't know Julie all that well, but she seemed every bit the capable employee of handling a lot more and being rewarded for it. She needed to step-up to it in my estimation. But that was none of my business.

As she explained her situation to me, it immediately reminded me of the same issues I had recently rediscovered in my Grandmother's cookbook essays and diary. It also brought back bits of memories of what my own Mother had always vexed about. All of them—Grandmothers, Mother and Julie, were touching on the same theme about *men in power*. They all discoursed how it angered them that men controlled *everything* but couldn't administrate *anything* without the women who propped them up. Some of them obviously had trouble bringing up the issue, choosing instead to complain into their hidden cookbook diaries or just stew about it silently and take it, or if they were lucky enough to have one, exasperate to fellow employees who had zero power to do anything about it. I wondered if every woman had always had the same angst buried within them. I concluded that they did. It was even more reason for me to modify my own recent behavior. I didn't want

Julie to lump me in with that kind of male ilk. For some reason, it started to matter to me that she didn't see me in that same inconsiderate light.

"Ok, not gonna bore you with my problems this time." Julie switched topics. "I owe *you* some time to *elaborate*."

"Elaborate? That usually gets me in trouble. But that's very thoughtful of you." I took notice of her gesture of fairness and deliberated how to begin. Truth be told, most people after unloading their drama on someone else, feel refreshed and unburdened, but the recipient feels weighed down. It's as if they found a sponge to absorb their bucket of dirty water. Keeping that in mind, I still questioned whether she was really interested in hearing my story. I tested her sincerity with the abridged version of it.

"Well, I'm divorced a couple of years now. Married 19 years. Got two kids. Pretty common reason—she strayed. Lured by the big money—jet set lifestyle. I found out. Devastated. Divorced. Shared custody now but she gets the most of it. Blah, blah, blah."

"Oh, c'mon, there has to be more to the story than that." She pursued.

Hmm, maybe she *was* interested in hearing the details. I continued. "So, we are, um, *were* the typical two-income suburban family. I worked for the International Genome Project. I was not in a capacity as a scientist or anything technical—just in the P. R. arm of the effort, along with some others. My job was to make sense of the wonky tech jargon and report on the science breakthroughs in press releases and news interviews for science journals, TV, and the like. I had to make it palatable to the masses. They seemed to think my efforts helped secure continued funding, and for the general public, it pumped up interest in the long-term project of mapping the human genetic code. It was a big deal, but it eventually wound to a halt—at least the initial phases of it. It's now at the boring stages of tedious specific research going forward."

"So, you left?" Julie asked. "That sounds like a much better job than this."

"No, the organization cut back in the second phase and didn't really need my services anymore. My dumb luck was that the recession and divorce hit at the same time."

"The fact is, that this company and others like it are kind of spin-off industries based on the results of some of that research we did. The possibilities of what they will find out in the future are unlimited." I started to sound like one of my own press releases. "Anyway, all that might have helped me get this job, I guess. But to tell you the truth, I don't think they really looked too closely at my resume. I think they saw the word, *genome*, and figured I knew something about what kind of work they do here. So, here I am."

Julie patiently allowed me to continue my thought before she interrupted. "I know, I was the one who pulled your app and resume."

It suddenly dawned on me. "Oh, right. I keep

forgetting that it was you I spoke with on the phone to set up the interview. Duh! Why didn't you stop me? This is no news to you. You're too polite."

"I guess my politeness and deference in this job came in my previous training as a domestic subservient." She smirked. "It's ok. You can skip past the employment stuff." She said with a glib laugh in that low octave voice. "But I will tell you, Mr. Orrin specifically handed me your resume and told me to call you right away. Continue."

"Really? Huh?" I was taken aback by that nugget of info. "Well, Lanie—the Ex, decided to go back to work once the girls were old enough for school. She said she was bored just staying home—which in retrospect, should have been a warning sign to me, and I agreed that we could use the extra money. We did ok when we both worked, but then my hours got sketchy at the old job and I've been scrambling for more dollars ever since."

"Their names? She asked.

"Oh, my daughters. I have two. The oldest— Elizabeth, she's 6 and Mary is 4. Good kids really."

"No doubt. Go on." She said in an interviewer kind of fashion.

"I only get them every other weekend. Anyway, before we decided to have children, the Ex worked as a bookkeeper for a CPA. After the girls got old enough for school, she landed a job with some venture capitalist firm. All was fine for the most part, but we fell into the rut lots of couples do with the demands of kids—too much drudgery of family stuff, and not enough time for each other. We grew into a distant marriage. I think that's kinda normal, but she drifted further away than me with the lure of the corporate jet-set world. All the excitement—none of the laundry. And she's a good-looking woman, so all the *swingin' dicks* in the office were playin' her up big time—especially the boss."

"*Swinging*—oh my Lord!" She burst out in a haughty belly laugh, then quickly tried to suppress it. "I'm sorry but I've never heard that one before. I should tell my girlfriends, but I'd die of embarrassment. Sorry, go on."

"Glad you liked it." I continued. "It didn't take long after she hired in. Lots of later-than-normal meetings into the evening past dinnertime. She was rarely there for bath time for the girls and they often went to bed without seeing her at night. There were a lot of harsh words between us about her not being around to help. Yada, yada. Finally, she was invited to this weekend business trip. That really made me worried and suspicious. It got the better of me and I did the unthinkable in a trustworthy marriage. I tapped our own home landline. I patched in an old cassette tape recorder. She called in sick to her job one day. When I got home and checked, there was a phone call on the tape with this guy at work—her boss, Jason."

Julie interrupted. "Another Jason? Huh, must be a common trait. You don't have to fill in the blanks if you don't want to."

"No, it's ok." I assured her. Now Julie was going to know how I felt when she unloaded her tale of infidelity on me. "So, I dreaded listening to the playback of the tape. It filled the entire side of the cassette. I only needed to listen for about 10 minutes to hear all I needed to know—all the crap they were gonna "do" to each other on the trip. My wife never even talked to me like that. I wanted to puke."

"Been there." Was all Julie said—probably reliving her relationship's gut-punch moment. Then she half whispered, "It hurts. What did you do?"

"Well, I wanted to *kill* her." I said a bit too loud as the word *kill* seemed to echo through the warehouse. "I've never been that hurt and angry before. If she had been there when I heard that tape, I might have. I don't know. My heart was crushed like I'd been kicked in the chest. I'm not sure which was stronger, the feeling of anger or hurt. I wanted to curl up somewhere and die, but reacting rather than thinking it through or talking to someone about it, I just gathering up as many of her clothes as I could from the closet, and dumped them in the driveway. I soaked em' in lighter fluid from the barbecue grill and set em' ablaze. It was a funeral pyre for my marriage. I didn't take the time to think about what I was doing and how it would affect my children."

"Oh!" She gasped.

I continued. "About that time, she turned into the driveway and was greeted by the bonfire in front of the garage. The kids were not with her and still in daycare—thank God. I'm not sure what that scene would have done to them. I'm sure the Ex recognized her wardrobe being consumed by the growing fire and knew the jig was up. As I came out of the house with another armload of her things to dump on the fire, she whipped the car around across the front lawn and raced back down the street and out of sight. I filed for divorce two days later."

Julie and I slowed our pace on the walk around the warehouse and then stopped, looking out onto the parking lot from the open door of the loading dock. "She got the good lawyer, a real shark." I groused. "I got one who talked a good game but did virtually nothing except cash my big retainer check. The whole thing was capped off with the case being assigned to a man-hater Judge—whom I am sure pronounced me guilty of every imaginable wrong the moment I set foot in her courtroom, simply based on my gender. I was decreed by the court to be a horrible father and husband. So, I only get every other weekend with my daughters except for rotating holidays. Almost every dime I make goes to child support—which she probably pockets and blows on herself, because her hot-shot, venture capitalist BF pays for everything."

"Hmm." Julie said in a knowing way—most likely drawing a parallel to her own recent relationship arrangement. "But you're *not* a horrible person, right?"

"No, of course not. The court and attorneys can sure make a person out to be evil though. Look, I'm flawed like everyone, but not horrible. I've made mistakes but never done anything malicious—well, aside from starting high-end fashion bonfires. I think I'm a good dad—friends say so. I'm kind of a doting father. My girls love me. I don't know."

Julie laughed at my self-convincing argument. "It is never fair. I'm sure that you are."

"Sometimes I wonder if it'll ever even out, Julie." I lamented. "But I'm a firm believer of what my Mother always said to me. *Things happen when you least expect it.* I get it that some of it will be good and some bad and it'll be served to you in ways you could never imagine, but it's all supposed to even out eventually. I'm just not sure if I can hold my breath that long. Eventually you gotta exhale. But who knows if you get another breath after that?"

"For nothing is hid, that shall not be made manifest; nor anything secret, that shall not be known and come to light." Julie summarized.

"Luke, right? So, you know your Bible?" I asked.

"I do. Luke it is. I believe every word in the Bible is the inspired word of God." She stated.

I thought to myself, Oh, one of *them*! And we were getting along so nicely. Well, I wasn't going to get into a religious argument with her now. Especially after she had been so nice in allowing me to let off some steam on her. Thankfully, I didn't have the time to joust spiritual forays with her as the coffee break— the *walk n' talk* as she had dubbed it was over.

"Unfortunately, it's time to close the curtain on this

discussion." I cheerfully said. "Back to some mind-numbing work."

"Same time tomorrow?" She shot back with an air of hope.

I was not expecting that. But then, I reasoned she was just being a polite co-worker. "Yes, I think I'd like some more stimulating conversation. Makes the day go by better." I said.

"I think I'd like that too. I'd like to think it's the *beginning*—uh, the start of a good routine—at work." She stumbled through her clarification with a bit of shyness and a *Mona Lisa-like* smile. She flipped her visor down and we retreated to our individual lab workstations to resume the grind of the workday.

I had to admit, Julie was continuing to make a favorable impression with me. Despite every precaution I held, there was something about her which inspired me to place a cautious trust in her. Our religious outlook was surely different and I'm sure there were other differences, but it felt good to finally tell someone my story. Up until now, I had refrained from telling anyone in my family or circle of friends about all the drama that had transpired recently for me. I had shut down, just wanting it all to go away. Outside of my interaction with my daughters, I had become somewhat of a hermit socially and emotionally. So, I silently thanked God for the therapy this Julie Douglas had provided me. She was not only a needed confidant but was rapidly becoming a real friend too.

Chapter 14.

Written in pencil onto letter stationary. It was saved in the book: The Eleventh Annual Report of the Secretary of the State Horticultural Society of Michigan – 1881

18 March 1950

The focus of our prayers was no longer as it had been for years. It had been 5 years since James had safely returned from Europe. And father no longer sat by the radio for news overseas. Our shared concerns seemed to vanish into our own thoughts and duties for work, family, and friends. We no longer prayed at night for the safe return of our son and the sons of the others I knew from the Ladies Auxiliary. One had lost her son and another a nephew. It was polite not to mention them should we hurt their feelings. We thought proper to reserve our own joys and griefs for private remembrances. In fact, we prayed for nothing together anymore. Father's health seemed to deteriorate with Diabetes, and he slept often— sometimes at the wheel of the car for brief seconds. Our distance was palpable at dinner and now even more so with the new television set which commanded our attention to maintain consistent vertical and horizontal hold of the picture and during the few programs on. We found ourselves staring at the test pattern between programs which further increased our isolation as a couple. But that was a symptom not a real cause. The ladies in my card club also complained about their husbands, their brutishness, ailments, and distance. I kept mine to myself other than scribing here. As Grandmother Chloe always taught; 'if you engage in gossip, you're just as guilty as the ones who spread it first.'

Helen Laurinda Wilcox-Phillips

The pattern of the *walk n' talks* with Julie continued every day now. Morning and afternoon break with her gave us some needed relief from the tedium. The lunch break of 30 minutes many times offered another opportunity to chat. I rarely brought anything to eat for the midday break or go out for lunch in order to save every penny so I could splurge on the kids when it was my weekend of custody. Julie never seemed to eat lunch either, so we logged significant time together. With that we grew more comfortable with each other. The topics varied. It rotated between my kids, favorite movies, food choices and our mutual love of 60's dance and rhythm and blues music. We shared rich laughs at our shared knowledge of things we both experienced as youths, and her propensity for expressing bad puns. My observations of our co-workers made her laugh out loud in that distinctive laugh of hers. We chit-chatted over superficial subject matter, but nothing overly personal about ourselves, other than the mutual dim view of our Ex's. I knew enough not to bring up the contentious topic of politics and I especially avoided religion. No sense pissing anyone off, because I knew from past experiences, I was out of the mainstream of accepted norms when it came to Christianity. I did not share the viewpoints of the ultra-conservative mindset in that.

So, we covered a lot of ground—both in topics and in laps around the warehouse. There was certainly nothing romantic developing between us. It was just a growing friendship—a true friendship, not one based on pheromones—which would invariably build up to an intimate liaison. Although on a base level, that might have been a good diversion and release, it wasn't a part of our work-place friendship. The lack of any the prospects of intimacy between us, I found to be refreshing. It was also apparent that neither one of us could handle anything approaching that sort of thing coming off bad relationships.

Since the devastation of my divorce, I had not moved on. I had been the diligent father and faithful husband. To tell the truth, I enjoyed being married and having a family. Honestly, in the 20 years of marriage, I never looked at any other woman for romantic purposes. If I were still married, I would never have given Julie a single thought. Nothing against her, but I was exceptionally happy in what my marriage provided. My focus had been on my children, wife, work, and nothing else. I was proud in being a boring dad. So, when everything fell apart in such short order, it was no wonder I now had no libido. I'm sure if I were to sit down with some psychologist, they would diagnose me as clinically depressed and prescribe some mood enhancers for me out of caution that I might become suicidal.

My "medicine" however, was to work through it. Working through tragedy or troubles had always been my family's way to approach things. There was no doubt that I inherited that character trait as well. Though, little did I know, that when I took a brief pause in adhering to the merits of independence and determination embedded in that family trait, it would get me involved in something I would regret and jeopardize my family's well-being. The situation would again confirm what my Mother had foretold. *'Things happen when you least expect them and in ways one could never predict.'*

Chapter 15.

Written on a Michigan Bell Telephone bill of $3.45 for a residence in Flint Michigan. Paid in January 1934. It was found in the cookbook, The Compleat Housewife, or, Accomplish'd Gentlewoman's Companion.

5 October 1949

It's thought-provoking how children can sense—for the most part, of a person's character. I hope I can always be the type of Grandma that the children will want to be near. I see some of Erma's grandkids are so distant with her. This is by no means their nature, so ensuring their trust and respect befalls on her.

Helen Laurinda Wilcox-Phillips

Attached to a page of the book: The Eleventh Annual Report of the Secretary of the State Horticultural Society of Michigan – 1881 with needle and black thread. Archived by Chloe Stevens, circa 1900.

"But whoso shall offend one of these little ones which believe in me, it were better for him that a millstone were hanged about his neck, and that he were drowned in the depth of the sea."

Matthew 18:6 - King James Version.

It was another long-anticipated Friday with the girls. Five o'clock and the workday was done. The transfer of the girls with the Ex was done with little conflict this time. There was just a sour look on Lanie's face—which was a standard feature of her now. I don't think she ever sported that image while we were married. Maybe the single, jet-set lifestyle wasn't turning out as good as she anticipated. Her grimace of displeasure toward me was a minimal response compared to what I usually got. The normal exchange usually included some snide remarks about, what was in her estimation, my shabby apparel. She also managed to work into the conversation the lavish plans she had with Brad, or Jason, or what's-his-face, this weekend. I had to listen to her schedules for skiing, a cruise, a big party, or other frivolous events she would attend with the other stuffed shirt, country-club types, and their trophy girlfriends. It saddened me that she was now considered one of them.

Our brief encounters usually ended with her unnecessary orders to me that I had to be here for the return exchange at 6 pm *sharp!* God, I was beginning to hate that word. There was no need for her to remind me. She knew I was the one who was always punctual in our former relationship. She on the other hand, was habitually late for everything. I guess in her mind, she was now in authority over our situation, but I viewed it as a pathetic attempt to throw what was left of her weight around—which was steadily approaching anorexic range. Though, arguing the issue was not worth the exchange of words.

Our Friday plans ended up like it usually did—The girls and I at the pizza place for takeout. While in line to order, I felt a familiar light tap on my shoulder. I turned and was surprised to see Julie behind us.

"Hey stranger!" Her mood was light. "I see we have the same taste in five-dollar pizza!"

"Hi Julie. Surprised to see you here. I thought you ate healthy."

"I do mostly during the week." She confessed. "But I cheat occasionally on the weekends. Pizza, a glass of wine and a rented movie is usually my Friday night."

"Ours too—except for the wine." I clarified. "These are my girls!"

Julie looked down, placed both her hands on her slightly bended knees and smiled generously at the girls.

"Well, it's nice to meet you." She said. "My name is Julie. What are your names?"

Both girls looked at the stranger with wide eyes. In response to her eager question, they gripped my hands and arms even more tightly and moved closer to and slightly behind my legs to shield themselves from this unknown person. When neither offered up an answer to Julie, I interjected.

"This is Elizabeth, and this is Mary," I said, respectively gesturing toward each child with my restrained hands.

Julie fawned over them as was common for any adult to do. "It's nice to meet you Elizabeth and Mary. You are both so cute. I like your shoes." She said pointing to their matching, pink canvas sneakers.

Still no reaction from either girl. Julie straightened and looked back up to me.

"They're a little shy around new people." I half whispered as if the girls couldn't hear me. It was something else all adults did around kids.

Julie slightly nodded and squinted, mouthing the words, "its Ok."

"Number 27." came a voice over a loudspeaker. Our order was up.

"That's us already!" I informed Julie. "A cheese pizza doesn't take long."

She let out a noticeable sigh. "Have a great night. It was nice to meet you both." Julie again stated to the girls in a heartfelt way. We moved to the front of the pickup line for our pizza. Passing her again on the way out after paying, she half whispered, "Maybe we can do this *all together* another weekend?

I paused. Hmm, *all together*? I cautiously thought but said positively, "That would be great! See you at work Monday."

"Ok, enjoy your weekend!" she replied as we exited the pizza place. I could sense a bit of sadness in her voice and could feel her eyes watching us as we crossed the parking lot to the vehicle. With the pizza in my left hand, my right-hand holding Elizabeth's, and as she held hands with Mary, we must have looked like the picture-perfect family to Julie. It made me especially cherish the relationship I had with my girls, but it also made me sad that Julie would not be getting that same feeling from her five-dollar pizza and bottle of wine. Loneliness is a terrible thing to feel yourself. It is even sadder to watch in someone else.

My thoughts continued a moment longer on Julie. I suppose I should take her at her word about wanting to share pizza *all together* some time. I made a promise that I would invite her for that soon. As we drove a few miles, it was quiet in the truck. My thoughts of Julie were interrupted from the back seat by Mary.

"Daddy, can my hair be *red* someday?"

Apparently, she had been thinking about Julie too.

"Oh, like my friend Julie?" I was curious as to what she was thinking.

"Yeah, and curly like hers. I liked it." said Elizabeth.

"Me too." said Mary.

"Well, I don't think so. Your hair is pretty like it is. Straight and brown is very pretty—like your Mommas. I don't think it'll turn red and curly like Julie's." I said.

The girls didn't seem overly disappointed by my answer. Their hair was indeed pretty as it was. Each girl had rich, shiny brown hair with auburn highlights—especially in the summer months when they spent more time in the sun.

"She's nice." stated Mary.

I was surprised she had assessed Julie's character and was willing to share it. "How about you Liz, you think she's nice?" I asked.

"Yeah," was the simple answer.

That was the end of any conversation about Julie for the remainder of the weekend. But I took note of the girl's interest in her. If the girls like her, that's another and particularly important plus in my book. Both of my girls were painfully shy around strangers and I was happy they were at this age. For them, a bit of caution around any unfamiliar adult is prudent, but I was sure I could trust my kids around Julie. As I reasoned this out in my head, I could feel a slight smile spreading across my face and felt a noticeable degree or two of increased warmth spreading in my heart. "Nice job Julie." I said under my breath.

Chapter 16.

Written on letter stationary. It was discovered in a blank envelope which was inside the cookbook, The Compleat Housewife, or, Accomplish'd Gentlewoman's Companion. It was adjacent to page 324 which had the recipe: To prevent Fits in Children.

4 April 1960

The grandchildren would sidle up to me for one of Gramma's back rubs. They took delight in getting them and I took delight in giving. I believe this new generation shows appreciation far better than the previous likely due to my status as senior member and matriarch of this clan. They always ask for and then wolf down my rolled-out sugar cookies which they claim to be 'better than Mommas.' I use the same tin biscuit cutter that's been in this kitchen for near a hundred years. Some of the cookies are out of shape but the children don't seem to mind. My own meals are spare affairs gathering the leftovers into what Janelle said were doctored-up meals. I thought it was being thrifty and they weren't so awfully bad. Not compared to times in the Great Depression when all we had was beans, onions and few carrots in the root cellar and a barrel of salt pork that always became rancid my March and the warmer weather. But we ate as it was all we had once the salt was rinsed and rinsed, and the lot was boiled long into a soup to kill any bacteria and most of the flavor. I would agree that was doctored. I only cook fancy meals these days for Thanksgiving, Christmas Day, and Easter. The pennies I save from Fathers pension I spend on sweets for the grandchildren which I keep in a crystal candy dish. They like the miniature chocolate bars best based on the number of wrappers I find on the floor around the rocker. I smile when I hear the telltale tinkle of the glass lid being lifted when little fingers help themselves. Parental warnings that candy will spoil their dinner go unheeded as my place as a Grandparent is not to enforce rules. I have earned the right to be exempt from them.

Helen Laurinda Wilcox-Phillips

A couple of weeks later the girls and I found ourselves in the same Friday night routine. But by Saturday mid-morning they found themselves a little bored. It was too cold for them to go outside and "blow the stink off them" as my Grandmother used to tell me and my siblings when we were younger. The girl's inside play had gotten too rambunctious and they were getting on each other's nerves with small skirmishes erupting between them. I think they were a little tired of me too. I wondered if they could use a third person in the mix as a diversion. I instantly thought of Julie. Not only would it be a different dynamic for the afternoon, but it would be nice for me to see her too, I thought. Our relationship at work had grown into something a little more than acquaintances and I missed being around her.

I questioned the girls. "How would you like it if my friend Julie visited us this afternoon and ate dinner with us today?"

Both stopped their latest dispute over their size of their "territory" on the living room area rug and stared at me. As was their custom, there was no immediate response from them. The prospects of unfamiliar people invading their surroundings made them freeze. They said nothing.

"Whadya say, Elizabeth? Mary? You liked her. Would it be ok?"

Elizabeth spoke first. "I guess."

"How 'bout you Mary?" I repeated. She nodded her head after first seeing what Liz's decision was.

"Ok, I'll call her in a minute and see if she's available—just for a couple hours. We'll have dinner with her and then we can have the rest of the weekend to ourselves."

"Ok." "Ok." Was the dual response.

I went to the kitchen, called her number and she accepted the invitation with enthusiasm. She had nothing planned and wanted to know if she could bring anything.

"Just yourself!" I said declining her offer. We agreed on the time of around four-ish. It would be a casual get-together, and I warned her it would also be a simple meal—explaining that the girls were picky eaters. She didn't mind. I did not go into the fact that there was not much in my cupboards anyway and it was too late to go grocery shopping. However, there was still a couple hours to get the house in order and give the girls a quick bath to freshen them up a bit.

Right on time, Julie knocked at the door, entered, and only briefly glanced at me. She went directly to the living room and straight to the girls. With a big smile she fawned over them again as she did at the pizza place. She complimented them on their still wet hair from their recent baths and adored their outfits. They wore nothing special. Both had matching but faded and well-worn blue jeans, little sweatshirt tops with unicorns on the front and pink socks. They smiled and looked at each item of clothing on themselves as Julie pointed them out with her commentary. I thought maybe Julie was a little over the top, but the girls didn't seem to mind the flattery at all since they were on their home turf. She was highly enthusiastic but not enough for the girls to retreat into their shyness. She walked the fine line between enthusiasm and adult fakeness. It was just enough to bring out some warmth in the girls.

I took in the scene and whispered to myself. "This might turn out to be a very good idea! Glad I thought of it."

"What do you girls want to do?" Julie inquired.

No immediate response from them, but I interjected. "The girls like board games. You three could play something at the table until dinner is ready."

They both nodded and proceeded to the dining room. The girls propped themselves up to reach the table by kneeling on pillows they had retrieved from the couch.

"I haven't played this one in years." Julie confessed. "It's my favorite. I was rather good when I was your age. I might win." She teased.

"You've got your work cut out for you." I said. "The girls play all the time. They beat me consistently."

"Yeah, but Mary cheats!" announced Liz. "I do not! Daddy!" cried Mary.

"Girls! Be on your best behavior," I said sternly. "No arguing, remember?"

I retreated to the kitchen to prepare the meal. "Nothing fancy for sure!" I raised my voice toward the dining room. "I hope you like chicken."

No answer. The game had begun and consumed their

attention. I heard the familiar popping sound of the plastic cube in the middle of the board game which shook the dice. That was followed by the tap, tapping of the game pieces to count out their advance around the board.

I continued the meal prep for what I knew the girls *would* eat—pan fried, breaded, boneless chicken breasts, green bean casserole with mushroom soup—as long as it had crunchy onion rings on top and instant mashed potatoes. I hoped it would be a passable meal for Julie.

In another 20 minutes, the casserole in the oven would be done. I walked back to the dining room and found that the board game had broken up and they had retreated to the living room floor. All three of them were laying on their stomachs—their elbows propping them up. Each had chosen a doll from the plastic toy bin and were in the process of changing their outfits and accessorizing.

They were oblivious to me as I again announced the menu. "I hope you like chicken." Julie looked up. "Sure. That sounds great. Huh, girls?"

"Yeah, I'm hungry." "Me too." The girls chimed in.

They went back to playing. I paused to absorb the tender, family-like scene before me. It was one I had forgotten how much I enjoyed seeing when I was married. I was jarred by how much I missed it and my heart sank a bit. In the good old days, Lanie did this kind of play with the girls often, while I was in my usual space, in the kitchen making dinner.

This scene however, seemed different. I got the sense that Julie genuinely enjoyed herself with the child's play and was not just going through the motions as Lanie seemed to at times. Julie was not just trying to be a polite guest entertaining the children, she was also expressing a kind of parental love for Liz and Mary as she chatted with them in their childlike language. I saw how Julie periodically stopped her play to reach out and lovingly brush back the hair from their faces or give them a quick and light rub on their shoulders or backs. The girls leaned into the attention.

I was impressed how Julie instinctively expressed her maternal instincts. It was equally evident that she was receiving invisible rewards of affection from the girls. The sinking of my heart, a few minutes earlier, was replaced with a realization of what was happening. It was clear. This dynamic of a *complete* family was missing from Julie's life, the girl's, and mine too. It was good on so many levels for all of us. I would have to think through this *revelation*. But I would do that later. Dinner was ready.

The sparse meal that followed was enjoyed by all three of them. I was proud the girls *ate big*—as we called it, without any prodding from me. Some of that almost always occurred at mealtime. In its place, however, smiles and laughter accompanied this dinner.

With the meal over and the girls excused from the table, they settled in front of the television and popped in a DVD animated movie.

"Can I help clear the table?" Julie asked.

"Sure. There's not much to clear though. Thanks." I was happy for her company.

"They are *wonderful* girls." Julie gushed. "I bet they miss their Mommy and Daddy being together."

Oh, wow, I thought. She had also been analyzing the situation. The family-like dynamic of this evening had obviously made an impression on Julie's thoughts too.

"Well, you would think." I sighed. "But sometimes I wonder if the Ex thought of that when she was making her decision to jeopardize it. These days I wonder how much hands-on attention they get from her to replace the loss of the family unit. They seem to be a little starved for it when I get them. Thank you for stepping in to provide some maternal care tonight, Julie."

"Oh no," Julie stepped back, "I would never interfere with their Mother's role. Maybe I shouldn't stay too long so I don't impose myself on your time together."

I interrupted forcefully. "No, no, I think the girls really like you. I so appreciate you being here. You're not taking anybody's place. It's all good. I don't know how to tell you this, but they took to you more than I thought they would. You've seen what they're like around strangers initially. They usually cling pretty close to me. But you're a natural with kids. You're great! I think they think so too."

Julie just smiled without any words, but her eyes moistened with tears. There was something else going on in her thoughts besides a reaction to my compliment. Not wanting her to cry, I quickly tried to move past the subject. Thankfully, her tears evaporated in few seconds. And her voice returned.

"Ok. You sure?" She asked.

"Oh yes, very!" I enthusiastically replied.

With that, a warm and inviting smile began to spread across her freckled face along with a bit of a blush onto her cheeks and neck. She was now slightly embarrassed from my gushing praise and pleased that she had passed muster from the girl's standpoint and mine too. She reached out and slipped a soft hand onto the top of mine with a gentle squeeze, softly saying, "I'm glad."

A bit startled by the physical contact, I replied, "Uh, I am too."

The awkward moment was broken up by Mary entering the kitchen with a question. "I'm still hungry. Do we have ice cream?"

"Yes, we do!" I pulled away from Julie's touch. "Give me a few minutes so we can wash dishes. There are no clean bowls. When we're done in here, we'll dish up some ice cream."

Satisfied with my answer, Mary went back to the video and Julie and I busied ourselves with the task of washing and drying dishes. Our efficient teamwork on this simple task also gave me a warm feeling, that frankly, I had never had before when married. Lanie never did dishes. Making dinner and the cleanup—that was my domain. It was nice to have a partner in the kitchen. My mind wandered to what *other* kind of *partner* Julie Douglas might make.

Chapter 17.

Attached to page 228 of the cookbook, The Compleat Housewife, or, Accomplish'd Gentlewoman's Companion with a woman's hat pin. That page had the recipes: The Lady Allen's Water, and Plague-Water. Archived by Chloe Stevens, circa 1900.

"For we wrestle not against flesh and blood, but against principalities, against powers, against the rulers of the darkness of this world, against spiritual wickedness in high places."

Ephesians 6:12 – King James Version.

Written on the top margin of the front page of the newspaper: The Dearborn Independent—which was considered to have published anti-Semitic content at times. From May 1920. The page was inside the back cover of the book: The Eleventh Annual Report of the Secretary of the State Horticultural Society of

Michigan – 1881

24 May 1920

The truth has always been out there for people to seek in order to lessen their stupidity, but they prefer to seek out only their known biases and those of their like-minded groups, published in their own prejudiced publications, thereby entrenching their stupidity.

    Helen Laurinda Wilcox

An excerpt from Helen's essay: Where Do We Find Ourselves Today?

"...the rich—who could afford to pay to compensate for their earthly transgressions, got in line in front of poor folk who were stuck with their sins. On account of the church wasn't accepting I. O. U.'s on a sinner's debt, the poor were left with the choice of either purchasing a ticket to Heaven or pay the mortgage with their take home pay."

It was another Monday—indistinguishable from any other. Julie and I began our afternoon coffee break walk n' talk around the warehouse portion of the building but barely got in a lap, when we were interrupted by the Hiring Manager, Mr. Welch, who handed me a folded and stapled piece of paper. It was the same kind of paper as the faded, old, green ledgers we used to log-in customer data. I opened it. It was a hand scribbled note that looked like it had been written by someone with a Parkinson's palsy. It was Orrin's unmistakable penmanship. It read:

> *Mr. Jacobs,*
>
> *I'd like for you to attend services at my church this Sunday. 9 am sharp! 3745 Linden Avenue. Please feel free to bring a guest. I look forward to your attendance.*
>
> *W. F. Orrin*

"Huh." I huffed. "It's from the old man."

"Mr. Orrin?" Julie asked in surprise.

"Yeah, he wants me to come to his church service this Sunday. It reads more like an order rather than invitation though." I scoffed. "Says I can bring a guest."

"You going?" She asked with a light tone to her voice. Was she offering to be my date to this?

I ignored the opening. I didn't want to drag another person into this. I didn't even want to go myself. "How can I refuse?" I reasoned. "If I don't show, he seems to be the type to hold a grudge. This is a lot of extra pressure I don't need added to me in order to keep this crappy job. Good thing it's not my weekend with the girls or I'd have to refuse the offer."

"Well," Julie explained, "it shouldn't be too bad. I'm sure it's a Christian service—born-again types I hear. You'll hear a charismatic *Amen* now and again, some organ music and classic gospel songs."

"Did he ever put pressure on you to attend? I asked. "You spend a lot more time with him than me."

"He did once, but I told him I was a life-long member of the Central Methodist church here in town. So, he let it drop. It'll just be an hour or so for you." She added forlornly. Her upbeat mood slowly faded from her earlier optimism at the dashed prospects of attending the service with me.

I ignored her mood shift. I could not imagine a first date—not that this would qualify as one, with anyone in an evangelical church. My thoughts were focused on how this additional hurdle in my life came about. What was it that I said to him? I must have been a little too enthusiastic about his *church mission.* Now he thinks I'm interested. I resolved right then and there, to never elaborate on anything again—whether in my resume or in person to anyone. Making my thoughts known always seemed to get me in deeper crap.

So, here I was again at a familiar juncture. I was again fighting to keep my head above the vortex that tried to suck me into the *just go-along-with-it* process—as some had called it in alternative media in the late 60's. *The Man* was again targeting a straggler like me with his relentless effort to indoctrinate into the *Establishment.* Well, now I could finally say I had met *The Man.* Turns out it was Mr. Wendell Francis

Orrin.

Chapter 18.

Sewn with needle and red thread onto a page of the Book: The Great Galveston Disaster. Archived by Chloe Stevens, circa 1900.

"Be not deceived: evil communications corrupt good manners."

1 Corinthians 15:33 – King James Version

Typewritten onto the front and back of a blank folded recipe card. It was in the pages of the cookbook, The Compleat Housewife, or, Accomplish'd Gentlewoman's Companion.

This inequality, being the exact opposite of where the real strength, responsibility and due respect should fall in our modern day is indefensible. The old wisdom still rules but it is hard pressed to explain why it should. I can cite countless ways that it is also the way in my family and has been for generations. I try to change the current of it but with little success. I should accept that there is little hope it will ever change. But steadfast in its inherent truth, I shall continue to pray for it anyway knowing that it will square with God.

Helen Laurinda Wilcox

Two days passed. Wednesday morning at punch-in time I was greeted by another page of green ledger flagged to my timecard. Reluctantly unfolding it, it read:

Mr. Jacobs,

Please see me first thing this morning.

W. F. Orrin.

My shoulders sunk in depression. "Now what?" I groaned.

I slowly walked up the flight of stairs to Orrin's office, knocked, entered, and was asked to be seated in the chair before his desk. It was like he never left from my last visit here. He had on the same suit and tie—or one just like it. Seated behind his desk, he was also wearing his black, frayed, and rumpled overcoat in the cold and clammy atmosphere. I swear he was shuffling the same papers on his desk as my last visit here. The only difference this time, the stack of customer checks on the right side of his desk was a few inches higher.

"You wanted to see me?" I meekly asked.

"Yes. Yessssss," he dragged out the word. "My

thoughts were interrupted the other day."

I silently agreed. Must have been caused by the trance he fell into when I departed his office the last meeting.

"As I was *thinking,* you have experience that I feel would be helpful to our very important work."

"Sure." That was my calculated reply—trying to find the sweet spot between mild interest but not over-enthusiasm.

"I think you will find it financially beneficial to you." He paused. "And to your *children* too."

My children? Why was there a mention about them in this conversation? And it was an unsettling emphasis on the word. How did he even know I had children? Did I write that on my application? Why would he hang on the word *children*? It sounded a bit sinister. I said nothing and let him continue.

"Your background as spokesperson for the International Genome Project would be helpful to us." He elaborated. "I've read your press releases and saw a few of your press briefings. They were presented in clear fashion and understandable without…" He paused to search for a socially correct word to describe his meaning that would not be offensive. After a long moment he continued his sentence. "…presented without an *accent.* You see, our clientele for this initiative is for *traditional* Christians." He smiled and paused again to make sure I got his drift. I did. It was for white folks only. If I hadn't gotten the message by now, I'm sure he would have laid an index finger to the side of his nose, winked and come around the desk to elbow me in the ribs with a "Capisce? Know what I mean?" That was not going to be necessary. I fully comprehended his meaning and his racist views. I suppressed my true feelings with my flat response. "I understand Mr. Orrin." All too well I understood.

Satisfied he made his point clear, he continued. "You would maintain your current status in the Prep Lab for now of course, and complete your current daily workload, but as our company needs expand, at a point when we launch our new initiative, I would then require you to take on the added responsibility of our public relations needs, in much the same capacity as you did for the International Genome folks. Of course, we would increase your compensation for this additional workload. I'll have Mrs. Orrin put through the paperwork for the increase in the next pay period. That's the way we do things here. We step up when called upon in a team effort. And for that our team members are rewarded. You wouldn't object to a bump up in pay, would you? I am looking at this figure for you."

He scribbled something on a scrap of paper and shoved it across the desk to me. It was done as dramatically as if he were someone in a high-stakes poker game when they shove all their chips in the pot as they call a bluff.

I choked when seeing the amount. "Guh, No! I wouldn't' mind." It was close to six figures. "That's very generous Mr. Orrin." Tossing aside any scruples I usually maintained, I replied, "I would be glad to help in any way I could in my area of expertise." That's what I said out loud. However, as I did, I felt the dreaded prospect of being more ingratiated into this company drop on my shoulders like a horse collar.

A larger question swirled in my brain though. How would I walk that tightrope of accepting more money here but not selling myself out to promote the goals of an obvious bigot? Was I to become a second "lap dog" like his mangy, four-legged Maltese, Zephaniah? The motivations seemed the same. Do what Orrin wants. The pet gets extra treats. I get extra cash. Quid pro quo. I would wrestle with the morality of it later, but for now, the bottom line was all I could think of. Don't look *a gift Orrin in the mouth!*

"Very well, thank you Mr. Jacobs." He went back to rummaging papers around on his desk. He said nothing else. I guess the interview was over and the deal with the Devil was consummated. I silently retreated from the room—glad for two things. One, the pay raise would help me make rent this month. And two, that I had developed a muscle memory in Orrin's office, which allowed me to retrace my steps and avoid stepping in any of Zephaniah's dog droppings on my way out.

I then began my workday in the Prep Lab cautiously optimistic about the prospects of increased income and responsibilities. I would mention the promotion to Julie at break to get her take on it but would avoid telling her about the pay increase part. I got the feeling that that would not go over so well.

Chapter 19.

Clipped from an older publication of the Bible and sewn with needle and thread onto a page of the book: The Great Galveston Disaster. Archived by Chloe Stevens, circa 1900.

"I will therefore that the younger women marry, bear children, guide the house, give none occasion to the adversary to speak reproachfully."

1 Timothy 5:14 - King James Version

Curiously written in pencil next to the above verse, in the margin of the same page, were two question marks. "? ?" The handwriting could be either Helen's or Chloe's.

Written on 8-1/2x11 inch composition paper. It was folded in half and found in the pages of the book: The Eleventh Annual Report of the Secretary of the State Horticultural Society of Michigan – 1881.

9 April 1944 – Easter Sunday

I had been shamed at our weekly card club into attending Esther's church for today's Easter service. It was not what I expected. Her comment about my dress put me off from the jump. Granted, it is a bit old, but I didn't see anything wrong with it and it was all I had in the closet to wear besides housedresses. It was a beautiful spring day and I thought the bright pink peony flowers on it fit the occasion. Esther said it was a bit flashy for church. I wondered whether I was attending a church service or a fashion show. I should rip the dress into strips, crochet it into a rag rug and give it to her. Then she'll have to look at it every day on her kitchen floor.

I was also put off by the sermon. I expected one to befit the day to be on the Good News of the Resurrection. But the Preacher jawed at us about Scripture saying a woman's place is the family and we should hold our tongues. Said our reward was having children and keeping house or you'll be helping the devil. Timothy says so. So, we shouldn't go a following anything the First Lady or her crowd says. I haven't read all of it, but I'm quite sure she's not mentioned in the Gospel. I've had four children already by myself at home with a midwife and I don't need Timothy or any other man telling me how it's done. I don't suspect we'll be going back.

Helen Laurinda Wilcox-Phillips

The Sunday of my first visit to Orrin's church was

sunny but bitterly cold. The clock on the truck dashboard read 8:45 am. I didn't want to leave the warmth of the cab, but I couldn't be late for the service since I was told in the Orrin fashion, Nine O'clock *sharp!* I accepted that this was now most likely to be part of my weekly work routine. Attend church—get paid bigger bucks! I crumpled Orrin's note and stuffed it into my pocket. Taking a deep breath and pulling up my collar tightly around my neck, I opened the truck door and made my way up the un-shoveled sidewalk into the back vestibule of the starkly protestant-style church.

Inside the sanctuary, I noticed the bland white walls and plain wooden benches with no other adornment of any kind. This was completely different from any Catholic church in my experience. There was just a single step up to a riser at the front of the church and a simple wooden cross behind it on the front wall of the building. No stained-glass windows—only plain clear ones completed the bare space. For all intents and purposes this might easily be mistaken for a VFW rental hall.

I thought to strategically seat myself near the outside of a pew near the back of the church in order to stay as inconspicuous as possible in the slowly filling church. I didn't want to appear too eager to be up front in the first couple rows or a complete slacker by choosing a back-row seat. From my position, I figured that no one would have to crawl over me to get in or out of the pew. As it turned out, with the sparse crowd, there was plenty of room in front and behind me.

Watching the procession of other attendees file into the building, I was struggling to hold back an anxiety I have always felt come over me in new surroundings with unfamiliar people. There's no doubt my daughters inherited that same trait. Finally, something about this orderly scene of the incoming church goers began to initiate something within me. I felt I had witnessed this all before somehow. My anxiety rose within me to an alarming level. The familiarity of the scene was about to break a dam of emotions that could no longer be held back, and I was about to be swept away from the reality of the moment and transported back in time to reliving a memory buried deep within me. This memory was something I had rarely thought of over the last four-plus decades of my life. As it now flooded to the surface of my thoughts in full force, I was again filled with every painful detail I had already lived through once.

Specifically, what triggered this feeling in me, was the orderly procession of unfamiliar men in their long dark overcoats as they entered the church. It served to release the buried memory of the single most consequential event of my life. This unfolding scene was all eerily the same as one I had experienced decades before as a small child, when a similar group of men had entered our home.

As I sat there in the church pew, just as back then, these men were unaware of me, but I could feel the bitter cold breeze brought in with them from the open doors. It was fanned by their long black overcoats as they brushed by me. These men—the members of the Church Council in their long "robes" entered first—

with their purposeful procession to the front two rows. This was a sign to all assembled of their importance and the rightful recognition they should receive from it. They were followed in tow by their nondescript wives in drab clothing with their purses and children—as if they were merely possessions of the men carried by servants. Each woman was outwardly expressionless, but I could sense that they all shared a mutual sadness—if you can call it that, from their second-class status of this arrangement. Every one of them was saddled with a burden of an accepted responsibility that their male counterparts did not have. To me, this was all a completely familiar scenario—in all its symbolism and sentiments, to one I had experienced a fateful morning over forty years ago. Today's Sunday morning pageant of conventional ritualism was a reenactment of that day—which brought forth every feeling of childhood fear and anxiety that I experienced on the day of my Father's death.

The feelings were overwhelming. They washed over me as if to drown me in this distant memory now resurfaced. My heart raced and I physically gasped for air while I shook my head in a futile attempt to clear it. However, the recollections of that fateful day persisted. They were as real to me, in this moment, as if it were happening all over again. There was nothing I could do now but to relive it.

Chapter 20.

Printed on a sympathy card to Helen. Received after the death of her husband in October of 1958. The words were circled in blue ink. The card was in the cookbook, The Compleat Housewife, or, Accomplish'd Gentlewoman's Companion.

"Now she that is a widow indeed, and desolate, trusteth in God, and continueth in supplications and prayers night and day."
    1 Timothy 5:5 – King James Version

Written in black ink on blank newsprint using a fountain pen. It is one of the earliest dated entries found in any of the cookbooks. It was inside the front cover of the book: The Eleventh Annual Report of the Secretary of the State Horticultural Society of Michigan – 1881.

22 May 1889

The grass hasn't even grown over the opening yet or allowed us to plant geraniums at the grave for Decoration Day. And here comes a letter from Veteran Affairs office in Washington D.C. Someone inquiring about Uncle Dilizon's Military Pension from the Civil War.

For many years he had been collecting a $12 dollars per month benefit medical pension until his death. Uncle said he come down with pleurisy damage in his left lung from sleeping on the cold ground at the *encampment of his brigade at Alexandria, Virginia. He had powerful coughing spells all the time he lived with us in his old age. I remember him telling us that. It was one of many stories he proudly told of his time with the 15th Michigan Volunteer Infantry.*

Truth be told, Uncle Dilizon was conflicted about marching for Lincoln's Army. On the one hand, he believed the States should stay in the Union, but emancipating the Negros was also an issue. No one should be a slave. Neither man nor woman of any color. But he also held segregationist views here in the north and that of men over women. He thought the south was doing what they thought was right for themselves about slavery and it was not the duty of the north to change that. Their way of living had always used slave labor and that is truly not plum with the Lord when it is their times to meet him at the Gates. We all knew enough not to discuss it with him as it would just cause a stir in the family. Uncle has his chance now to explainin hisself before his Lord.

Now here I gets this letter says a woman named Sarah is trying to claim his pension because they were married years ago by a preacher in a church she cannot remember and then Uncle abandoned her for the War.

It is true, she is from Livingston County and that is where he lived back then around age 20 before he enlisted. But her description of him is all wrong in the application to the Veterans Affairs. He has always had sandy brown hair, blue eyes, and a fair complexion and only about 5 foot, 7 inches tall. This woman claims he was over 6 feet tall, thin, and dark hair and mustache.

I feel sad for this woman. I understand she is a widow and indigent like so many these days. $12 dollars a month is a lot of money and would be a blessing to her. Even though it is against the Commandments to steal, I won't blame her for wanting to claim the pension. There is not much help for a widow of 67 years other than charity.

    Chloe Stevens

I could see it all so vividly again. On a cold December morning in 1958, my Mother was attending to her four children. I was the second oldest at age three and a half. My older sister would have her fifth birthday next month and my two other siblings were ages two years and five months respectively—both still in diapers.

I was sitting on the linoleum floor playing with my truck. It was a metal navy blue jeep with a star on the hood. This was no "army" jeep. My Father was a veteran who served on a Navy destroyer in the Pacific in World War II. He wouldn't think of having *army khaki green* in his house. He proudly rooted for Navy over Army every year while watching the game on our black and white console TV. I was told he was quick to brag to his fellow workers who were Army vets when Navy managed to win.

Suddenly a gust of bitter December wind entered the

kitchen and swept across the floor, followed by a procession of men entering the small house. Their ominous long black overcoats brushed over my head. They paid no attention to me, but I scrambled to the safety of under the kitchen table to avoid them. What soon followed would be the defining moment of my life and that of my family as well. To this day, it plays the most significant part of what shapes and challenges me.

The men in their long coats continued to file into the tiny kitchen. One by one they entered and crowded together but no one said anything. My Mother, with my baby sister in her arms, came to the kitchen with mouth agape at this site and stared without saying a word. She was incapable in the moment to utter a syllable about what was happening. Still not one man said anything. Their eyes uniformly avoiding my Mother's anxiety filled gaze.

Then, emerging from the center of this mass of men in overcoats and grim faces was the Parish Priest dressed in his vestments of a black hooded Alb and the traditional black biretta hat. Seeing my Mother, but staying a relatively long distance from her, he removed the biretta from his head, paused, and then flatly stated, "I am sorry to inform you that John was killed earlier this morning in a vehicle crash while he was at work."

The facts were plainly stated to my Mother. There were no additional words added to the announcement to soften the shock. There was no physical embrace to comfort her by the Priest or any of the other men who had gathered for the announcement. My Mother, still clutching her youngest in her arms—even in this moment of unimaginable tragedy, had to continue in her responsibilities of nurturing and protecting her child. She stood in stunned disbelief and said nothing.

A voice from one of the men in the middle of the crowd offered only a few more details. "John's delivery van apparently ran into the back of a tractor-trailer parked on the side of the road in the pre-dawn hours." Other particulars of why and how it had happened would never be known by any of us.

My Mother, still with no words or noticeable emotion, slowly sank into a chair in the hallway just outside the crowded kitchen and my older sister and I rushed to her lap.

With the completion of their initial duty of informing my Mother of the devastating news that my Father had died that brutally cold morning, it must have been the cue for the men in their long robes, led by the Priest, to recite a Rosary for the repose of the soul of the deceased. The Priest began the cadence and the men repeated the refrain of the lengthy prayer. Now, some of the men's faces became recognizable to me. They were men who served along with my Father in the Knights of Columbus chapter associated with the Parish. I remember seeing them in church.

In the middle of their Rosary, came a secondary wave of women into the crowded kitchen. Most of these women were familiar to my Mother, sister, and me. They were comprised of our Grandmothers, Aunts, and a couple of the neighbor ladies. They had heard the awful news and descended upon our house—but not before they somehow had the time to produce food to bring with them. It was like they were arriving for Thanksgiving dinner or a picnic with a dish to pass. Each carried a bowl of potato salad or macaroni and cheese or desserts.

They entered the kitchen but did not immediately advance toward my Mother to comfort her or shed tears with her. For most of them, you could tell that they had been crying. They wore the awfulness of the news upon their faces. However, my Mother was still without tears or outward emotion. She was unable to calculate the depth of her grief.

The reason the women had paused in their arrival or to make any efforts to comfort my Mother was because it would be improper—even at this devastating time, to interrupt the saying of the men's prayer. Thus, they stepped back, bowed their heads, and prayed along with them.

One Aunt finally did slip through the room to a back bedroom to bring forth the other child, my brother, from his crib and place him on my Mother's lap with the rest of her children. Her thinking must have been that it would be a shame if he missed out on the intended blessing that this sterile reading of church supplication would surely bring to us.

At the end of the seemingly endless formality, the men looked around at each other waiting for their next cue. The Priest again stated how sorry he was for our loss and would be in touch with Mother soon for funeral arrangements. He put his biretta back on his head, bundled himself tighter in his vestments and left—leaving the kitchen door slightly ajar, which allowed another icy blast to flood the room.

The men, their ceremonial duties of informing the widow officially being over and seeing the bowls of food the women had brought, moved toward the kitchen counters. The women scrambled to accommodate them in this impromptu buffet with plates and forks retrieved from cupboards and drawers. Newly washed ones—still in the rack on the sink drain board, clattered as they were retrieved for lunch service for the men. Someone started a pot of coffee—its smell filling the tiny kitchen and mixing with the competing odors of men's colognes.

With their official duty of bearers-of-bad-news ended, the men dined—all still with their overcoats on. They huddled in groups of two or three and engaged in small talk. A few of them mumbled comments that they apparently wanted none of the womenfolk to hear. Some suppressed light chuckles. All of it having nothing to do with the reason that they had assembled. None of it would be of any help for my Mother to cope with what had just transpired to radically change our existence.

Mercifully, after completion of their first responsibilities to the men in long robes, a couple of my dear Aunts did slip in next to my Mother on the edge of her chair to offer hugs, tears, and soft words of comfort. But they too were soon summoned back to the kitchen to meet the insignificant needs of providing second helpings, more clean plates, or refills on coffee for the men. This priority of ritual and hierarchy took precedent over consoling my Mother, and it continued that way until the last of them left.

Then the women, one by one, said goodbye to my Mother. All shed a few more tears, shared a few more hugs and pledged assurances that she could call them if she ever needed anything. Words of encouragement were offered by each. "Don't let yourself fall apart." "Remember you have the children."

Although I'm sure the words of support were said with good intentions, they rang hollow. They were nothing more that platitudes—things people often say upon their exit from a sad situation. The words are used to fill the void left when there is nothing that can help mend the situation or make any difference at all.

Was there anything that my Mother needed?

Yes! She needed her husband. She needed the Father of her four children. She needed to know what she was supposed to do now. She needed an answer as to how she would provide for her family. She needed help on how to get through the next days, hours, minutes and even her next breath, without completely collapsing and giving up. She needed for this to all be just a bad dream. However, coldly, unemotionally, it was not. What she *would* need in order to survive, she would have to find out largely by herself. And remarkably, this challenge—which settled upon her so suddenly, was not unlike the same kinds of challenges that so many other women—in my family and countless others, had to endure before her. That is because society and the established roles of men and women had already been defined in that way thousands of years before.

As the last of the cars departed the driveway, the house was left with an eerie silence. The winter morning was again as it was about 90 minutes earlier. My younger brother and sister were unaware of the implication of any of the earlier activity. They were back to their immediate needs of diaper changes and baby bottles of formula.

Still in the same chair, Mother looked down at her previously spotless kitchen floor. In our home, it was expected that everyone removed their shoes and boots and leave them on a rug at the back-door landing before entering the house. Most of the men in long robes couldn't have known that house rule. However, those that did—who had been to our house before, never bothered on this occasion to abide by it. My Mother would have to be the one to mop up the salt residue and puddles of water left by the melting snow that they had tracked in on their footwear. It was up to her as there were no other women to help in the resumption of life in this house. The ones who were here earlier couldn't help. They were needed in their own houses to prepare their husband's dinners— which were expected on the table at their regular time.

Although my younger sister and brother were too young to grasp anything that had occurred, my older sister and I knew something terribly wrong had just happened which would surely affect us, but we too failed to comprehend the extent of it.

In our innocence, we were unaware of the complete gravity and meaning of a *vehicle crash*. What was the significance of the entrance and exit of so many strangers in their long, dark robes? We knew nothing of the things they mentioned. What were, funeral arrangements, life insurance, workers compensation benefits and more? Why were all the women crying at various times, but not Mother? The lasting lesson for us from this experience was that some men in long black robes had entered our lives briefly and ceremoniously. They presented troubling news, and for that they received respect, reverence, and a meal—which was solely reserved for them, and then they left.

In later years, I would learn that what I had witnessed as a three-year-old, was a long-established cultural norm that took precedence over even a mother in her moment of anguish. It would be the same types of established protocols that she would repeatedly have to rise above and negotiate through, with truly little help from any man or anyone else in the immediate future, and for decades to come.

My Mother just had everything in her world of importance to her—the dynamics of her immediate family, change in an instant. Yet, that fact wouldn't cause a ripple of change on the surface of that stagnant pond of previous behaviors or attitudes of men in leadership.

Reflecting to that day, I was astounded that the men had completed their limited duties and were duly rewarded for their meager efforts. But for the ones whom you would think would also find it in their duty to take some additional responsibility for the plight of those who were now left vulnerable, or offer a modicum of help in the aftermath, sadly for most it would be business as usual. There would be a continuation of what humankind had established millennia ago. Namely, that some—most of them men, assume the leadership and ceremonial roles but stop short of anything consequential. The rest—most of them women, must fend for themselves.

For my Mother, she knew she would have to alone draw on her generations of inherited strong-willed fortitude for survival and knew enough to not expect anything from anyone.

The recovered memory began to fade. As it did, I was reminded that I had read about such things in my Grandmother's cookbooks.

Chapter 21.

Attached to page 300 of the cookbook, The Compleat Housewife, or, Accomplish'd Gentlewoman's Companion with a straight pin. The page had the recipe for: A New Method for curing the Venereal Disease. Those instructions were scribbled over with a fountain pen to obliterate the text. The following Bible verse covered it. Archived by Chloe Stevens, circa 1900.

"But avoid foolish questions, and genealogies, and contentions, and strivings about the law; for they are unprofitable and vain."

Titus 3:9 – King James Version

A handwritten note which had accompanied a gift to Helen from her Grandmother, Chloe Stevens, for her Sweet Sixteen Debutante Ball, March 1916. The note was saved in the book: The Eleventh Annual Report of the Secretary of the State Horticultural Society of Michigan – 1881.

Happy Sweet 16 dear Helen.

I hope you will always remember me and the following sentiments whenever you wear this heirloom broach, which was given to me at my Cotillion dance so many years ago.

Be always mindful of whom you associate. Ask yourself if they are worthy of your time. Question whether their choices and causes strive for love, kindness, and a desire to nurture, or are they motivated by hate, mean spiritedness and seek to tear down? Those should be your guiding principles.

Love, Grandma Stevens

The unsteady B-flat on the keyboard of the groaning

organ served as a punctuation to the completed narrative of my flashback and caused the vision to evaporate completely. I was once again just an uneasy member of the congregation.

The service began with several old-timey gospel songs, which were poorly played and unenthusiastically sung. The pall created by the assembled and morbid long black coats, which initially triggered all my depressing memories, returned to their current significance. They were simply a bunch of old men in rumpled overcoats who had filed in and plunked themselves down in the first two rows, which were reserved for them, the members of the Church Council in this stark assembly.

For the remainder of the service, not only did I now have to quietly deal with the emotional aftermath of reliving that most tragic day of my life, but I also had to choke down the stale aftershave fragrances these old dinosaurs seemed to have applied to their overcoats at some point in the distant past. It filled the stuffy air of the gathering and served as a lingering reminder of my flashback, as does the odor of Sulphur after a match is extinguished.

Just when I thought the worst of this morning was over, matters would again become almost unbearable for me. There would be multiple aspects of the subsequent sermon that were all related—at least in my view. And all of them aggravated me.

First, today's sermon would concentrate on a pet peeve of mine. It was one that always made me bristle based on the history of my family and had consistently put me at odds with what I call the *Incontrovertible Bible Believers* crowd. It was the issue of *Women in Leadership*—or lack thereof, and the continued pithy reasons supporting the status quo of it in this church and others that may subscribe to the same doctrine.

Secondly, the sermon also directly reflected upon the events in my Mother's kitchen four decades earlier. The Preacher's words would serve to underscore the atmosphere present that day of a widow's plight and the men in long robes who took advantage of it— paying her only lip service.

And finally, the sermon's substance would also harken back to the themes I had most recently read about in the rediscovered pages of essays and diary entries in my Grandmother's cookbooks. What were the odds of all of them converging at the same time on this Sunday morning? Again, my Mother's words rang true as a prophesy. *Things happens when you least expect it and in ways you cannot predict.*

"How could this setting and experience get even worse?" I mumbled to myself. My anxiety level once again spiked as the service continued, and I closed my eyes in a desperate attempt to escape from it. I did my best to regulate my breathing to encourage a meditative state within me. I repeated my mantra of *for my two girls* several times—which helped to cleansed me of some of my anxiety, but none of my displeasure regarding what I was hearing. I would just have to tough it out.

Fortunately, I had regained some composure to bolster me for the duration of the church ritual. As it turned out, it probably was not needed. I don't think anyone in this assemblage of zombie-like attendees cared what was going on around them concerning anyone else. There was apparently no community spirit in this congregation. It was just their duty to be here.

The minister—another haggard dinosaur in grungy vestments began. "It is in the Bible—the word of God, so it not to be questioned. 1 Timothy 2:12 states in the King James Version: *But I permit not a woman to teach, nor to have dominion over a man, but to be in quietness.*"

My voice filter engaged to thwart a revolt. I bit my tongue as a precaution to halt any reaction I might want to express. The Preacher continued the sermon stating the case for the continued second-class status of women to be maintained. I'm paraphrasing. I squirmed in the pew and clenched my fist.

"In today's modern, sin filled world, women—some of those who are members of this church—especially the younger ones, want to be treated equally. But I say unto you, their roles have already been defined by the Almighty in the Bible in Timothy and elsewhere. They are told by God they should not seek leadership roles in the church. They should have babies and that should be their reward." He paused and scanned the crowd for either some nodding heads of approval or better yet, an answer to his question, "Can I get an Amen?" He got a couple of half-hearted ones, then continued. "They must leave leadership to men."

I sat appalled. I can't believe he's quoting God for *that*? Ugh, this is what fries my bacon. The insistence of the orthodox church that the words some *scribe* in the First or Second Century said is somehow attributed to be the Word of God. Who certified that? It was the Church authority in the Third and Fourth Century. That chain of logic is unsustainable by any thinking person but that is what has been enforced on believers for hundreds of years. Does no one see that? Even I know that God *himself* did not say that. It was Paul who said it in a *letter* to Timothy—one of his ministers and assistant leaders in the emerging Christian church of the First Century. Instead of an "Amen," I would have liked to shout out. "That is being a bit fast and loose with the facts of who said what!" But of course, like the rest of the congregation, I did not point out his glaring discrepancy.

Previously, I always discounted verses like these in the Bible as just a reflection of the conventional roles of women *at the time*—two thousand years ago! Sure, I can see how it was then. But now? C'mon. How can anyone justify the same oppressed roles women had back then as legitimate for today's times?

Most churches I have attended in the past know enough to gloss over these kinds of troubling passages from Scripture or avoid them altogether for the subject matter of a sermon, because they know there is no way to explain away the plain meaning of what those words say and mean to anyone in the modern world. In the ancient world, for centuries, they got away with it because the words and meanings remained obscured in Latin—where few could read it and fewer would be able to confront it had they objected. Yet, right in front of me, in the 21st Century, this church was underlining the passage in Timothy and advocating for it forcefully.

To top it off, the pithy justification for this church's stance on the issue was reasoned out by the fire and brimstone Preacher as, "Women should not be jealous of the men with their God-given role of leaders in His church, because men hold no jealousy because of a women's ability to have babies."

I considered the Preacher's reasoning to fall into the category of what some call a *False Equivalence* argument, but I like to call it the, *'Well yeah, but'* defense. For example, someone might say, "Why do *you* get to choose the restaurant?" The answer, "Well, yeah, but *you* got to choose where we parked the car in the lot." How is that a fair exchange?

The Preacher continued his performance of warped logic with more quotes from the Bible. By doing so, it served more to show his ability to memorize the verses rather than act as a defense of the church's posture toward woman. And nothing he said acknowledged that he was aware we were now in the 21st Century. On so many of his proclamations, I wanted to stand up and say, "Come on! Are you kidding? Are you listening to yourself?" But I held my tongue firmly between my teeth to avoid it. Squirming in my seat, I assessed the situation.

Speaking out any objections about the sermon would bring on the definite prospect of pissing off my employer who was in the front row. On the other hand, if I just sat absorbing this blather of outdated dogma—as all the others in the room seemed to be doing, I might be giving the impression that I was ok with it, and then I'd be expected to listen to this kind of twisted doctrine on a weekly basis in order to stay on the good side of my employer. Either choice revolved around the dictates of Mr. Orrin.

How could I drag my feet to keep from being subjected to this as part of my job? I had already accepted the pay raise and front man status for his Mission at work. How was I to avoid being force-fed into accepting ancient conventional wisdoms—the intent of which, was to keep the womenfolk down to maintain the status quo? Is this what I must go along with every Sunday for the sake of staying employed? Ugh, the quid pro quo I had been sucked into was iron-clad.

Ashamed I had briefly compromised my principals in Orrin's office, which allowed myself to get into this predicament, my thoughts drifted back to the scene of my Mother and the perfunctory, uncaring group of men who prayed the Rosary in our kitchen that *awful* day. I might as well have been one of them. After all, I was on the brink of being indoctrinated into their long-standing fraternity of bad behavior toward women. I thought of the words in my Grandmother's cookbook essays of warnings and exasperations dealing with the same kinds of anti-woman issues, and now, here I was participating in what amounted to one of their rallies—disguised as Sunday church.

Mostly though, I thought of my mantra—*for my two girls*. What kind of example would I be making for them by being a part of this? How could I ignore the heritage of lessons learned from my female ancestors, in order to subject my children to this kind of crap—all at the direction of *men who desire to walk in long robes*, as they are identified in the Gospel of Mark. The answer: For money! I'd be willing to bet a dollar of that money the Preacher won't quote *that* verse! It would be self-incriminating.

As I stewed in my thoughts without trying to show any emotion, what struck me numb was that I did not observe one woman in the audience raise any objection to the views being espoused. Not one whispered disapproval or shifted uncomfortably in their seat with the pronouncement from the pulpit that they were forever sentenced to a subservient, second-class status—limiting them to housekeeping and baby-making. They just rolled with it. All I could think was that these were not my kind of people—not today or ever. I also asked myself, how could anyone be in a relationship with a woman like that?

Finally, I could take listening to this no more. Rather than make a scene, I quietly excused myself from the pew and headed toward the back of the church under the pretext of using the restroom.

Standing alone in the back vestibule of the church I was faced with the instinctive choice of *fight or flight*. I decided not to hang around. I exited the building, went straight to my truck, and wheeled out of the parking lot. However, by choosing *flight*, the farther I drove away from the church, the more I realized I should have stayed and toughed it out by plastering a fake smile on my face, shaking hands with the others after the service and played nice, instead of what I would have liked to say to them. Though, I figured the odds were, that if I hung around, instead of niceties coming out of my mouth, I would say something I would regret later—like I normally do. That would be a fatal error. So, I took off.

"Damn!" I exclaimed and pounded my fist on the steering wheel. "Why does everyone always want you to conform to their stupid ways? Can't they leave a man alone? They leverage a man's paycheck, in order to bend him to their will. It's a page from the oldest playbook in the world. God! human beings in power suck!"

The rest of the weekend, my thoughts were filled with different scenarios of how I was to handle the eventual meeting with the boss on Monday. The best outcome would be that he didn't even see me there, or if he did, he missed my premature exit. I practiced all sorts of excuses, but experiencing a sudden illness seemed the most plausible in case I was questioned. Most other excuses came up as pathetic, and in my estimation, would easily be exposed as B. S. I hoped in the next 24-hours, Orrin would have forgotten the whole thing, and would be on to more urgent needs— like making a taller stack of $99. checks. My best bet was to go to work, keep my head down, and hope the whole thing would just blow over.

Chapter 22.

Undated. It is estimated to have been written in the mid 1920's based on Family Genealogical birth records. It was found between the pages of the book: The Great Galveston Disaster.

My cousin Beatrice finally told her Ma and Pa that she was with child. It was a secret that would eventually tell itself. She is going to stay with her new in-laws after a private Justice of the Peace service until the day of the newborn's arrival. They are hoping for a girl but of course will be happy in either outcome if a healthy child. Her betrothed's parents seem less disturbed by this potentially socially embarrassing event than her own. Mistakes and passions can happen, and I wish her parents would be more supportive. But I hear tell her in-laws, the O'Brien's, are overjoyed for the arrival of their first Grandchild. Love should be shared equally to all—in all circumstances, and not subject to anyone's inconveniences.

    Helen Laurinda Wilcox

On time and punched in at 830am *sharp*! I already

dreaded this daily ritual because it signaled the start of the workday. Now, there was also an additional palpable fear associated with it because there could be a note from Orrin attached to my timecard—which would be a bad sign. Thankfully, there was none. I burrowed into my workstation hoping not to be noticed by anyone. I breathed a sigh of relief at my seemingly good fortune, but it would not last long.

Julie stopped by for the 10 am walk n' talk, and I was anticipating her first question to be about the Sunday service. She didn't have the chance to ask. On an overhead warehouse speaker came the cackling voice of Mrs. Orrin. "*Michael Jacobs, please come to Mr. Orrin's office immediately. Michael Jacobs, please come to Mr. Orrin's office immediately.*" My head sank to my chest.

"Well, it was nice working with you." I glumly said to Julie.

"What?" She said, clearly not understanding.

"Call me later, I'm sure I'll be unemployed and home by noon."

She stood there motionless and I turned and made the dreaded trek up to Mr. Orrin's loft. Each step up the rickety stairs mocked me with the creaking oak floorboards saying "You're." "Fired." "You're." "Fired."

Knocking twice on the door, I heard the familiar, "Come."

Orrin sat slumped in his chair, his head and shoulders could barely be seen above the clutter on his desk. His dog, Zephaniah was on his lap. The office floor was still strewn with random dog food and dog crap.

"You wanted to see me? I inquired, acting like I had no idea why I was summoned.

"Mr. Jacobs, I didn't see you at the end of the Sunday meeting." Orrin quizzed me. "Someone said you excused yourself to the restroom but never returned."

Geez, I must have a *heretic's bullseye* on my back, I thought. Or maybe someone had attached a tracking device to me while I was in the church. They know my every move. Why was my presence at that service so important to Orrin? My thoughts turned briefly to how I really should update my resume and start searching for a new job.

"I'm sorry I missed the rest of the service." I explained. "I was a little nauseous. I think I started coming down with a bug Saturday night. I'm better now." I said, including a slight cough for effect. "A hot bath and a good night's sleep did the trick."

My practiced excuse sounded better than I thought it would. I added to the believability of my performance of the made-up ordeal, by also feigning the look and sound of exhaustion.

"Well, I'm glad you're on the mend" He replied in a tone that said he didn't believe a word of it. But he didn't call me out on it either. He just breezed past my falsehood and got to the point of this meeting.

"Mr. Jacobs, I've been reviewing your resume and it says you worked on the International Genome Project. Is that right?"

"Yes, that's correct." I said hesitantly with a feeling of déjà vu. Didn't we already cover this last meeting? I thought.

He continued, "You obviously have some expertise that we at this company could use to the benefit of our Missions."

Ok. Again, he said *Missions*—plural. And again, we already reviewed my resume. Is he that forgetful? I hope he remembered he promised me a raise last time. I'd hate to have to remind him of that. I'm not even going to consider doing what he wants—whatever it is, without the extra money.

"Sir," I explained, "You are aware that my expertise at the Genome Project was in a public relations capacity. I'm no scientist. My job was to take the wonky, scientific jargon of the reports and breakthroughs and periodically reshape it into something more palatable to the general public in press releases describing the progress being made. It was for the purposes of promoting and securing continued funding for the massive project. I really have no actual science training—other than the basics I've picked up during my time here."

I felt I had to clarify this to him in case he initially didn't look too deeply at my resume and previous job title. In the moment, I could not fathom how either my being a former PR guy or currently opening boxes and cataloging specimens for the *real* scientists here might help further achieve his company's Mission—or *Missions*—no matter how many there were.

Mr. Orrin would have none of it.

"Yes, yes, of course." He said brushing past my explanation. "But I would like you to lend your expertise to my yet unveiled project here—which not only benefits my business Mission but also that of the Mission of my church. I was going to introduce you to our Church Council of Elders at the end of the service yesterday and they were going to give you a briefing of sorts. But again, you *said* you were ill." He emphasized the word *said*—clearly reminding me that he did not believe my excuse. "We can reschedule next Sunday."

"Next Sunday? I'm not sure I will be available." I scrambled. "It's my weekend of custody with my two daughters. I'm divorced." Now *I* was repeating myself from our first meeting. "We may be out of town on Sunday."

"Yessssss, your *children*." He dragged out that word too. "Well, instead of the Church Council, I can take the time now—even with my full morning schedule, to give you a brief outline." Clearly irritated, he added, "I suppose."

He pushed a pile of papers to the side of his desk, folded his hands upon the cleared space, leaned forward and began. "Mr. Jacobs, I have—I should say, *we* have a project underway in my church community, in conjunction with the business we do here, in which I believe you could help promote to a select clientele list we are now compiling from the data gathered in the general work you and the others in the Prep and Final Labs are now doing—along with a future select clientele that, with your help, we will be soliciting as part of a new initiative."

That may have been the longest, most confusing, and would prove to be the most consequential sentence I have ever heard. I could only respond. "Sir?"

He followed it with a curious summary. "Mr. Jacobs, we are identifying a threshold base of customers and God willing, an exciting number of potential new customers needed, which will help us achieve our efforts to define the *final few*."

Now, I was completely lost. "Define the *final few*?" I asked.

Just then. a light tap, tap came from the door of the adjacent room on the north side of his office, which interrupted his cryptic explanation. Mrs. Orrin cracked the door and peeked in to inform him that his overseas call from Belgium was on hold.

"I'm sorry Mr. Jacobs, I have to take this call." He announced.

I knew the routine, I excused myself. Only getting these little drips and drabs of info from this guy was driving me crazy. On the way back down to the Prep Lab, I wondered what he meant by his church's mission, *to define the final few*. I decided I needed to do some research on what that might mean and, if it were available anywhere, do some snooping on Mr. Orrin himself, as soon as I could.

Chapter 23.

Clipped from the page of an older Bible. It is attached to a page of the book: The Great Galveston Disaster with thin hand spun wool yarn which has been deteriorated by moths. It is believed to have been archived by Chloe Stevens, circa 1902.

"And I looked, and, lo, a Lamb stood on the mount Sion, and with him an hundred forty and four thousand, having his Father's name written in their foreheads."

Revelation 14:1 – King James Version

The words in the above verse, "*an hundred forty and four thousand*" are circled in pencil. Also, written in pencil along the margin of the same page are the words, "W*ho is conducting the count?*"

I began my investigation into Orrin the next morning with Julie during our coffee break walk n' talk. "So, what you know about the old man?" I questioned her.

"Old man?" She said. "What old man?"

"Orrin. He's a strange bird."

"Oh, yeah." Julie admitted. "He's kind of creepy in a weird-old-uncle kind of way. But he's harmless. Certainly, the cheapest guy I've ever seen."

"And that old car he drives. It's a relic like him." I said. "What does he do outside of work? And his wife? Strange couple!" I listed my observations in bullet points.

"Not much besides work." She continued by confirming the rumors. "I think the only other thing is he's into big-time is his own church."

"Yeah, that's a tiny old building—pretty plain inside. Not much of a neighborhood around it either."

"By the way," Julie interjected. "Did you enjoy the Sunday meeting?"

"Hmm." I responded. "What denomination is it?"

Julie frowned at my one syllable snort. "I think its independent. A little, poorly hand-lettered sign out front of the building says, CHURCH OF THE *SIX LIV*." Julie sounded it out. "I think that's what it says. The sign is faded and the paint on it is peeling off it so I'm not sure on that exactly."

"Six Liv?" I repeated it phonetically. "What's *Six Liv*?"

"I'm not sure, and I never had the nerve to ask him."

She admitted.

"How is *Six Liv* spelled—with an S?" I pursued the question.

"C, X, L, I, V, I think." She said. "All in caps."

Astonished, I proclaimed, "Wait, C, X, L, I, V? If I know my Roman Numerals, that's the number 144,000!"

"Oh, right!" Julie paused and laughed. "Of course!" She was now completely familiar with the significance. "That's a reference from the Book of Revelation." She began. "It's mentioned—I think three times in it. Some religions believe that only 144,000 souls will ever get to heaven based on those Scripture quotes and the rest of the saved ones will have to live out eternity here on Earth after the apocalypse. They believe that most of the 144,000 are already in heaven."

"Huh. How many left before they reach 144,000?" I asked.

"Not sure that's established. Could be a few thousand, a few hundred—maybe only a handful." She stated. And then Julie offered a tantalizing clue. "I'm not sure how many are left to define, but if you're a literal Bible believer, I'm sure they're all pretty coveted positions."

Ahh, it started to all make sense. Orrin mentioned identifying a threshold base of customers from our collected data and a potential number of new customers to define the *remaining few*—the *few* remaining in this 144,000! Was he and his church making efforts to be the "kingmakers" for those coveted positions to expand his congregation and to somehow monetize it all through the work we do at his company? Quite the bold business venture.

But how would he make that work—based on his say-so? How would that alone gain any more traction with believers than the hundreds of other church leaders in countless congregations over the centuries who worked to cultivate followers and direct contributions to the collection plate each Sunday? I pondered the prospects.

His little congregation was pretty small compared to the mega churches. He didn't have the charismatic charm of any of their leaders. He had no TV, radio, or internet savvy for an electronic ministry. So, was Orrin banking on something he alone knew, which would exponentially draw in more followers and tap a new source of revenue? What was it that Orrin had—besides his delusional rhetoric, that would attempt to corner his portion of the market on Christian Faith? How much of it had to do with what was going on in his Final Lab with the secretive Shadow Brothers? Time would tell.

However, far more frightening to me than any of that was Orrin's insistence that I was going to be the front man for a marketing effort to draw in his select clientele for his soon to be unveiled enterprise. I could kick myself for taking a first step on that slippery slope by agreeing to be part of his plan.

Morally, I wanted nothing to do with it. Financially, yeah, I did. Well, I just had to be on guard for what may come next. I could always quit. Then again, I rationalized. How much of my soul would I actually have to sell for my new six-figure salary?

Alas, the complete details on Orrin, his church and his business project were not going to be sorted out during this walk n' talk with Julie. Break time was over.

Chapter 24.

Written in the blank spaces remaining on a picture postcard of the Grand Teton National Park, Cloudveil Dome. Addressed to Helen from a woman named Regina who writes, *"Wish you were here!"* Postmarked August 17, 1932. It was found in the pages of the cookbook, The Compleat Housewife, or, Accomplish'd Gentlewoman's Companion.

Father keeps telling me if I spare the rod, I'll spoil the child. Their tears are brief but mine seem to last when I am forced to use the fly swatter on their behinds.

Helen Laurinda Wilcox-Phillips

It was another weekend with my girls, and I was looking forward to it. But frankly, they were a little on the grouchy side. I was not sure if they brought it with them as a carryover from the last two weeks with their Mom, or it was due to something else. There seemed to be a little more sibling rivalry between them this weekend than previously. Maybe it's a phase. Maybe its cabin fever brought on by this gruesomely long winter and they are tired of each other. Maybe they were tired of me. The scheduled dentist appointments for their regular six-month checkup Saturday morning was most likely causing some trepidation in them too. I could see that.

It didn't help that their Mother's last words of warning to them before the exchange was, "Don't forget you have early dentist appointments tomorrow morning!" It made the girls anxious and it pissed me off too. These things were supposed to happen on the Ex's timeclock. Why would she make appointments for them on my weekend? I had so little time with them as it was. I'm sure it was her way of sticking it to me and to free up more leisure time for her when *she* had the girls. "I bet she shoves them off onto babysitters all the time." I groused.

So, after the dentist visits and their continued unruly behavior, I was forced to order a mandatory nap for the two of them on Saturday afternoon as a little attitude adjustment. It would do them good and during their down time I would be able to spend a couple hours online trying to find out all I could about Genome 23 History and other similar companies, along with investigating any emerging technologies in this scientific field. What might be looming on the horizon of genetic research that I might be called upon soon to market in my new role for the company?

Putting on my reading glasses, I dug into numerous articles on the tremendous upside in the field of genetics. From the things I scanned online, the scientific community was salivating over new possibilities—just as they had in the buildup to the International Genome Project. This was despite the nay-sayers doubting that anyone could successfully map the entire human genome's three billion variables. But with a lot of hard work and considerable time, the nay-sayers had been proven wrong.

In my online investigation I did some window shopping for the newest diagnostic equipment used in genetics—hoping it might give me a clue as to what might be going on in our Final Lab. I visited the websites of the largest genealogical companies that did what we did, but it was all basic stuff. They didn't show any of their proprietary methods and none of it would have given much insight to my non-scientific mind anyhow. My brief time online during kiddie naptime had just scratched the surface of any real research. As suspected, there was nothing on the web about Orrin. He had no profiles or web pages. I could have guessed he wasn't one to post to social media. I basically drew a blank on him.

The rest of the weekend slipped by all too quickly as they always did. However as planned, the girls Saturday afternoon nap recalibrated their sweet dispositions and we enjoyed board games, mac n' cheese and make believe. They dressed up as princesses while I played the part of the mean ogre who would jump out from under the couch cushions to grab them as they strolled the castle gardens. The ogre attacked them with ogre kisses—which they claimed were poison and would cause them to faint to the ground. As with all kids, we had to reenact that same scene dozens of times—complete with their high-pitched screams and lots of laughter. It wore out both the princesses and the ogre, and we all slept soundly that night.

The girls clung to me even tighter on the return exchange Sunday evening. I was not overly concerned by that because their reluctance to leave me happened every time we parted. But this time, as I strapped them into their seat belts in the back seat of Lanie's car I caught a faint whiff of alcohol. I had no time to inquire about it as the car sped away.

Chapter 25.

Written on letter stationary. It was stapled to one of the last few pages in the book: The Eleventh Annual Report of the Secretary of the State Horticultural Society of Michigan – 1881.

10 May 1925

Some men are so predatory and condescending. Why is that their nature? I guess they always have been.

I remember when I was a girl the day an older man came to the screen door. I was coloring a picture at the kitchen table, so I could hear Grandma and him. He wanted to speak to the man of the house and Grandma said he was not here, and she could help him. The man said he'd rather speak to a man because it's about farm equipment and it's more something a man would know about.

Grandma's hackles were raised by that attitude. She told him 'There ain't a word you know that I haven't heard before. So, you can tell me.'

He said. 'I'll come back another time when your husband is here. When would be a good time for that?' He insisted.

Grandma wrinkled up her forehead and said, 'Sir, my husband has passed. This is the Wilcox household. Mr. Wilcox is my son-in-law. He and my daughter are away visiting a sick relative and tending to their dairy farm. Not till next month.'

The man got a crooked smile on his face and said, 'A pretty woman like yourself must be lonely without a man around.'

Grandma took a quick glance at me and stepped out of the kitchen and down the drive a few yards with the man so I could not hear their conversation. I looked out through the screen door and saw Grandma pointing down the lane and then the man also pointed in that direction and she nodded. Then she said something, and the man got all red in the face and his crooked smile turned into a frown. He turned and walked away as fast as his old legs could a carry him. Grandma watched until he was out of sight and came back into the kitchen. I asked her what he said."

'Nothing much child. I did most of the talking.' She said.

'What did you say?'

'Oh, this and that, dear. Nothing you need to hear.' But Grandma then checked to see if Papa's scatter gun was still behind the pantry door.

> *Helen Laurinda Wilcox*

Saved in the book: The Great Galveston Disaster. It is a portion of a letter written to: Alma Wilcox, c/o Theda Harris, Dagget Road, Howard City, Michigan from her mother Chloe Stevens. Inside the envelope was a drawing in crayon of Peony flowers on construction paper.

16 July 1912

That child of yourn' is a born newspaper reporter with all her questions.

The farm Implement Salesman from Saginaw came calling the other day and was fresh with me, so I stepped out of the house and sent him packing.

Helen was persistent in wanting to know what he was about, but I didn't go into details for her young ears. If not for her age it would have been a good lesson to be wary of his kind. I was tempted to tell her exactly what I told him and that would have been, 'See down the lane to that big hemlock tree near the road. He pointed to the tree and said he could. I told him that that was the property line and he should start heading for it. And when he got to it, he should just keep a going and not come back.' I hope you were not in the process of purchasing something from him.

But what I did tell Helen was, 'Now, Helen, you don't need to tell Papa about this when he gets back from visiting kin. It'll be our little secret.' I didn't want her to be alarmed—and I should have known better than to walk over to the pantry door while she was looking, to see where Papa's shotgun is. That started a whole new round of questions from Miss Persistence.

I changed the subject as best I could. 'That's a pretty picture of a flower child. How on earth are you such a good artist' I told her. 'Can I send that one to your Momma in the letter I'm writing her?' She started drawing, but I could tell she knew my story had more than I was letting on. But that man's kind worries me for the safety of me and the youngsters. I wager it would be a good thing for you to keep it all to yourself about it too. No sense upsetting Frank about it. You know how can go on about things. Enclosed is Helen's drawing of a Peony flower.

I must close now. Be safe in your travel back come next month.

> *Love, Momma.*

Monday morning—the start of another workweek.

"So, how was church this weekend?" Julie asked.

"Oh, um well," I attempted to explain, but Julie interjected. "That bad? Why?"

"No, I had the girls this weekend. I didn't attend church."

"Oh!" She said surprised. I sensed her feelings were hurt that I had the girls and didn't invite her to join us. I felt bad about that, but we had the dentist appointments on Saturday morning. That ate up a lot of quality time for me and there was too much on my mind to entertain another person. In retrospect, the girls would have liked her company. I admit, I would have too. It was an opportunity lost.

Julie persisted with the interrogation about the church. "But you *have* been to the church. Besides 'Hmm,' what were your first impressions of the service?"

Ok, I wanted to let it drop, but knew Julie could be persistent with her questioning when she got interested in something. Changing the subject to something else would not satisfy her curiosity. So, rather than keep playing this game of 20 questions with her, I decided, true to my form, to open-up and let her know exactly how I felt.

"Julie, if you must know, I have been forced into a *religious corner* again. I'm not sure if a 15-minute break is enough time to explain it, but I had to excruciatingly sit through a sermon based on the mindset that promotes a view that women are second-class citizens. It was all so old-school that it's not relevant to me."

"What? You're kidding me." She laughed.

"No, I'm serious—all too serious. During my first and hopefully my last visit there, they focused on the issue, that apparently some upstart young woman in the congregation raised with the Church Council, of why women were not allowed in the leadership roles. The church's response, in a nutshell, was that women are just to focus on having babies and leave the leadership roles to men because it says so in the Bible."

"It does not!" She emphatically stated.

I could see this impasse would not be fully resolved in the remaining time we had left on our walk n' talk.

"Listen, why don't you come over tonight after work and I can explain it all." I said. "We don't have time here."

"You're right!" Julie agreed. "I'd like to hear the details of the sermon and your explanation. That makes no sense to me."

"Ok, plan on eating dinner with me. I'll put something together. I just have leftovers."

"Leftovers are fine."

"Stop by around 6?"

"6 it is."

Chapter 26.

Undated. Written on the back of an envelope addressed to Helen. No return-address. Postmark illegible. Saved in the cookbook, The Compleat Housewife, or, Accomplish'd Gentlewoman's Companion.

I will always tell someone the truth, unless it's something that might hurt their feelings, unless it be for their own good which will outweigh the hurt.

Helen Laurinda Wilcox

An excerpt from Helen's essay: Where Do We Find Ourselves Today?

"...today we are left with some troubling conventions of the Christian tradition that are unsettlingly explained in the circular logically way: It is the way it is, because that is the way it has always been. Oh, and do not so much as question it, because of the tradition of forbidding that too."

"You may ask yourself, what is it about us humans—and especially male humans—who are the ones who mostly had their finger in the above kettle of soup, got the rest of us to where we are today?"

Julie arrived right on time. There was no serious talk during the meal. Both of us seemed to want to enjoy the moment and somehow avoid the difficult topic that was the *elephant in the room.*

We finished the meal, cleaned off the dining room table, and settled onto the couch.

"So, about the service." I began. "Woman are second class citizens and should stay in that role because they say it's in the Bible."

Julie said, "I don't think that right. I never read that."

"It most certainly does—even though I'm paraphrasing a bit." I gently argued. "In fact, the Bible has quite a lot of unsavory, out-of-step with the times proclamations in it. Some of them are ones that no one should take seriously anymore. Take Paul's letter to the Ephesians. Some say it pretty much gives legitimacy to slavery in how it addresses the dynamics between masters and servants."

"Where on earth did you read that?" she stated with incredulity.

"Chapter 6. It's all in there depending on the version of the Bible you read. Some have the word *slave* as *servant,* or they mean *bond slave*—like someone captured in a war, but they all decipher that same way in my opinion. Slavery *was* a "thing" back then. Even some in this country in the 19th Century—in the run-up to the Civil War, argued against the Abolitionists saying that slavery was acceptable since it was referenced in the Bible.

Julie sat with her mouth open—a look of disbelief on her face.

"And in Paul's Ephesians 5 it says, *Women are supposed to submit to their husbands on everything— **everything!***" I said digging deeper into her beliefs. "Have you ever read Paul?"

"I'm sure I've heard it in church." She said.

"You've heard *all* of it in church?" I quizzed her. "Have you read it yourself or just had the church's version of it read to you? Was it even mentioned at all?" She didn't answer.

"To go further." I stated. "The Bible's passages in Timothy about keeping women in a second-class status is an uncomfortable topic to explain to a modern church audience. I was surprised they broached the subject head-on in Orrin's church. They read from First Timothy and then expounded on it to make it clear. But then again, they're a conservative bunch and in favor of the literal translation. I can tell you that those verses in Paul and Timothy are not sections of the Bible that any progressive modern church focuses on. If they were to, their women attendees would run for the doors. You should read it sometime."

Holding her obvious ire, she said, "Go on."

"It seems pretty plain when you read it." I continued. "That's why I don't want anything to do with his church. And Orrin is pressing me to be a part of his M*issions* he keeps saying. Missions for both his business *and* his church. They're tied together somehow. I would like to stay as far away from both as possible but I'm not sure I'm gonna be able to. My plate of drama is already full. In fact, it's overflowing right now with the girls, dealing with Lanie and trying to keep my head above water in this economy."

My explanation and reasoning did not penetrate her. "It never says that." She flatly stated.

"Hmm, you haven't answered my question Julie. Have you ever *read* First Timothy or Ephesians?"

"Well," she paused. "I can't say for certain if I remember."

"Why not? I persisted. "I'd be willing to bet a dollar—because it's all I can afford, that in your church experience, those passages and other uncomfortable ones have been glossed over. I mean, c'mon, in this day and age, *women shouldn't hold dominion over a man*, because it's in the Bible?"

"I just don't believe any church would believe and say women are second-class citizens, never hold leadership roles and should stay home and have babies." She implored.

"It does in *his* church. And they point to that verse in First Timothy as their proof!" I stated.

"I find that hard to believe." Julie persisted.

I was beginning to get vexed. "I've got news for you, Missy. Here's the thing. If you are among the many who has been led to believe that every word in the Bible is true—that it was inspired by God and must be followed to the letter, then you gotta go along with the program—the *whole* program. You can't be a cafeteria Christian—believing some of the Bible but not all of it. They don't allow for that kind of radical, logical thinking in a verbatim congregation like Orrin's. And part and parcel to professing to belief in *every* word of the Bible—including Timothy and Ephesians and other troubling verses about women, slavery, and the like, you gotta subscribe to all of it. That would include mixing linen and wool together in your clothing!

"What?" Julie asked incredulously.

"Look it up in Leviticus! By the way, isn't your coat a wool and linen blend?" I asked rhetorically.

"My coat?" She protested in a manner that said she thought I had lost my mind.

I blew past that observation. "Julie, you repeated the church establishment's line to me once yourself. Let me paraphrase. '*It's all inspired by God and every word is true.*' I just don't read it that way or accept that mindset."

Julie sat there stunned and finally offered. "I did say something to that effect. It was how I was raised to believe in the Bible." Then, as a defense, she posed a question that I had heard many times before from the *born-again* crowd when they had reached their limit for further discussion on the topic of religion. It always came out when arguments against their way of thinking began to challenge their sensibilities and start to make sense to them. "Don't you believe in the Bible?" She questioned me.

I had relatively held my tongue until now, but I could no longer.

"Ugh, let's unwrap that." I began. "What do you mean by *believe* in the Bible? Are you asking me if I *believe* it is a compilation—a bound book of select gathered manuscripts by early church authority, that they believed had validity on the question of Jesus and his divinity? Yes! Do I believe that *every* word by *every* author on *every* subject and *every* interpretation they addressed and was selected for inclusion in the Bible by that authority that existed way back when is true? That they're all true when you take into account all the various translations that have taken place since the originals—which by the way are not in existence anymore—from Aramaic, then to Greek, to Coptic, to Latin? Well, some of it—with a fair amount of skepticism! Should I believe it is all 100% valid for *today* in its application? Should I go along with all the add-ons and opinions and conventional wisdoms of *their* day and give them the same weight as the core teachings of Jesus? No! I especially don't believe the writings they selected for the Bible comprise a final word on Jesus and his Message when you consider the volumes of other, so called apocryphal writings, that were also available but not chosen to be included by the authority of the church in the first few centuries of the Christian era because those— arguably equally valid ideas and writing, didn't suit their orthodox ones."

"Julie, put it in perspective. Why should Paul's or Timothy's or the Orthodoxy's opinions from back then be any more relevant than any current religious scholar's writings on the subject? In fact, some of the more modern takes on Christianity that I have read, should replace some of the original ones where their old ideas don't speak to truth these days. That way it can be kind of an *evolving* Bible. Ya know, keep the basic message from the Principal Himself. Update the rules and regs for today's society."

"And going further, Julie. Are you asking that question; *Don't I believe in the Bible,* because that's what the established religious higher-ups have instructed the "herd" to ask when you confront someone like me who is more of a free thinker— albeit a free thinker who also happens to be a Christian?"

Julie did not answer.

"Listen, I've dealt with the same question before from others. Over my life, every time I've heard it, it has always been directed at me with the eventual purpose to exclude people like me from participation in your group of the *included* ones, because admittance to that group is an all or nothing proposal. I might not fit in the group with my current thinking and my willingness to express it. They don't want to hear that. They immediately label it as blasphemous. They require that a person must believe in all of it or you just won't fit in. The group does not want a troublemaker who might point out some discrepancies in their doctrine."

I mocked the reasoning of that to Julie with a hillbilly sounding twang. *"If'n ya start parsing the Bible, it'll fall apart and then where'll we be? We'll have ta start thinkin' fer ourselves. Then there'll be no need fer the Institooshin' to exist. Folks will be able to be a Christian on their own. Preachers will be floodin' the unemployment line."* That clearly angered her.

Then Julie posed the second question I have always heard in tandem with her first about belief in the Bible. "Don't you believe Jesus was the Son of God and died on the cross to forgive our sins and make it so we can go to heaven?"

I did a slow burn before answering. "I reject even acknowledging that question from you, Julie. I won't even consider answering it. You should know I believe in the basic core tenets of my Faith. I reject that question because that's not what you really want to know. You weaponize that question to define me as someone to keep out of your group—not your *brand* of Christian."

"Julie, what you're saying is that unless I agree with the institutional litmus test, in your view, I have no right to be with my God at the end of my life. That's what that question is telling me. That's what you are defining as my either-or choice—and that's just like the conundrum I find myself at work. I must pledge to Orrin's Missions—even though I don't really believe in them, or I'm on the outs! However, the pressure to make me conform is so great it bends me to them. Do you see how coercive and insidious those methods are? Do you see the similarities?"

Julie fumbled for a response, "No, uh, I was just wondering where you stand."

I was on a roll and no sense stopping now with my captive audience of one. "And to my earlier point, Julie. Do I believe that far too many of this same orthodox church hierarchy—whether it was the original group back in the day, or the ones right on up through today, are populated with an abundance of hypocrites who are more concerned with preserving the institution than providing for the individual? Yes, Mam! Do I think far too many of them use the Bible more of an enforcement tool and business plan rather than a spiritual guide, by cherry-picking parts of it that are favorable to their continued control and financial gain—while ignoring some of the plain directives—that would actually do some good for humanity? No doubt! Their behavior in leadership has never changed. It keeps people like you down in their system and excludes people like me from it. Their control of the Message is all done for their benefit—not yours or mine. The original Message of Jesus is not used as a guide for their flocks to live a better life. To them, it's just a means to *their* desired end."

"I'm sure you misread things in the Bible or misunderstood the meaning. I'm sure a Minister could explain it to you with their interpretation." Julie would take none of my rationale.

"That's a slippery slope, Julie. So, you're saying the Bible is subject to *interpretation*?"

"By some!" Was her unsure answer. It came unsteadily as she realized she was contradicting herself about her stance on the incontrovertibility of the Bible.

"Well now, who's qualified to interpret?" I questioned her. "Just some guys from way back when—the *scribes in long robes*, just 'cuz they're from way back when—even though most of the ones picking and choosing what's in the Bible came along centuries after Jesus? How do they know any more or can interpret any better than you or me?"

"They've studied it…I assume." With that statement, she put her other foot in her mouth.

"Who has studied it?" I persisted. "Can you even name anyone from the first few centuries of the Christian era who were in on the study or explain by what measure they used to interpret and select any of the writings for inclusion into the book? You can't!"

"Well…I uh." Julie struggled with the barrage of difficult questions and could only repeat her earlier defense. "You must have misunderstood."

"No chance!" I remained steadfast. "I can read Julie. I don't need some minister to massage what is plainly written to mollify my conclusions. When this book was being codified as the Canon by the orthodoxy sixteen hundred to two thousand years ago, most likely I and 99 percent of the population would have been illiterate and had to go by what they said. The education was limited to the elite of the society. Those were the clergy and kings and rulers and rich folks. I don't even know all of who *they* are either, but *they* controlled the belief system, and in their view, all the acceptable writings of Christianity. And, on the subject of women—all those accepted writings I pointed out serve to reinforce their already established roles, which to this day *treats the entirety of womanhood as but a second-class citizenry*."

I stopped my discourse suddenly. I had just quoted one of the most prolific phrases in my Grandmother's cookbook essay. Wow, I thought. Powerful words can sure stay with you and surface when you least expect them at most inappropriate, or in this case, *appropriate* times.

No time to reflect further, I continued. "And the church institutional hierarchy of men keeps on keepin' on with the afore-mentioned mentality regarding you women—right up to the present."

"Here's the philosophical conundrum in a nutshell, Julie. It is a human paradox. Someone comes along, filled with self-importance. With their status, yet limited human knowledge, they feel they have somehow been imparted with the unknowable nature and knowledge of God himself—which is unquestionable and unlimited for Him, but certainly not for us. Regardless of that glaring discrepancy, by the simple virtue of their own absolute earthly authority, they then go on to enforce their limited and questionable human intelligence with a declaration or two that what they say is the infallible and final words authorized by God." I paused. "Are you following me Julie?"

Her one-word response was, "Hmm." I took that as a *yes* and elaborated.

"Then the upper crust of the church think that they must dumb it all down even further, to explain their inferior human knowledge in even more simplified concepts to the even less knowledgeable than themselves. Chew on that for a while, Julie!" I could see the light of continued engagement with me on this subject fading from her eyes as her face showed no emotion.

I lowered my voice. "Julie, men in power are more than happy to keep women uneducated and uninvolved. They continue to keep you in the role of home makers and baby makers and perpetuate the mindset that you couldn't possibly *lead* anything other than maybe a choir. That norm has somehow survived for two thousand years, despite advancements in equality for women and available education opportunities for them."

"I'm not telling you anything you don't already know, Julie. Look at you working for Orrin. I hate to say it, but you're second class in his mind. It's just that you haven't fully accepted the truth of it or spoke up about it. And as long as you don't beef about it, he's more than happy to let you wallow in it. That's why I don't subscribe to the Bible as 100 percent all true and incontrovertible. It just isn't. Most of it is inspirational and a great guide for living a virtuous life, but there's an awful lot in it that's just unfair. And most importantly, I don't want my girls subjected to the unfair parts of it by anyone. What gets me is that people can read these days, but it seems very few do."

My condemnation had hit home with her. My words had clearly insulted her based on the dour look on her face. I had gone too far—again. It was familiar territory for me. I tried to soften my blow.

"Julie, What I mean to say is that those sections of Paul and Timothy—those are, for lack of a better word, *opinion pieces,* as I call them. They don't further Jesus' core Message or change the original facts, but what they do accomplish in large measures, is ensure that the institutional bureaucracy of the religion will survive, and those in power, will stay in power. That does not do one damn thing for you or me." I could see I didn't need to keep going because she had already stopped listening.

Julie sat as if frozen and looked at me the same way

so many others had over my lifetime when this topic of religion came up. Her eyes said, "*You're a heretic.*" And her chilling demeanor said, "*Let me start the process of excluding you from my life as a friend and even an acquaintance. You don't fit in with our group of likeminded believers. We can't have a free thinker amongst us or one who could potentially poison our views of the orthodoxy. For you see, when free thinkers like you enter our polite conversations— ones where we all agree with everything we have been told, we are taught to react to the intruder by closing ranks and push them away and close our ears to heretical talk, rather than consider the ambiguities in our own beliefs. That's tradition! That's the way it has been for two thousand years. That's how our church group maintains its flow of income and control over its congregations by controlling the message in its doctrine. We can't have any dissidents around to upset that harmony.*"

That's what Julie was saying to me without uttering a syllable. I'd seen that look and attitude in so many others, so many times before. It both angered and disappointed me.

Thoroughly peeved that our friendship had fallen into this familiar path and ended up at this inevitable conflict of beliefs, I went one step further and said, "And I'm surprised a modern, self-sufficient woman like you—who aspires to *now* be independent, would look the other way from the glaring ambiguities in your belief system, and maybe invest a little of your time in discovery of some truth. It might be beneficial to you. You may have been recently in your last relationship, but you don't seem to be the type of woman who wants to take the words, actions and directives of a bunch of men with their own suspect personal agendas to be your guiding principles."

I should have bitten my tongue before uttering that last sentence. If I could've retrieved the words from the air before they reached her ears, I would have. However, it was a fraction of a second too late and I immediately knew it was a cruel thing to say to a friend. Temper is an awful thing when it's not directed in a righteous manner. Innocent people get in its way.

"Well!" She gasped and then just stared at me for the longest time.

I could feel her friendship and warmth ebbing away. She stiffened in her staccato response with little emotion.

"Perhaps, we should call it a night. It's getting late. Thanks for the wonderful time."

And with that, she put on her coat, said good night, refused my offer to walk her to her car and she drove away.

With the last glimpse of her taillights disappearing down the street, I said aloud, "Well, ruined that friendship with my big mouth. Never see her again."

Chapter 27.

Written in the margin of page 247 of the cookbook, The Compleat Housewife, or, Accomplish'd Gentlewoman's Companion. That page had the recipe: For any Man or Beast bitten by a mad Dog.

3 March 1927

I reach a certain point when I cannot argue anymore with Erma when she says, 'You have to believe what's in the Bible, because it says so in the Bible.' I wonder if she's ever heard of the fascinating concept of circular logic.

Helen Laurinda Wilcox

An excerpt from Helen's essay: Where Do We Find Ourselves Today?

"For the vast majority of the rest who are the followers, the pressures to conform to the whims of the scribes come in many methods. Some are subtle. Some are overt. Efforts to coerce conformity can make us change our looks, alter our actions, and often bend our beliefs in order to remain in a state of favor, so we can continue to be included in our modern groups and relationships. The pressures to conform are systemic and incremental. They all lead to fatality of our individualism."

My thoughts turned inward. I asked myself familiar questions. Why do I keep getting pushed to this same limit again and again by people all wanting me to change to their way of thinking? Even with people I like—with people who know me and should respect me, I must inevitably confront this issue and then get pushed away. Why is my way of thinking so evil to them? I try to follow the Beatitudes. Isn't that enough? Doesn't that qualify me as a Christian? Why must I also have to pass additional requirements? Damn it! You can have wonderful chemistry and incredible conversation with someone, but you also must pass a religious litmus test of conventional beliefs in order to get along with 'em. Otherwise, you're just not good enough. The sad thing is that those applying the test to you have little or no insight or context into the meaning of what they ask of you. They can only reiterate the centuries old rhetoric that marginalizes people rather that include them. That is so antithetical to the ideals of *inclusiveness* that Jesus preached about and how he lived his life. "You can look it up!" I shouted out to no one.

Retreating to my inner thoughts, I mimicked the opposition's arguments against me, while pacing the floor. "*Oh, no! Don't want to be around that kind of thinking—even though it's true. You've upset my sensibilities. To fit in with our group, you can't be a free thinker. Just go along with our beliefs. Even though I silently agree with you in private, for the sake of the public show, I can't be seen with a religious revolutionary. So, it's been nice knowing you. I'm retreating to the comfort of my other fellow sheep where our bleating voices all sound the same."*

Slightly calming after that rant, I re-doubled my vow to remain steadfast in my beliefs *for my two girls*. How could I do otherwise? Moreover, I was deeply saddened to find out that Julie, at least in part, was no different than Orrin at their core. Ninety-nine percent of my beliefs were the same as theirs. The core tenets of my Faith—the same as theirs! I was galled that a one percent difference in how I looked at my beliefs and how I applied them to my life, were slapped back in my face. I was again being ostracized by someone I thought was a friend. "Because of *that!*" I shouted angrily, while gesturing in a backhanded way toward my family Bible that sat on the bookshelf.

Fully disgusted, I walked to it, picked up the book and threw it across the room—knocking over some picture frames on an end table. Instantly, I was awash with a horrible chill and deep regret for losing my temper. I feared Almighty retribution that I might be struck by lightning at any minute or the roof would cave in on me with the wrath of God for my blasphemous act of tossing His book. I then stopped in mid-thought.

Wait! Not ten minutes ago, I was criticizing Julie for having this same irrational reverence for *everything* in that book—regardless of some of its content not being capable of holding its own water in today's world. See how it is? I'm still suffering from the centuries of cultured indoctrination of reverence regarding the Bible. It's just a book! I thought.

"The Bible!" I groused aloud. "You can't criticize it. You can't interpret it. Be very afraid for your eternal soul if you do! That's the mindset that they have ingrained in me too. Man! It is so frustrating! Isn't there a reasonable middle-ground?" I asked myself.

I continued the argument by presenting my case to the empty cottage in the woods. "Look, God! I agree the Bible has wonderful accounts of miracles and the key element that provides a basis for Faith—my Faith! But honestly, the outdated opinions like the ones I pointed out to Julie from Timothy and Ephesians and others—which promote inequality that the likes of Orrin and his ilk cling to, should be abridged or foot noted or just debunked. Can't somebody fix that? It makes no sense to embrace those odious ideas today. Why can't people see that, God? Why does the idea of common sense and fairness offend them?"

I returned to silently processing the situation. I spoke my mind like I always do and now I found myself at a familiar place. I won't have a friend to share with anymore. There will be no bright spots in my life other than the too infrequent times I share with my girls. I'll only have work by itself with no interaction with anyone there to distract me from the loneliness and despair I'll carry with me. And now my job will have an even greater ominous shadow over it because I agreed to be a complicit advocate for the same untenable ideas and practices embodied in Orrin's damn church that I abhor. All for a little extra money. I felt just like Judas.

Trying to sort it out in relative terms, I rationalized

that by comparison my dilemma was not nearly as challenging as many others in my own family had to endure before me —although it would basically require the same dogged determination by me to work through it. However, as a man, I would be generously compensated for succumbing to the conformities forced upon me. Others in the past were not so fortunate. So often they all worked themselves to exhaustion to carry out their burdens to completion without proper compensation or even thanks.

My goal, however, would be the same. I would follow their examples to do what I had to do for the sake of my children. I would have to accomplish it from a position of subservience to the orthodoxy of this company and that church, and to the person who controls it—all while trying to avoid falling into a crippling depression that didn't seem that far off.

That was all in my future unless there was a way out of this. Could I negotiate my way out of this predicament? Orrin was probably a reasonable man I deduced. He must have raised a family before. He would understand. Yeah, right! I couldn't even convince myself of that. But I had no choice but to make the attempt to appeal to his *better angels*—if they existed.

As soon as I could, I had to set the boss straight on everything I felt. But it would have to wait a bit as there was no Orrin in the building for the rest of the week. The rumor was that he was out of town—out of the country, on a business matter for the company in Belgium. That was all anyone knew. It made me wonder, as I remembered Orrin getting that urgent call from Belgium during our last meeting. That call and his trip had to be related. It also made some sense that his sudden trip was part of the new initiative for the company. It had to be. No one had ever remembered Orrin missing a workday.

My confrontational talk with him would have to wait till next week. However, in the interim, I was on the hook for another obligated Sunday service at his church. His spies on the Church Council would surely rat me out if I failed to show. I kept telling myself, I can get through this one more Sunday. When Orrin is back, I *must* say something. I hope I had the courage to do so when the time came.

Chapter 28.

Written on letter stationery. It was found tucked inside the back cover of the book: The Great Galveston Disaster.

22 February 1959

It has been a difficult last few months. Word came from my oldest son that Father had passed on the way to work. His diabetes had gotten so bad lately that he could not drive himself and we were worried about him falling asleep at the wheel. So, the neighbor, Harold, had begun driving him to work as they were on the same shift. He was too stubborn to take a sick leave and would still punch in on time every day. It was his final way of defying the disease. Harold said his heart gave out on the way. A stop by McAlbin Emergency room and a shot of adrenaline to his heart had been no use.

Unlike, the sudden loss of Janell's husband which has just befell this family, I had been expecting something like this for Father soon. My heart is twice broken now. They say deaths come in threes. I worry about whom I might know next. The Gospel says we should be thankful in all circumstances. I know that it is true but the proof of it in my spirit is hard to come by right now.

Helen Laurinda Wilcox-Phillips

It was another snowy Sunday in this endless winter. I settled into a pew just a little closer to the front of the church this time. It was only a calculated game I was playing. I thought this shift forward would show a subtle increasing interest to the rest of the congregation on my part—even though I had none. I maintained a respectable distance from the front few rows. Those were clearly reserved for the respected Church Counsel—with their dutiful, silent seconds stationed in the next couple pews behind them.

After my first Sunday here and the flashback I experienced then, I would now also be saddled with the lingering traces of that memory each time I was forced to view the cluster of stately but ominous, long dark coated men displayed in front of me. Looking at them, I wondered what the group would be wearing in the summer months when this non air-conditioned space would be sweltering.

As with each Sunday, the shaky hands of the organist tried their best to perform the tried and true melody of a pentecostal standard.

Then it happened. It was another one of those, *at a time I could not have expected, and in a way, I could never have predicted* type events.

To my astonishment, from the side entrance of the church, in walked Lanie with a man, and to my horror, my two little girls. Elizabeth and Mary were dressed in matching outfits of plain black dresses without adornment and simple pill-box hats on their heads. I was so shocked that I thought I might be experiencing another flashback or vision, but it was all too real.

My girls were led to a third-row pew by their Mother on the opposite side of the church from me and they quickly blended in with the other second-class attendees of women and children. I could see they tried to hold back and were reluctant to enter the unfamiliar surroundings with all those strange people around them.

I was dumbstruck. As they entered the pew, the Ex and the man did not see me initially, but Mary looked in my direction and recognized me. She was forced to quickly averted her eyes back to the front of the church after a hard tug on her arm by her Mother.

That was followed by an evil glance in my direction by Lanie. I immediately realized I was somehow being *played* in this church gathering, but for some unknown purpose.

A jumble of thoughts raced through my head. How did Lanie know I was going to be here? It was obvious the girls had been forewarned that I'd be in attendance and that they should not make any contact with me or recognition of me. That was evident based on the corrective action taken on Mary's arm to redirect her attention to the front. What in the Hell was going on?

The organ continued to play as I sat there breathless and I began sweating as the temperature began to rise under my collar. I felt flushed with rage at this spectacle.

Here they were, my daughters, dressed like little clones of the Church Counsel's second team. They were led in without my say-so as if they were sacrificial lambs to the indoctrination of this cult. This would have never happened on my watch under my custody. How could Lanie do this without my permission?

What was I to do now? Would I get up, rush over to them, grab the girls and make a dramatic exit? Would I stand and shout at them—cursing at Lanie at the top of my lungs for this grandstand play in this house of worship? Those were the types of things to which I would usually gravitate when things like this would set me off in the past. Or, this time, would I die right there of a heart attack—overcome by the sheer magnitude of this development? I felt as if I was on the brink of one.

No, in fact, I would do nothing. I *could* do nothing! I was in a trap controlled by the norms expected of one being in a Church. This house of worship, like all of them, demanded my restraint and respect for the proceedings—which held authority over me and everyone else in the building. Even though I knew what was unfolding before me was wrong on every level, I had to sit and take it—no different than everyone else.

My stomach churned and my head ached. I just had all my parental control over my own children subverted. My parental rights were disregarded, and I was on hold for the remainder of the service, with no way to respond. I was crushed.

For the next hour, I paid no attention to the service. My every thought swirled around the question of how this had happened. Why had the Ex decided to attend this church, of all churches, on this Sunday? Amid my barely manageable rage, I quickly concluded that Orrin's fingerprints were all over this. But what was the motivation for it and what was I going to do in response once I got out of here?

I didn't get the chance. At service's end, Lanie and the girls quickly exited the building, and my attempt to get to them was thwarted by a large group of parishioners who were slow to exit the pew and blocked the aisles. When I finally reached the parking lot, they had already driven away. The rest of the day, frantic attempts to call Lanie went directly to her voice mail. I drove by her house twice, but there we no cars in the driveway and no one was home. I prayed for direction and was left with nothing else I could do but cry myself to sleep.

Chapter 29.

Clipped from an older publication of the Bible, believed to be archived by Chloe Stevens. It was attached with a straight pin to page 342 in the cookbook, The Compleat Housewife, or, Accomplish'd Gentlewoman's Companion. That page had listed the recipe: An approved Remedy for a Cancer in the Breast.

"Greater love hath no man than this, that a man lay down his life for his friends."

John 15:13 - King James Version

Again, as things seem to happen that no one could predict, a few days later, in the middle of the night, something did happen that was at first terrorizing and then offered a direction. It was the *direction* I had consistently prayed for since the breakup of my marriage. This new and unexpected direction upended the entire custody agreement I had with Lanie.

In a dream filled sleep, I was awakened by a phone

call around 2 am from someone identifying themselves as Officer Barnes of the County Sherriff's Department on behalf of the Child Protective Services Agency.

Panic immediately rose in my throat. "Children! Police! Oh my God, what happened?" I frantically asked.

"Your children are safe." The officer calmly assured me. "And your Ex-wife is safe. However, they are at the Sherriff's Office with our staff. We'd like for you to come down immediately and take the children home. We are turning the children over to your full custody, so please bring your ID. Again, they are all ok Mr. Jacobs. We'll see you soon. Please drive carefully."

"Thank God!" I exhaled. "What happened? Never mind. Yes, I'll be there as soon as I can get dressed and come down. It'll be about 20 minutes."

My truck came to a screeching halt and I sprinted from the parking lot into the Police Station. The girls were just exiting an office off the lobby and we ran to each other. They were crying and wearing those mylar emergency blankets that rescuers provide for survivors at disaster situations. To my horror, they looked just like the TV images of disheveled migrants in border detention centers. Another wave of panic rushed over me and this time I could not hold back a wave of tears. I buried Liz and Mary in my arms. Right behind them was Officer Barnes. "Mr. Michael Jacobs?" She asked.

"What happened? Are they alright? Yes, I'm their Daddy. What happened?" I flooded the Officer with questions as I sobbed in my breaking voice.

Redirecting my attention toward the girls, I tried to lower my voice so I wouldn't frighten them even more than they already were. "It'll be alright girls. Daddy is just upset. Its ok. Don't cry." I sobbed in gasps as they clung to me with all their might.

"Why don't we all step back into the office here." Officer Barnes suggested. "I'll fill you in and we can gather their belongings." We entered the room, closed the door and she gave me the details.

"Your ex-wife, Lanie Jacobs, was pulled over for a broken taillight early this morning by one of our patrolling officers. The report says that it was 1 am. He noticed alcohol on her breath, and she failed the roadside sobriety test. He also noticed that one of the girls was not wearing a seatbelt. Because of the dangerous conditions she presented for herself and for your children, she was arrested, and the girls were placed in our protective custody until you could be contacted."

Filled with anger, I demanded, "Is she here? I want to talk to her!"

"No, she bonded out. Her friend—a man, paid the bond and she will be waiting a court date. From what I could gather, she said that she was leaving a party and had too much to drink. Sadly, we see this kind of poor choice to drive impaired happening far too frequently and too many times it ends up tragically.

They're lucky."

It then hit me. I knew I had smelled alcohol in her car on the last Sunday exchange of the girls. Damn her! How could she be so reckless and foolish?

"I'm sure the rest of the story will unfold for you in the next couple days," The Officer continued. "But these girls are under your full custody now and for the foreseeable future."

"There's no problem with that. I take good care of them. I understand. Thank you. They'll be ok." I rambled through a litany of affirmations. "Where are there coats? Where's Liz's other shoe?"

"Um, oh, I'm sorry." The officer confessed. "I guess maybe the officer left them in your ex-wife's car. That was impounded. The shoe might have come off in the patrol car. That officer went right back out on an incoming call. We'll radio him to do a search when he's able. For now, the emergency blankets should keep them warm. We'll get their coats retrieved as soon as we can, but it'll probably be later today when the impoundment lot opens. You might want to warm up your car first before they get in. If there's anything you need, please call me. Here's my card."

The police station seemed as disorganized as I felt.

I carried both girls in my arms to the truck at the same time. I placed them in the back seats of the truck and made sure their seat belts were fastened securely—maybe a little too snug, but it was an overreaction to

Lanie's irresponsibility. I put the heater on full-blast and all the way home I kept looking in the rearview mirror to check on them. Soon after leaving the parking lot of the police station, both were fast asleep. It had been a harrowing evening for them. The clock on the dash read 3:45 am.

On the rest of the drive home, I made a concerted effort to calm down as best I could. For me, it was miserably hot in the vehicle and it only added to the anger boiling under my collar. What the Hell was Lanie thinking—driving around drunk with my girls in the vehicle? No seatbelts! Oh, how I wanted to throttle her. I also wanted to break down and cry, but I couldn't. That would be wasted effort. I had no time for anguish. "I gotta keep it together *for my two girls*." I whispered. "Remember, I have the children...*I have the children*." Why did those words sound so familiar?

My mind raced. I thought of the worst outcome. Oh, God. What if they had gotten into an accident?

"Ok, wait, wait...wait!" I said to out loud in an incoherent, murmuring ramble to calm myself. "There was no accident. Just a taillight out—just a taillight. The girls are safe. Nobody's hurt."

I momentarily regained some focus, but then realized the only clothes or provisions I had for the girls at my house would be the clothes they had on their backs. There were no spare winter coats for them. I don't even think I had a pair of their pajamas in the dirty clothes hamper. I suddenly felt completely alone and helpless.

Then the surreal nature of it all dawned on me as I gasped. "Oh my God! *Remember I have the children!* That is exactly what Mom was told and had to face all those years ago." Now I too was suddenly all alone to protect my children. There was no other help. The panic of it was engulfing. I felt as if I couldn't catch my breath. But wait! Was I truly all alone? If only I could reach out and talk to *someone*. But I only had one person whom I could talk to. It was far too early, but I called Julie. She answered in a groggy state after the fourth ring.

"Hello, Michael? What's going on?"

"Everything is alright." I tried to assure her. "But can I ask you a favor? I just had to pick up my girls from the police."

"The police!" she shouted.

"They're both safe. Don't be alarmed. Both are safe but I just had to pick them up at the police station. Long story short; Lanie was arrested for drunk driving. The girls were in the car."

I fired off a series of short statements to Julie. "Protective custody. They called me. What a mess. But I have no extra clothes for them. No pajamas, no socks, no underwear. Oh, and Liz lost a shoe. Could you do me a huge favor? I know it's a lot to ask but sometime later this morning can you stop by a department store and pick up a few things for them? I just wanna get them home right away and not take them anywhere. When they wake up, I want their surroundings to be calm and familiar and as normal as possible, and for me to be right there next to them. I'm a mess. I'm sorry. I shouldn't ask you for anything after our falling out. I'm sorry for waking you."

"No, no, it's fine." Julie objected. "I can pick up what you need and be there in an hour or so."

"No, you don't need to do it now. It can wait till later this morning." I objected.

"Nonsense!" Julie said. "You need help now. There's a big box store just down the block. They're open 24 hours. And there's no way I can go back to sleep now. It's fine. You can fill me in when I get there." Julie then took the reins of the conversation like an experienced therapist. "They're alright Michael. That's the main thing. Thank you, Jesus! But you need to calm yourself too. You ok?"

"Yeah, I'm calming down." I assured her but was really lying. "Um, their P.J.'s. They don't have any." I said. "I can wash the clothes they're wearing. No, you'll have to get some laundry detergent for me too. I'm out. I'll reimburse you for all of it and buy gas for your car."

"No, it's no problem. Don't worry about it." Julie reassured.

"God, they don't even have their coats!" I suddenly remembered. "They left them in the cop car or Lanie's car or somewhere. They can't check Lanie's car at the impoundment lot for them until they open later this morning. I'll have to somehow get down there and retrieve them at some point. But I can't take the girls because they don't have coats. Crap! Why is this happening?"

Julie assured me everything would be alright and ended the call with a stern declaration. "Michael! I'll take care of *everything*. Don't worry about it now. Just focus on them. That's all you need to do. I'm here for you. Things happen for a reason. I'm praying for all three of you—and Lanie too. I know you're upset with her, but this must be awful for her too." She added with a hopefulness in her voice. "It'll be ok, Michael. You'll see."

Those were just the words of comfort that I needed. I felt like I could breathe again. I was so thankful I had a friend in Julie—*thankful in any kind of circumstance*. I now understood what that verse from Paul in the Bible meant. What would I do without Julie?

Chapter 30.

Written on the back of a Sunday bulletin for the Vienna-Pine Run Assembly Church. It was saved in the cookbook, The Compleat Housewife, or, Accomplish'd Gentlewoman's Companion.

24 December 1932

Just because I felt it was something I needed to do. I volunteered this Christmastime to gather food to provide Christmas meals for the under privileged families in the area. The local Christian church on the corner had canvased the area to create a list of families that were needy.

We were told there would be nearly 40 families who would need our services. It seemed each year there were more and more of them during the hard times of the depression.

Each volunteer would gather food from the participating grocery stores who would donate some and the rest we would purchase from monetary donations and then deliver the meals. I had a list of five families, but on the page one of them was crossed off.

I inquired about why it was crossed off and got no immediate explanation. But later, the rumor was the church society determined that the family's religion was not truly Christian. It was of a certain sect that was at odds with theirs.

I kept my thoughts to myself and filled the order for that fifth family anyway out of funds from my own pocketbook. I never mentioned to them that the church had crossed them out. That would not be in the Christmas spirit. I also said nothing to the church that I had delivered a meal to them anyway.

Helen Laurinda Wilcox

Just as she said, about an hour later, Julie arrived at my door with her arms full of packages.

Noticing the girls fast asleep on the couch, she whispered, "Everyone ok?"

I nodded and paused to take in the vision of my guardian angel—my *saving* angel. She had an almost comical look to her. Julie had wasted no time in coming to my rescue—not even combing her unruly, bright, curly red hair that was even more bushy than usual caused by a severe case of bed head. If I wasn't so glad to see her, I might have laughed out loud. Aside from the brief comic relief, what her arrival did do, was raise a lump of gratitude in my throat. Because of her generosity and kindness, it sparked the beginnings of what I can best describe as a *fledgling love* for her in my heart.

We quietly opened the packages. Not only had Julie purchased warm pajamas for the girls, but she had also purchased all sorts of accessories. There were ample undergarments, socks, and two matching winter coats with fur collars. The coats were a collage of pinks, light blues, and lavender. Under any circumstances the girls would love them. I admit, as a man with a limited sense of fashion, they wouldn't have been my choices for them, so I appreciated Julie's mindfulness in this area. She had even purchased shoes for both girls—and in the correct sizes.

"How did you know what their shoes sizes were—I never told you?" I asked.

Julie confessed she took note of their sizes while they were all playing dolls on the living room rug the time she dined with us. "Just doing some research in case I thought about getting them a gift for Christmas." She said.

"Julie." I marveled. "That is maternal instinct personified!" She blushed while I continued the compliment. "I would have never even thought of doing that."

"Sure, you would have." She contradicted me. "You know what you're doing with these girls. I see you pay attention to them and their needs."

As each package was opened, I wondered how I would pay for everything without busting the budget. I had just enough cash in my wallet to reimburse Julie, but then that was it until payday. She argued that it was not necessary to pay her, but I insisted.

"Julie, this is the reason credit cards exist. I will lean heavily on my credit limit for now *and* Faith when the bills come due next month."

Chapter 31.

Written on the back of a Christmas card. It was saved in the book: The Great Galveston Disaster.

15 December 1947

Each year, for the past four or five years now, I have received a most mysterious Christmas card like this one in the mail. There is never a return address, and it is never signed, and each year it has been postmarked from a different location. Manchester, Ohio, Delmar, Florida, and a few other states. Besides the printed verse inside, the handwritten note usually says something to the effect of, 'Thank you for all you did for my family. May God grant you a joyous Christmas season.' I haven't the foggiest, but it makes me feel blessed.

   Helen Laurinda Wilcox-Phillips

The next several days, the circumstances of Lanie's DUI arrest and the hearing for custody of my children would play out in Family Court. As a result, Lanie's and my role would completely reverse. The Court ordered for the next several months, that it would be me who would get the girls most of the time with exception of every other weekend visits with their Mother. She was not allowed to drive them anywhere until she completed the State's extensive program for DUI offenders—which also carried a hefty fine. This was the harsh ruling handed down by the Judge—who happened to be running for reelection and had campaigned hard on the issue of drunk drivers. By chance, Lanie was to be her *example* case. Now, I thought, it was her turn to face the consequences from a "hanging judge." Julie's prophesy of, "things happening for a reason," was unfolding.

Amid the changes, I found that the parental role reversal did help correct the injustice I had received in the matter at the time of our divorce decree. However, this also created a new set of challenges for me. I now had the responsibility to make sure the girls schedule was not interrupted. There was the required planning of three-square meals a day—not to mention covering the cost of that. I had to make sure daycare, pre-school and school was onboard with the parental changes. My duties would now include attending *every* PTA meeting, *every* assembly, volunteering for school fundraisers and help organize the girl's upcoming Christmas concert with the other parents. I was going to be swamped with activities. It was a big change for a bachelor's life.

Through it all, my hero, Julie, was there more and more to offer help. We resumed our walk n' talks at work. They evolved into discussions on what was going on with the girls and less of our past injustices with Ex's. We made plans together *as a team* on how best to coordinate every change. To have a fully committed partner for that part of child rearing was new to me.

Julie was unquestionably a Godsend. Her concern and care for the girls was genuine! She was there often for their bath time, school project assignments and play time. All the while, Julie was ever mindful of the role she played in their lives and mine and went out of her way to "stay in her lane" and not to try to replace their Mother. She took it upon herself to only fill in *temporarily* for the things that Lanie was not there to provide for the girls. I appreciated that.

First and foremost, with this new parental arrangement, I did not want the girls to be distanced from their Mother. Although I doubt if the circumstances were reversed, the Ex would reciprocate in the same way. Lanie could be vindictive. Julie, by comparison, was generous as a Saint. In many ways, Julie had managed to slip in comfortably between the role of surrogate Mother and big sister for the girls.

Things were working so well. I admit I found myself at times forgetting that Julie was still just a good friend to me and not my spouse. She fit in so nicely with us. We shared in every way a married couple with children would—except for anything intimate or even remotely romantic. We knew enough not to take that step or even broach the subject in conversation. That was simply not the focus of this understanding.

A couple of times, I found myself slipping toward ungratefulness for what Julie was doing for us. When I realized that drift, I felt ashamed and was made acutely aware that my behavior was all too like the *men in long robes*. When it happened, I course-corrected by remembering my Mother and Grandmothers. Their legacies outlined in those precious cookbooks, always starkly reminded me how wrong it would be for me to treat Julie in the same manner as they had been so often over the course of their lives. I vowed to never to do that.

Throughout all this upheaval in our lives, one question kept nagging at me that had never been resolved. How did it come to be that the Ex and my girls attended that Church service? How did she know I was there? Who involved her in that group of people and for what purpose? I never directly confronted Lanie about it. At first it was because she would never take my calls, but after her arrest I figured she was under enough stress, and I'm sure the discussion—or rather an argument, would add to it. So, I avoided the issue, and thus was never given a clear answer. But each time I contemplated the question, I knew it had to be Orrin who was the one spinning the web. I concluded that he must have done a deep dive researching *me*! Although, on the surface he seemed a distant and a doddering senior, he was in fact, calculating and devious. He was the epitome of a frugal megalomaniac and master manipulator who always got what he wanted.

I think I had it figured out. Since Orrin was a man of single-minded purpose, he had made up his mind that I was the one he needed to further his business-church scheme to the general public. Beyond the big pay raise—which would normally be enough for anyone to submit to his designs, as added insurance, after sensing my resistance, he had accessed my personnel file where Lanie was listed as the emergency contact. He then reached out to her, inquired about my children, and invited them all to be at his church, as a way of leveraging my reluctance to participate.

To me, the most horrifying aspect of Orrin's scheming was the most personal method he used to get what he wanted. In my mind, his orchestrations were no different than those employed by terrorist organizations. I've read the reports that reluctant suicide bombers are ultimately convinced to strap on explosives to blow up a crowded restaurant with the added incentive that their family members were being held hostage until the deed was done. The terrorist organizations had *men who desired to walk in long robes* too.

Chapter 32.

Handwritten with a fountain pen inside the front cover of the book: The Eleventh Annual Report of the Secretary of the State Horticultural Society of Michigan – 1881. The penmanship appears to be Chloe Stevens'.

"This is my commandment, that ye love one another, as I have loved you."

John 15:12 - King James Version

Julie's willingness to help through the drama of Lanie's DUI, the custody issue, and the genuine love she showered upon the girls seemed to smooth over the religious rift that had flared between us. I think we both tried to pretend the earlier contentious discussion and the way that evening ended had never happened. We never again mentioned our religious differences.

But because of her willingness to unselfishly help, I wanted to express my gratitude to her in some special way. I still had a *little* margin left on the credit card limit, so the next day during our walk n' talk, I invited her out to dinner at a nice restaurant. I wanted to give her a special thank-you for all her invaluable help.

In hindsight, reflecting on Julie's immediate response to my call, I recognized that she embodied the essence of a true Christian spirit. Rather than try to go it alone—which I feared I would have to, out of desperation, I had made the decision to chasten my pride and ask Julie to take a big step into our lives. It was the best decision I have ever made. There was no doubt that my consistent prayer for direction was what guided me to reach out to her. Previously, without prayer—or at least contemplative thought, my usual choice was to insist on complete independence—which lately had seemed to make things worse. By admitting vulnerability and seeking help, I believe it was a sign of *my own* growth and maturity. Imagine that after 50 plus years. Besides, it was nice having someone to share with—someone who was a constant source of comfort, security, and joy.

Yes, I believe there is a built-in desire to be *included* rather than stand alone. After all the recent events, I recognized that need in me and I suspected Julie benefitted from our arrangement too. From her outward expressions of determination, I could see she felt the same way about sharing my challenges. They had become her challenges. But that arrangement was patently unfair. There was a huge imbalance to it. It harkened back to all the injustices I had learned about in those cookbooks. It couldn't let it continue that way and I intended to make sure that Julie knew I was there for *her* too. Thus, the thank-you dinner.

So, that night, we got a babysitter for the girls. It was one of Julie's married girlfriends who had been slyly hinting to us of late that we should take the plunge to advance our friendship beyond just being pals. We always ignored her playful taunts.

That evening, I don't know if it was the culmination of all her girlfriend's urgings to us, the exceptional wine, the atmosphere of the restaurant, or Julie's elegant makeup, dress, hair and ever-present intelligent conversation, but in my dense, manly ways, I realized I had never contemplated her in this light before. It hit me out of the blue and settled onto my heart. I loved her. To be clear, I was not sure at what level, but I did, and it was more than the *fledgling love* I had felt for her earlier.

However, in that moment of revelation, I couldn't sort it all out in my mind and I couldn't find the words to express it to her in a heartfelt but subdued way without saying those *three little words*. I knew they were a relationship lynchpin. In my recent experience, those words were only reserved for my daughters, and for them, it had a different meaning. Those words had last been said to an adult woman when I was married. I knew what they meant with Lanie. Frankly, I never expected to feel that kind of romantic love or use those words in that way with anyone else again. And I wasn't completely sure now. So, I was at a loss, and let my newly realized feeling for Julie go unannounced. Instead of my usual behavior of, speak first and worry about the consequences later, I pushed the feeling back to the recesses of my heart and mind, where it would lay silent. I needed lots of time and prayer for God's direction on this one.

Chapter 33.

Archived loosely in the cookbook, The Compleat Housewife, or, Accomplish'd Gentlewoman's Companion by Chloe Stevens, circa 1900.

"For the mystery of iniquity doth already work: only he who now letteth will let, until he be taken out of the way."

2 Thessalonians 2:7 – King James Version

Written on the margins of an 8-page publication: Argosy All Story Weekly, circa 1925. Price 10 cents. Archived in the book: The Great Galveston Disaster.

11 June 1925

Gosh Doomit! Roger gets so possessive of even the sparest of change. My lands! To have a brother that is such a poor sport when it comes to playing a hand of pinochle is embarrassing. Every penny bet brings out the worse in him. He gets so angry when the cards do not fall his way that I am fearful the vein in his forehead will burst. Telling him to calm himself only makes matters worse. And there is no owing him his winnings. His mind is made up. "I want my 35 cents and I want you to pay up now." My stars and garters, he takes all the fun out of a game but insists I play. I refuse to take the 35 cents from my pocketbook to settle my debt. I expect an argument at some point when he counts his jar of coins on his nightstand.

Helen Laurinda Wilcox

With all the recent events of Lanie's DUI and my new family obligations, I pushed the issue of my developing responsibilities at work and Orrin's dual missions to the back burner. But the time had come for confrontation. I could avoid it no longer. I knocked on Orrin's door and entered the dingy office with the intent to set the record straight about me, my interests, what I was willing to do for him and his church and what I could not. I would try to deftly back out of my quid pro quo with the old man. I don't think it had ever been done before, but I would try to successfully return my "*30 pieces of silver*."

While practicing the words that I would use in addressing Orrin, I reread some of my Grandmother's cookbooks content for inspiration—even memorizing some of her most eloquent phrases so I could draw upon them in order to sway him. I knew they were always so empowering, and I thought that they might give me the foresight to walk a fine line between saying words that would allow me to keep my job or ones that would find me back in another line—the *unemployment* line.

I began. "Mr. Orrin, I have thought about this long and hard. I don't believe I'm the man for your job. Frankly, with all due respect, Sir, I do not feel comfortable within the tenets of your church community. And I believe I am within my rights not to be subjected to it in order to stay employed. And I strongly object, with all due respect, that my children should not be a part of this. I know you had something to do with their invitation to attend your church. I appreciate the Christian gesture, but they have been through a lot lately, and I'd rather not complicate their lives currently—especially at their age and with their current needs. I'm sorry. I hope you understand. I have full custody of them now and it's all I can do to raise them properly to face the challenges of today's modern world. Again, I hope you understand. I honestly don't have the time that you should rightfully require of me to perform to your satisfaction the added functions you have in mind for me. You have every right to expect that and I know I would meet those expectation if circumstances were different."

I was not interrupted by Orrin, so I continued. "I will relinquish the pay raise you generously gave me and request that I remain employed in my previous capacity of Prep Lab rat—uh, I mean *associate*." Oh, that was an unforced error. I hoped he didn't notice the faux pas.

So, now my excuse to him was finished. It was said without ambiguity or nuance and with complete sincerity, but I had to admit there was a lot of rambling near the end of my delivery. My fate was now in his hands.

Orrin sat there without reaction. It was possible that no one else had ever spoken to him in this manner before. How would he react? I couldn't get a read on his temperament, but that was nothing new. He was an enigma. I knew full well that he was used to his toadies cowering before him—knowing his authority controlled their livelihood. I understood he was a man who got what he wanted, and I had just shown the audacity to deny him. What would be his reaction?

Then, what I had feared most began to happen. After an uncomfortable amount of time, his stunned expression slowly morphed into one of seething rage. Like an overfilled tea kettle, he quickly built up steam and boiled over in a sputtering barrage.

"You! You've been accepting *my* money I gave you as part of our agreement!" He began to rise from his creaking chair with great difficulty. "You! Under false pretenses, *you* agreed to work on my Missions. The project is in motion. And now you have a change of heart? It's not that easy Mr. Jacobs. I have spent *my* valuable time and *my* resources on this project. You!" His voice raised an octave and became even more agitated as he stuttered and struggled for words.

"P-p-p, people like you who think they know everything about the modern world. *That* is your God instead of the true God—holding your family's needs above those of the Lord."

The stammering continued. "Lu-Lu-Luke 14:26 says, "If any man come to me, and hate not his f-f-father, and mother, and wife, and children, and brethren, and sisters, yea, and his own life also, he cannot be my d-d-disciple."

Instinctively taking a step back from his onslaught, I assumed his "Messiah complex," had now kicked into what I thought was full force. "You! are trying to undermine the Lord's and *my* Missions that he has charged *me* alone to do! You will burn in Hell!" I thought that should be his crescendo. However, he was just warming up.

"Revelation 12:11 says, "And they overcame him because of the blood of the Lamb, and because of the word of their testimony; and they loved *not their life* even unto death." He shouted at the top of his lungs.

After that burst, I heard the door to the adjacent Executive Secretary office, which had been slightly ajar, click shut. Obviously, Mrs. Orrin, didn't want to hear or have anything to do with what was going on in the boss' office. Orrin's dog, Zephaniah, also sensing the change in the atmosphere of the room, had already known enough to jump from his lap onto the floor and stood there shaking. He then sought cover under a blanket in his wicker dog bed as Orrin continued his painfully slow rise from his chair.

I didn't think the verbal assault could get worse, but it continued to gather a volcanic eruption amount of force as memorized quotes continued to spill from Orrin's lips in an endless tirade of Biblical threats. I stood dumbfounded and was admittedly a little scared by this disproportional response to my request. Sure, I had a penchant of saying the wrong thing to the wrong person at the wrong time—which could piss people off, but I could have never expected this kind of rage caused by my meager objections.

"You are *not* among the 144,000!" Orrin almost shrieked! "You will be cast to the sixth circle of Hell! Six circulus ex inferno, haereticus reputandus."

Whoa! Now that salvo sent a chill down my spine, but at the same time I was kinda impressed that this Orrin guy also knew his Latin and was thoughtful enough to provide an English translation for me too.

Orrin continued the struggle to get up from his chair to stand erect. Finally, managing to get to his feet, he staggered from around his desk toward me as he continued to spout a blur of religious babble in an old-English-King Jamesian style—at one point sentencing me to one of those burning tombs in Hell reserved for Heretics. I'm almost certain, wedged somewhere in between his references to the Four Horsemen of the Apocalypse, I heard the words: "You're fired!" I had been *dissed* by the religious self-righteous before, but never with so much outward vile condemnation.

Fight or flight? Those were my immediate options again. I chose flight as I backed toward the door seeking a quick exit. "I'm sorry! I didn't mean to imply." I tried to interject something to assuage his geriatric assault. "I think you misunderstood, Mr. Orrin!" But it did not deter him in the least. He pointed his bony finger in my face, still spewing a Biblical "word salad" of anger and vitriol.

Still not sure that I had in fact been fired, I said, "I better get back to work." Turning to the door—almost sprinting the last two steps toward it. I slipped through and shut it quickly. In the relative safety of the hallway, I realized that my developed muscle memory of avoiding dog droppings in his office had failed me while I was under assault. I had stepped in a recent fresh pile of Zephaniah's crap. I couldn't blame the dog, I thought. I had almost crapped myself too. Then for some reason, an odd question popped into my head. Who names a *dog,* Zephaniah, anyway?

The thought vanished as soon as it appeared, and I grimaced while wiping my shoe vigorously to remove the nastiness on the welcome mat outside Orrin's office. I then ducked down the hall to the men's room where I paper toweled the remaining excrement off the bottom of my shoe. Washing my hands thoroughly with as much soap from the dispenser as I could hold in the palm of my hand, I stood there looking at my reflection in the mirror.

"What have I done?" I gasped. The words: *My big mouth just cost me this job* kept racing through my brain. I should've just gone along with it—been the corporate stuffed suit. Just compromise everything I believe—everyone does it. What difference does it make anyway? What's the point of standing up for what you believe? You only get screwed and I should have known you can't reason with someone like that old man. How did I think I could? I've been canned. Now how will I pay my rent? What about my girls and their needs, their dentist bills, their Christmas presents? Had I seriously considered any of that before deciding to confront Orrin?

The person that I saw in the mirror, now filled with regret, questioned me. Was I only selfishly thinking about myself? No! Absolutely not! I just couldn't go along with it! Orrin's Missions were not going to be good in the long run for me or my children. That was the bottom line. I was justified in butting heads with him. My reasons were valid. It was the *principal of the matter* I told myself. But the *principal of the matter* would cost me big time. My mind shifted from one bad fallout of my actions to the next and it all sloshed around in my brain, with no answers rising to the surface which could provide direction.

"Well, I can't hide in this bathroom all day." I said. So, I beat a hasty exit down the stairs and returned to my cubicle in the Prep Lab—terribly shaken, but no one in the lab noticed. Out of habit, I sat down and started rummaging through the next batch of specimens to process, not really knowing what to do.

A few minutes passed and then suddenly the door of the Prep Lab swung open violently with a bang as it hit the casing. It was Orrin. Apparently, he was not through with me. He advanced menacingly toward my cubicle. I rose to the threat.

But then he stopped abruptly, and his demeanor miraculously changed. He got this wry look on his face and a half-smile of a Cheshire cat. In a voice loud enough for all in the lab to hear, he announced. "Well, Mr. Jacobs, at Genome 23 History we pride ourselves on providing the best work environment for all our employees on our team, but if you feel you *can't* work under these conditions here—everyone says they're the best—the best job conditions. They tell me, Sir, this is better than the previous employers we worked for. Everyone thinks that. Wouldn't you all agree?" He spoke as if he were at a political campaign rally and was waiting for applause. His question turned out to be a rhetorical one because no one in the lab spoke up. All pretended not to be startled by the bizarre scene unfolding before them. They cowered silently in their cubicles hoping he didn't call on them individually for their opinion.

With no reaction from his audience, he redirected his performance to me. "Mr. Jacobs, as I was saying, if you don't like it here, I'm more than happy to accept your letter of resignation—which you have just submitted and is *on my desk*. I had hoped you would have enjoyed it here. I had big plans for you. Good luck to you in your future endeavors." And with that, he turned to leave and headed for the door.

That bastard! That cheap bastard! I thought. He was trying to make it seem like I quit rather than him firing me. He was trying to beat me out of any unemployment benefits I had earned by saying I quit instead of being fired. Now, what was I to do? Unemployment benefits would be my safety net. I couldn't let him get away with it—not for the sake of my children's welfare. And what letter of resignation? I never submitted one, but he says mine is on his desk. A forgery?

Then it hit me. It was now abundantly clear what he had done. That clever S. O. B! I now understood the reason we all had to sign a blank piece of paper in our new-hire employment pack. He just used mine to create my signed letter of resignation. I'll bet he's having Mrs. Orrin type in the text of the letter right now.

"Quit?" I shouted. "You just fired me upstairs. You fired me and now you're trying to beat me out of unemployment with a forged letter of resignation! You bastard!"

Hearing the insult—and who wouldn't be able to in this tiny Prep Lab, he turned to me but brushed off my comment. "I don't know what you mean, Mr. Jacobs. You just gave me your *signed* resignation. I have it on the desk in my office." Then he smiled again, turned, and continued toward the door—his long black coat flowing behind him like a judge's robe as it would if he were exiting a courtroom after sentencing.

Over his shoulder he said, "Mr. Welch in H.R. will conduct your exit interview in a few minutes and escort you from the building. You should probably pack your belongings in the interim. I think there are some extra boxes in the shipping area. Feel free to take one. I'll waive the policy that prohibits the taking of company property from the building—this one time only. Have a blessed day." He continued his unsteady gait to the open door.

I had just been played like a pawn by a chess master. But, true to my nature, I couldn't let him get away with it without saying something—*something* memorable.

So, I disengaged my voice filter and my big mouth kicked in. What could it hurt at this point? I also amplified my response loud enough, for not only all in the Prep Lab, but also anyone or any vermin in the warehouse to hear. This performance was going to be epic. It was something that I had practiced before for such an event—if one ever materialized. Now it had. I would draw heavily from the prose I had memorized from my Grandmother's cache of essays tucked away in those precious cookbooks. Her words would prove to be spot-on for this rare occasion.

As I took in a deep breath, I was confident that Grandma Helen never had the opportunity in her lifetime to use the forceful words she had penned. I'll bet she could have never predicted that two generations later, her creative writing would be appropriate for an employee's exit from a genetic testing company. But the time was now to utilize some of her choicest prolific literature. The curtain rose on my performance. As Orrin reached for the door handle to exit the lab, I began.

"Orrin!" I shouted. "When a religion becomes more of a cult of self-righteousness—like *yours*, rather than the trans-formative purpose for living—for which it was intended, people like you—filled with your hubris, should really step back and fully view the intolerance you have for other people." I belted it out to the backrow. "The inherent ugliness of your twisted belief system is on display for everyone outside of the other like-minded sycophants in your cult! Yes, I said *cult*!"

Then, really feeling my oats, I adlibbed the rest in a style I believe any Shakespearean actor would approve. "*You*!" I said, mimicking his diatribe in the office. "*You!* and your ilk, in your long black overcoats—your *long robes*, you are so far removed from the basic core tenets of Christian Faith that its laughable! It's not funny, it's *laughable*! People like *You!* ruin it for *real* Christians!"

I had finished. It was a presentation worthy of taking a bow upon completion. Though, that would have seemed pompous on my part without any applause—and there was none of it being offered up from any of my fellow Prep Lab cohorts. Truth was that my contemporaries were still too scared to react to anything they were witnessing.

Facing away from me, at the crescendo of my performance, Orrin stopped in his tracks. His shoulders quickly rose and tightened as if someone had hit him in the back of the neck with a two by four. He angrily turned toward me and rapidly closed the distance with his bony index finger waving and pointing in my face. I instinctively backed up into my cubicle—nearly tripping over the rolling office chair. My backside crashed into the desk, scattering the materials on top of it in all directions.

Orrin unleashed. I was hit with another barrage of apocalyptic pronouncements like the ones I had fielded in his office. This time I couldn't distinguish their origins because I was too focused on survival mode. But they all had that *Armageddon* kind of vibe.

At the height of his recitation of vitriol and unleashed rage, just inches from me, he suddenly stopped cold. He stopped breathing. His mouth gaped open and his eyes rolled up into his head. He clutched for the cubicle wall, paused momentarily and then fell over backwards to the floor with the dull thud of a half-filled trash bag. The gasp of his last breath wheezed from his lifeless rumple and the room stood quiet for a split second.

This was a nightmare come true. I had previously envisioned, during my own frequent bouts of anxiety caused by sleep apnea, what it might be like at the very end of life—in the moment of *my* last breath. Now I was seeing it firsthand in Orrin. It was every bit as terrifying as I had imagined.

"My God! He's dead!" came a voice from behind me.

I stood there frozen over Orrin's body. "I just killed him. I just killed him." I said in a bewildered chant. Bodies began scrambling toward the commotion. One of the other employees in the lab who was a weekend paramedic for a fire department immediately loosened Orrin's tie and began chest compressions on the gray and lifeless form splayed out on the floor—while muttering a 120 beats per second song, just like they teach you in a CPR class to maintain compression rhythm. Someone else had already called 9-1-1 and was rapidly giving directions to EMS along with a thumbnail sketch of the scene and what had transpired. I staggered back and slumped into my cubicle again. Sitting stunned on the edge of my desk, I remained there silently for what seemed like an hour—but was only a few minutes. I had a ringside seat to watch the EMS personnel perform their lifesaving efforts until one of them pronounced Orrin dead. They tossed a sheet over him, lifted him onto a stretcher and carried him away to the ambulance. No one moved. I could hear concerned murmuring from my lab mates, and the distinct sound of Julie's voice sobbing from her cubicle, but no one said anything to me. Now I knew what it was like to be a pariah.

People started gathering their belonging and slowly exiting the lab with embarrassed and fearful quick glances toward me after the H.R. manager came in to announce that we should all go home for the rest of the afternoon. That was a first. An early end of the workday had never happened before in the history of employment here. Authorities said they would contact each of us if they had any questions. Mr. Welch tried to reassure all of us, in a surprisingly unpassionate, perfunctory tone, that Mr. Orrin was old and very frail lately. "It was his time." He said. I wondered if I would also hear a proclamation from him that, "The King is dead. Long live the new King!" I did not.

Leaving the Prep Lab with the others, we all reacted as if we were rescued animals being released from captivity—gingerly taking tentative first steps out of a cage. I filed out to the parking lot with them and headed to my vehicle, put it in gear and slowly drove to nowhere in particular.

Chapter 34.

Written in black ink on blank sheets of newsprint using a fountain pen. It was in the book: The Eleventh Annual Report of the Secretary of the State Horticultural Society of Michigan – 1881.

16 August 1892

Ralph is never overly generous with anyone, least of all the Turnbull's next door. They had words over the property lines and a fence placement. No one was paying for a survey to be done to establish the lines properly, so no one was happy where the fence landed. They say fences make good neighbors but not this one. So, charity was not discussed when our neighbors fell on hard times from Mr. Turnbull's surgery for lumbago. The rumor was that he hurt his back when pulling stumps by himself after the squabble and Ralph would not lend him the steam tractor for the job. He should be ashamed of his stinginess.

Dear Ellie would not have accepted charity in any form anyway. I knew that. She was proud as most folks around here and did what she could to make ends meet for the family throughout her husband's infirmity by selling eggs to passers-by from a wooden ice box on their front porch.

They ran it on the honor system as most folks do. I must admit I saw some take without paying for them. Petty theft in this case is far more hurtful that the thieves know. But despite Ralph's outright dismissal of helping the Turnbull's and his direct instructions to me to not offer them any of his precious money, I decided to do what I could without discussion with him on our differences.

Each Sunday morning while the Turnbull's were attending church, I would gather as many fresh eggs laid from our chicken coop as I could carry in my apron and took them over to their chicken coop to supplement the few on the nest laid by her scrawny, underfed and underproducing hens. She would then have more to sell. I'm sure she wondered how only half a dozen hens could lay all those eggs every Saturday night when she comes to gather them after Sunday services. The math had to be even more curious to her when they were forced to start culling a hen a week for the dinner table.

I had to stop the clandestine egg delivery when the last of her hens were consumed. To go beyond that would surely have been Divine intervention and a miracle.

Ellie never has said anything about this egg phenomenon, but I think maybe she knows better and who the culprit was. When we are both out tending to our flower gardens, she always smiles so affectionately, with knowing eyes, as she reaches out to hold my hand to chat for a bit, over that damned fence.

Chloe Stevens

After about an hour of aimless driving around town, my cell rang. It was Julie.

"Are you alright?" She shyly inquired.

"Um, yes, I guess." There was nothing reassuring in my voice.

"How did that all happen? She asked. "What went on in your office meeting with him?"

"I'm not sure." I explained. "I just spoke my mind. I told him about my beliefs—about *religion*." I said disgustedly.

"Oh, that topic again?" She said in a similar tone.

"Now what's that supposed to mean?" I asked but didn't wait for an answer. "I told him how I felt about his church and how I couldn't handle all the extra responsibility he had in mind for me because I now have the kids fulltime. I don't know. It set him off. I always get in trouble when I speak my mind— especially about *religion*." I again emphasized the word in an agitated way.

You got yourself let go over *religion?*" She asked.

"That's about the size of it." I groaned. "You can blame me for his death. I can tell everyone in the lab does."

She cut me off trying to reassure me. "No, that's not true!" She objected. "He was old, frail. You heard Welch say it. It was just his time. It's sad but there's nothing you or anybody could do to prevent it. It's not your fault. Just shouting at him—regardless of some of those awful things you said to him, shouldn't have killed him." She took a deep breath and then sighed. "I'm more worried about you. What are you going to do for work? What are you going to do for your girls?"

"You would think I would have thought all of that through before I pissed him off and killed him," I said in a snarky tone.

Julie agreed with more than a hint of scolding. "Yes, you would *think*." And then added. "Are you ok for money? I have a little saved. It's yours if you want it."

I was humbled by her generosity, despite her lecturing tone. "No, no that's not anything I could accept." I told her. "I have a little money saved too." That was a lie. "Listen, I passionately believe things happen for a reason. There's gotta be a silver lining in this—although right now I haven't the foggiest what that might be. I'm sure He—and by He, I mean God, will take care of everything in the end. I have good family precedent to believe that."

"Well, ok." She said—only half believing me. "You sure?"

"I'm fine. I just feel so bad about the old guy. Not my favorite person—sure, but I never knew I would set him off and it would end him."

"So, I'm still confused. You quit? You were fired? Which is it?" Julie wanted clarification.

"No!" I stated emphatically. "I tried to keep my old job and back out of the new part of it—the promotion part of it he offered. But like a dummy, I had already passively accepted it—I say coerced into it. A little of both I guess. I just couldn't do it now with all the duties I now have with the kids. I don't have the time. And his stupid dual Missions of work *and* his church. Ugh!"

Julie was not convinced with my answer. "Is it *that* difficult to go to church? She asked with incredulity. "You couldn't go along with it for the sake of your kids? You couldn't sit there for one hour every Sunday for the sake of your girls?"

She just wasn't getting my reasoning. I knew why. It went right back to the religious confrontation we had a while back. Julie, like so many, in so many religious flocks, was conditioned that everyone must attend church. Her thought process was: If you don't go, you'll go to Hell. Oh, and by the way, you can't just let it go in one ear and out the other. While in attendance, you also must believe everything they espouse. Oh, and one more thing, until the time that you do accept all of the church views, the inability of the rest of the flock to understand your reasons for disdaining regular church attendance or believing everything, will force us to ostracize you. You won't fit in. So, for the sake of financial security, just go along with it. It's a universal church-goers flow chart that eventually spits out people like me who don't.

Julie's insistences on the topic and her objections were nothing new to me. I had attempted to explain my reasons numerous times before to many people, but no one ever understood. But, since I considered Julie a friend, I'd try again. I lowered my tone.

"Listen Julie, I don't think you know the half of it. It's more than just being inconvenienced or uncomfortable in Orrin's church. I can't allow myself to be a passive member of it for an hour each week and then go about my life. I'll be sucked into his church's doctrine and then must promote it through his business project—which I still don't know what it is. I'd have to be the face of it in public by pushing his business-church agenda for his financial gain and my survival—which is bad enough of a compromise, but I'll also have to drag my kids into his same orthodox, B. S. That kind of systemic indoctrination will push them down. It'll groom them into what I don't want them to be. Hell, I've read about members of my own family that have had that same kind of stuff shoved down their throats. They fought against it and suffered from it for generations. The only thing they could do to resist it was to write about it and then stuff their thoughts into cookbooks so they would be hidden. And I've seen firsthand when I was a kid how the progression of that mindset affected people I love. So, I know what I'm talking about. That path of indoctrination goes against everything that I believe or want *for my two girls*. They've already been dragged into one of the church services. So, I *am* thinking of my children. Don't you get that?"

Julie's end of the conversation was silent. I wasn't even sure the phone call was still connected. "You still there?" I asked. She said only "Yes." Her one-word answer failed to indicate if any of my justification was penetrating her, but I continued as I tried to hold my frustration in check.

"I tried to reason with him, Julie. I offered to go back to the Prep Lab—even give up the pay raise. Nothing doing. He blew up and fired me in his office—which I heard him say, I think. Hell, he was babbling so much."

"You think?" Julie asked.

"Well, he told me to go to the sixth circle of Hell! I think that counts as a firing. I doubt I can commute from there. He said I quit just to be a prick—said I submitted a letter of resignation, which I didn't. They wrote it. Yeah, I signed it, but that was when I hired in. It was only a blank piece of paper with my signature on it then. They filled it in. D'ya get it? That's gonna ruin any unemployment benefits for me. That's what set *me* off."

I began losing my lower tone of voice and my anger rose. "He's vindictive. His pompous B. S. about me quitting was all for your benefit in the lab. Guess he thought he needed witnesses, but I think it was more for my humiliation. You heard him."

"So, let me get this straight." Julie persisted in

needing more clarification. "You didn't quit, but he fired you because you put your foot down. You couldn't do what your employer asked of you? You'd rather put yourself and your family at financial risk?"

"Ugh, no! That's not it." I shouted. "I have tried to explain it to you. I'm outta words, Julie! The only thing I know is that I'm 100% certain that my signature on that blank page—the one we all had to sign when we hired in, was so he could fill it in later with a letter of resignation and postdate it to today. It is his insidious way of always being able to get what he wants from everyone *or else!* His old lady in the next office probably already notarized it. I knew that was suspicious when I hired in. I'm so screwed."

"Hmm." Julie paused. "I signed one of them too." She considered the fact. "I think everyone has to when we hire in. That's not right if it was used the way you say. I'm sorry for that." She reluctantly said.

"Look, I'll be fine, Julie. I hope. I have to keep telling myself that. I can't let myself get down to the moment of despair, give up and do something stupid or a knee-jerk reaction. And no, all that with Orrin was *not* stupid or a knee-jerk reaction! I know you think it was but believe me it's not in the long run. I know in my heart I'll be lifted—eventually. I've seen it done before." I took a few deep breaths to try to reset a civil atmosphere on the call. "Sorry I yelled at you. I wish I could explain it better and make you understand. I'll just have to face the gorilla at the Unemployment Office to fight this."

I could tell she began to form a response, but then

hesitated, not understanding the reference to a gorilla. "Well." She tried to soften her defiant mood. "Don't worry. It'll all work out in the end." She insisted. And then reluctantly added. "And...I'll be praying for you."

"Thanks Julie. I appreciate your concern." The call ended. I repeated the same words I said the last time we had a falling out. "Well, probably never see her again!"

Thank God this was not a Friday when I'd have to pick up my girls. Lanie would have them this weekend. I could only imagine what they might say.

"What did you do today Daddy?"

"Oh, not much girls, I just killed my boss."

Chapter 35.

"But I know that even now, whatsoever thou wilt ask of God, God will give it thee."

John 11:22 - King James Version

The above verse, cut from an older publication of the Bible, was originally archived into one of the cookbooks by Chloe Stevens, circa 1900 with needle and thread. It was subsequently paperclipped to the following composition. The date of the composition happens to fall on Helen's birthday.

13 March 1953

Mother was near the end. She would take no food or drink and only opened her eyes occasionally in the fever. She wasn't aware of any of us who had gathered. It seems like we had to change the linens on her bed every hour. Her body had shut down from typhus and consumption. She was 89 and had lost half her weight in two weeks as an invalid. I was overwhelmed with the demands of her care not even having the time to cry. I asked Father if he could take an armful of the soiled linens to the basement and soak them in a wash tub as we were running out of them. He said that was 'women's work' and he'd ask some of the ladies in the Eastern Stars Auxiliary if they could help. The men receded from the house and were gone for several hours. They only returned when they had figured enough hours had passed so the angel of death had visited and left. They smelled of beer and had spent the time waiting at the corner tavern. One groused that there wasn't any supper prepared during all the fuss over Mother.

I was too tired and too filled with sorrow to argue the callousness of the comment. At the end, I only had time for a short prayer for her. I still needed to prepare Mother for the visitations. Relatives would be arriving soon after hearing the news to pay respects. This was not the kind of birthday I had imagined for myself. Things happen in ways one can never expect.

The next day, I stood alone in my little living room, pacing back and forth for what must have been hours, trying to grasp what had happened and what was to follow. It started to sink in that I should have handled the whole thing differently—should have never said what I did. Ahh, *regret*—my old friend. There was a knock on my door. Standing there was Julie.

"Can I come in?" She meekly inquired.

"Sure. Never thought I'd see you here again after our last phone call." I said.

"I never thought I'd be here either." She replied. "Can we talk?"

"Of course." My guard was let down. We both sat on the couch and simultaneously said, "I'm sorry."

"No," I repeated. "I'm sorry. First things first. I want to apologize. I should have learned my lesson over the years not to discuss religious differences. Hell, the difference just killed someone. It's your right to believe whatever you want, and I have no right to diminish your beliefs or how you practice them. I wouldn't want anyone to do that to me. I didn't want Orrin to do that to me."

"When it's happened to me in the past, I've been pissed and disappointed in people." I continued. "Sometimes they pushed me away, sometimes I did the pushing. Too many times it was mutual. But I shouldn't be doing the same thing to you—e*specially* you. You have been such a good friend to me and a big sister and surrogate mother to my daughters. I don't know how to express how much that has meant to the three of us. Instead of appreciation, I've treated all your kindness by insulting your religious traditions. That was simply wrong of me. I should know by now that my beliefs on the subject are outside the norm. So, please don't think I'm lumping you in with the likes of Orrin. You are not like him. I don't believe you are filled with that kind of delusional hate and intolerance. I'm sorry I was so short with you on the phone too. Again, please accept my apology." Her response surprised me.

"Let me apologize too." She said. "I admit, that after our last phone call—and going back to that time I left here abruptly after the first time we discussed the same subject, I was angry with you and disappointed by your attitude about Christianity. It didn't seem to match what I *thought* I knew about you. It confused me, and in the moment, it hurt my feelings. I reacted by bolting for the door, rather than listening and trying to understand from your standpoint. Even now, I'm not sure I fully understand, but you have the right to feel as you do, and I should have at least given you the chance to explain. And I still had a hard time with it on our last phone conversation. I almost hung up on you, but that wouldn't have been fair to you based on the position you're in with the loss of a job. I fear that my attitude was helping to ruin our friendship. When I left here the last time, and after the phone call, I said to myself, "Well, I'll never talk to him again.""

"I said the same things about you." I laughed.

"Two stubborn peas in a pod." She summarized our mutual reactions. "Then there was the thing at work yesterday. Oh my God, it was so awful. I saw it all in front of me and I couldn't believe it was happening. He died right in front of us. I've never witnessed that before. It was such a shock to me."

"It was for everyone." I agreed.

Julie continued. "So, after our phone call earlier, I was so confused. I know what I've always felt and what I've always been taught about religion. And I know you tried to explain what you feel and what you've been taught and learned from your family's experience. I couldn't make them both jell in the same universe. It upset me so much, I went straight home and curled up under an afghan and closed my eyes and prayed for direction."

"That's exactly what I do." I said.

"I was afraid for you." She continued. "The position it puts you in without a job. I feared for those precious little girls and wondered how you were going to be able to support them. But I also I felt like with you gone—from work *and my life*, I was the one losing something too. It made me afraid for *me* for some reason."

"I don't understand Julie." I said.

She repeated. "I closed my eyes and prayed for direction. I must have fallen asleep for a couple hours, but I woke suddenly with the clarity of thought that I needed to do something. I got out my Bible and turned the pages to Timothy and Ephesians—the ones we argued over. I don't think I ever read some of them before, but I did thoroughly this time. I read them. And I read them again and again. Michael, you were right. The words are plain."

"I even read them out loud to hear how they sounded." Julie explained. "From Ephesians 5 it talks about, *'Wives, be in subjection unto your own husbands...to their husbands in everything.'* And later stuff about fearing them. That's a license to exploit relationships, Michael. And in Timothy it said *'Let a woman learn in quietness with all subjection. But I permit not a woman to teach, nor to have dominion over a man, but to be in quietness.'* I read the verses in Timothy about slaves having to respect their masters and searched online for commentaries of scholars about that. They strained to try to explain it away that the word *slave* should be interpreted as *servant.* But I researched more and discovered in the earliest translations--in the old koine Greek, the word *doulos* meant someone bound to another with no rights—in other words, a *slave.* I know that real slavery was a common thing back when it was written and right up until the mid-1800's in this country, but that kind of slavery has no place in today's world. So, turning a blind eye to its reference in the Bible as an acceptable thing for today is wrong anyway."

"But the part about women you mentioned." She continued. "I had read those before but never dwelled on them. I tried to think that *you* must be misinterpreting it somehow. But I couldn't. Why hadn't I ever been exposed to its meaning or applied purpose and contemplated that before? How would I have felt if I had read it earlier in my life and really analyzed it? Would that have altered my beliefs or how I thought of my place in the world or who I hung out with? You're right. It all makes no sense to cling to that mentality in the 21st Century. You said Orrin and his church *did* promote those ideals and openly preached about it in services. I had a hard time believing you since I wasn't there to hear it for myself, but after reading it for myself in the same book that he does—well, did before he died, I realized I can't subscribe to it. And like you said, you can't understand anyone who would. That was what you said to me, Michael."

"I did. But I didn't mean for it to be in such a mean fashion." I apologized.

"No, Michael. Before, I was reluctant to believe what you said about Orrin and his church. But after reading about it but more importantly, *praying on it*, I was enlightened. I agree that kind of stuff in there only serves a purpose for those who control the contents of that book—the churches and those institutions. They use it as a set of rules to enforce the status quo to restrict some from leadership roles—and that's *women*. I feel like I've been a victim all this time."

"Michael, I think I understand you. You had read those things in the Bible, understood its meaning, and then compared the written words to the reality of your life. You rejected those ideas for you and your daughters. You couldn't subscribe to it because of the way it would dictate to you and oppress those you love. So, you stood up for yourself to Orrin. I understand that now. Michael, that took—pardon my language, balls! In your shoes, I would have done the same for those babies. You were being forced by Orrin to choose his church and business ways over your family's best interests." She concluded. "It was no contest for you. I get it. But…"

There is always a *but,* I thought. And here it comes.

Julie ended with a criticism. "The practical fallout from your adamant belief is that you have jeopardized your family's wellbeing over a principal."

"Well, yeah." Was my un-elegant reply to her very thoughtful and eloquent appraisal of the situation.

"Again, I can see why *you* say it's important to you, but I don't understand fully." Julie said, "You mentioned your family and the past. You said something about a diary and a cookbook and what you saw firsthand. What is it specifically in you and your family's past that makes you feel this strongly? I want to know. Because I've never stood up to…" Julie gulped on her next words. "…*pressure* from people." Can you share your story with me?"

I could see Julie was not here just to deliver an apology. She was struggling with something else. Rather than simply blowing me off as a friend, as so many others have done when they discovered that my religious views don't line up with theirs, she was in the process of coming to grips with some of the troubling discrepancies in her beliefs and how they had left marks on her life.

"Ok." I said softly. "Julie, I tried to explain on the phone, but I see that was not enough. You took the time and effort to be here. So, it must be important to you. I think you need to know the complete story. It's the only way you'll fully understand why I feel as I do. And I want to share it with you. You mean a lot to me and my girls. Now, I've never told this story to anyone before. It's too painful. I've never mentioned this to other friends—never even discussed it with any of my siblings." I took several deep breaths to alleviate the anxiety building within me.

"You see, Julie," I began. "Unlike to most of my male peers growing up, it wasn't taught in my house that the man was the head of the family. We didn't have one. In my world, the women of the family were always the ones who had to step-up, take responsibility for the welfare of everyone in the household and keep the family morally directed, safe, fed, and clothed. The men mostly got a pass on that—outside of making a paycheck. However, simply for that reason—and for a few of them, not much of any other contributions, they were still considered the *figurehead* boss of the family. The only thing that kept them in that position, was some ancient opinions in the Bible that have been continually fostered in our Christian society—like the ones in Ephesians and Timothy. The men took advantage of those traditions and never thought they needed to step up."

"So, it was up to the women to provide the family

"compass" as best they could from their second-class status." I said. "My Mother, my Grandmother before her, and from what I've read in those cookbooks, I'm certain my Great Grandmother and Great-Great Grandmother had to perform the same kind of deference to the man's authority in their times. Go back through history. That's the way it was. My family's circumstances were not unique in that kind of arrangement."

Then, for the first time to anyone, I proceeded to tell her the painful story of the day my Father died when I was three years old. It was a story I had rarely thought about over my life, but it had all come back to me in that flashback while I sat in Orrin's church the first time I attended. It surfaced then for a reason. Maybe this was it.

I explained to Julie that although I never dwelled on the memory, but when I thought about it, the tragic implications of that day had always been with me to direct my life. I determined the consequences of that day, and all those compositions I had discovered and read in the cookbooks, were weighing heavily on the recent events of the last few months.

I concluded my story to her with, "I will not under any circumstances become one of those men who *desire to walk in long robes*—not to my family, not for Orrin or anyone else."

I peered deeply into her eyes and said it as slowly as I could to emphasize every syllable. "And I won't compromise my ideals just to *please some men in their long robes and thereby abandon my children* for the sake of convenience and survival."

Julies eyes widened. She sucked in a deep breath and a sudden wave of anguish and grief washed over her.

"Ugh, that's what I did!" She gasped. That was immediately followed by uncontrolled sobbing and a torrent of tears. Her voice began shaking. "I've already lived through that and…" She stopped mid-sentence, covering her face with her hands, and wept, unable to continue for some time.

I was taken aback by the emotion she had suddenly released. I had no idea that the explanation of my situation would hit her so hard and would bring on this type reaction. I reached out, put one hand on her knee and placed the other on her shoulder in a meager attempt to console her. She tried to continue but failed through the readily flowing tears. No, it was not the explanation of *my* situation causing this outburst. There was something else that was making her fall apart.

Julie tried again to complete her thought with a thick and shaking voice. "You have told me so much about you, I want you to know something about me. Something I haven't told anyone either." She retrieved a tissue from her purse and wiped her eyes and nose. Through the tissue, in a muffled voice she began.

"When I was a young girl in high school, I was dating a boy. He came from a respectable family that attended the same church we did so my parents approved of him. Well, we—*I* found myself pregnant.

Michael, ever since I was a little girl, I've always dreamed of having a family, and the thought of having a baby someday always filled me with an incredible feeling of anticipation for the future, that was—well, hard to explain."

"Despite how elated I felt on one level—knowing my dream to be a mother was coming true, it took me many days to get the courage to tell my parents. My Stepmom, a teacher, was supportive at first, but worried that me having a child at such a young age would interfere with my education—which was everything to her. My Father was against me keeping it. He was disappointed in me for allowing it to happen. '*How could you allow this to happen to us?*' were his words to me."

"In his eyes, it was all my fault." She said in a tone of resentment. "In his twisted reasoning, the boy had nothing to do with it. Turns out my Dad was more worried about how it might look to his co-workers and his Church community. I loved him but he was so sanctimonious about it. That saddened me. But despite that, I was thrilled and filled with a joy I had never felt before. You wouldn't understand that feeling being a man, Michael. Not to be critical, but you wouldn't."

"Oh, I get it." I reassured her. "Not that I would presume to know what you or any pregnant woman feels. I know what a *fatherly* pride feels like—like when my girls came along, but I think I get what you're saying."

Satisfied that I did, she continued. "So, in my heart, I

wanted to keep the baby, get married and have a family. That would have been the right choice for *me!* But they put so much *pressure* on me—*pressure* to get an abortion. At first, I resisted. But they were relentless. I still lived at home, but my Dad stopped talking to me—ignoring me for the next couple weeks."

"I had always been extremely close to my Father after my own Mother and he divorced. But the way I was treated now made it seem like I had to make a choice between my Father's love and the unborn child growing in me. I felt abandoned." Julie lamented. "Meanwhile, it was my Stepmother who did his bidding. She kept telling me it would be better if I waited to start a family when I was better situated in life. I don't know how she could speak with any authority on the matter, since she had never had any children of her own. So, In the end, I caved. I didn't do what I thought was right for *me*. I felt I had no choice. I did what *they* wanted."

"I'm so sorry Julie," Were the only and horribly inadequate words I could find to console her.

"So, afterwards, I tried to put it out of my mind and block the sadness." Julie stated with determination. "I never dealt with the loss. I concentrated on school and convinced myself I *would* have a family someday. So, I moved out, met Jason—the one I recently broke up with, and *lived the life!* Fancy parties, the cruises—it was carefree. I figured I still had plenty of time on my biological clock. Occasionally, I brought up the subject of having a family with Jason. He always pushed off the discussion. He said that a child would get in the way of his career. So, I let the clock tick and threw my entire focus on him, trying to make the relationship work, with hopes that my dreams would eventually come true."

Julie's tone softened. "After a while, I found that *living the life* did not replace the void in my heart. Then after about a year came the diagnosis." She paused and took another deep breath. "Ovarian cancer."

She then began to cry uncontrollably. "If I had only had someone to talk to back then. Talk to someone who had seen the bigger picture and would have shared it with me. I needed someone who would have held *me* up—even in my moment of my despair. Now, I am never going to be blessed with my own children."

I reached out to grasp Julie's hands, but she had run out of dry tissues and had resorted to wiping her eyes and nose on her own sleeve and palms of her hands. She was distressed beyond anything I had ever seen. So, I retrieved a box of tissues from the bathroom and gave it to her in a futile attempt to stop the tears.

Blowing her nose, she whimpered. "And just now your words; *please some men in their long robes, and abandon my children*, cut me to my core." She became more agitated and angrier. "I tried to please my Father and Jason—for the sake of *their* reputation and *their* careers. I thought of *them* first. I didn't do what I should have done for *me*. I never chose what was right for *me* and I was never even allowed to grieve in the aftermath. And now I'm the one who suffers. My Father couldn't comprehend my loss. He could only comprehend his inconvenience and was of no help to me. With Jason, I'm sure he was relieved when I couldn't have children. Then I was replaced by him anyway. His inconvenience was over, and it was on with his career as usual. Those bastards!"

I said nothing and helplessly sat back and watched as she continued to unload every bit of her resentment as her voice became more frantic.

"And then, Michael, you came along, and I met your most amazing and wonderful children. Elizabeth and Mary are everything I could ever have wanted in children of my own—except maybe one of them *could* have had red, naturally curly hair."

I wasn't sure if she was serious or trying to make a joke, but it didn't come out humorous at all.

"And I always dreamed I would have *girls*." The word *girls* came out of her mouth in a long, sorrowful wail. "Then we had our differences and I feared that our friendship would be over. That was just like I felt when I was pushed away by my Dad. It was like I felt when my relationship with Jason was over. Why is the penalty for me always the same? I lose a child!" The intense sobbing began anew upon her confession.

Through her tears and thick voice, she forced out. "I wrongly substituted your children for the one I *abandoned*—without first dealing with the guilt and grief of my horrible decision. So, when we had a falling out, I reacted by being mad at you for your beliefs and for making the right decision for your children. I was jealous of you for having children, and not me! I know that's wrong! It turns out I'm not angry at you. I am angry at *me!*" She buried her face in her hands and the muffled words leaked out. "I'll have to live with my choice and deal with it forever." Her voice faltered in her unrelenting sobs. "I wish I had known your Mother. I wish I knew how she found the strength." Now the floodgates had opened fully. Tears continued more powerful than before.

Her story and this spectacle before me stung my heart and it brought back a memory of when my Mother had finally allowed her own flood of tears and grief to wash over her. Should I tell Julie about that too? Julie's lament could not continue in this way. I feared a complete emotional breakdown for her.

Chapter 36.

Archived in one of the cookbooks by Chloe Stevens, circa 1915. It is a verse from Scripture written in pencil on the back of a recipe card for the confection, Divinity. In the list of ingredients, the word: *sugar* was crossed out with the words: *secret ingredient, corn syrup* added. It was around the year 1915 that many recipes for Divinity started to call for corn syrup instead of sugar.

"Behold, I tell you a mystery: We all shall not sleep, but we shall all be changed."

1 Corinthians 15:51 - Revised Version, Standard American Edition, 1901

Julie's crying was not about to stop without intervention. She had reached full-on grief and I was witnessing her moment of utter despair. I had seen something exactly like it only once before in my life.

"Julie," I said, "I know what you're feeling. I've seen it before. I trust you to tell you this. When I do, you'll know what gives me the strength to feel the way I do, and I think it will offer you some perspective too."

Her anguish now overflowed. I could think of no other way to help her but share the most private event of my life with her. I hoped it would offer ultimate clarity to Julie and it would answer her question of how my own Mother found strength when she needed it most. Maybe by telling it to her, she would find it too.

"Julie, Julie, listen! There's two parts to the story, Julie." I held her shoulders—almost shaking her to get her attention.

I had already recounted the first part of my story—the flashback about the day my Father died that I had experienced in Orrin's church. I explained to her in painful detail of how those in leadership—the *men in long robes*, abdicated their responsibilities to my Mother in her time of grief and overwhelming need with their ceremonial show and nothing else. I told her that I had solemnly promised never to do that to anyone or be like they were. Now as she experienced *her* ultimate, *bottom of the exhale* moment, I could not act like they did and leave it all up to her. I had to make every effort to be there for Julie—to lift her up.

I repeated her last coherent sentence before the onslaught of tears. "Julie, you said, *I wish I knew how she found the strength.* Well, this is how she did."

Gaining her attention, I began. "Julie, I've never told this to anyone before. I never have, because it always hurt so much to remember it, and by sharing it with anyone, it might have embarrassed Mom if she found out we did. It may have even caused some of her relatives to think badly of her. I'm sure she never knew I even remembered it. It was something that showed how deeply painful and lonely it was for her, and how much weight was on her to survive for her children."

"Like you, Julie, she was allowed no outlet for her grief and was left to navigate the tragedy of my Father's death all alone. I saw it all and I remember every detail. You wouldn't think I could at age three, but I did. What I experienced—watching my Mother go through it, taught me a lesson that engraved a deep scar on my heart. The lesson I learned was the one placed on her by a bunch of ceremonial men—who in truth cared little for her plight. They were the very essence of the *men who desired to walk in long robes* from Scripture—the verse in Mark. I'll bet you've read it before. Those men showed up for ceremony and public prayers and made long speeches and received their honors the day my Father died. They took from the widow's house, but then would largely be absent for the real work that would follow. A short time after that fateful day, for my Mom, it would be her moment of the *bottom of an exhale and the feeling of despair that the next breath might not come*."

That analogy somehow penetrated Julie's distraught condition. She regained some of her voice and expressed a knowing and mournful, "Oh."

I nodded and continued. "Julie, I think it was kind of miraculous. Even from a position of weakness in her moment of grief, I saw her find and draw on a hidden well of strength. I've thought about the source of that strength for years. I believe, with all my heart, it's a strength that does not exist in our temporal world. It could only have been endowed upon her in that moment by her Creator. It is the strength reserved for times when there is nothing else left to save a good and faithful person—when Hope has vanished. For her, both the tragedy and then that strength arrived at a time and during circumstances no one could have predicted. And because of the next part of the story I'm about to tell you, I put my trust in that strength—that it will be there for me and my girls. It's there for you too, Julie!" Finishing my preface, I would shortly revisit the scene of forty plus years ago for her.

Chapter 37.

Verses from the Bible sewn with needle and thread onto the same page of the book: The Eleventh Annual Report of the Secretary of the State Horticultural Society of Michigan – 1881. Believed to be archived by Chloe Stevens, circa 1900.

"Rejoicing in hope; patient in tribulation; continuing instant in prayer"

Romans 12:12 – King James Version

"Watch therefore: for ye know not what hour your Lord doth come."

Matthew 24:42 - King James Version

"Julie, it was on one of those long, dark and cold winter afternoons a few weeks after the funeral of my Dad. Relatives and friends had expressed their sympathies and said their goodbyes. Long stretches of time alone now, my Mother had no choice but to set aside her anguish and throw herself into the family chores of caring for her children. The diapers needing changing. Baths needed to be given. Preparing meals for little mouths refusing to eat was a constant difficult task. This was in addition to attempting to keep house in her meticulous, Dutch-housewife tradition. Plus, there had to be grocery shopping with two babies and while dealing with a three and four-year-old doing what three and four-years-old's do. It was an impossible burden. Can you imagine taking four children those ages grocery shopping?"

"In the aftermath of death, there was also the responsibility of dealing with life insurance policies and worker's compensation claims, in addition to the mandatory requirement of writing thank you notes for the mountain of sympathy cards she had received— most of them containing the shallow and insincere platitude of the sender, *If you need anything, let me know.*"

"During the relentless obligations of all that, Mom was never given an opportunity to grieve. Eventually, there had to come a time for it, and I was there to witnessed it."

"On that winter afternoon, at the height of turmoil and alone with her children—just for a moment, she slipped from the burden of her tragic reality and the chaos that surrounded it, and shouted out, 'Daddy's home!' This immediately ceased the crying, tantrums, and every activity. The atmosphere in our world stood still. Even the two youngest in diapers stopped fussing to this revelation."

"The words; 'Daddy's home!' had always been the daily cue from her for us to run to the dining room window and look out onto the driveway, where we would see our Father's blue sedan pulling in at the end of his workday. It was a herald to her that no matter how challenging the day had been to that point, there was relief and joy with the return of her partner, along with order, security and a purpose to her family, which renewed her strength."

"But on this day, there was no blue sedan. There was no Daddy waving from his vehicle to the little faces pressed to the glass. This time the words, 'Daddy's home!' would have no joy, but would stand as her inevitable outpouring of despair that had been held back till that moment. My older sister and I turned to our Mother. We didn't understand. We wondered, had she just lied to us by this pronouncement?"

Julie's face showed a similar bewilderment.

"Let me explain, Julie. As children we had not attended the funeral. The adults thought the spectacle of it would be too much for us and for Mom to cope with. We stayed at home with Grandmother—leaving Mom to attend funeral rites by herself with all her Catholic in-laws—where they insistently propped her up to be strong through the visitations, Mass, and graveside service. So, our concept of him being gone had not made the impression of permanence upon us that it had for every adult. We knew nothing of accidents and funerals. Maybe Daddy was just gone for a few days and was just now returning. It wasn't uncommon for all of us to be in bed sleeping by the time he got home if he worked late or if he had stopped first to have a beer with the boys. So, it was common for us not to see him for long stretches. Thus, we were confused when there was no Daddy pulling into the driveway when she said there was. No tire tracks in the snow. No blue sedan—just drifting snow to underscore the horrible reality."

"Years later she would relate to me that on the day of the funeral, she had wished her 'Momma were there with her,' rather than staying home with my siblings and me. It would have allowed her to 'fall apart and cry.' If so, that would probably have been her moment to fully grieve. But without that kind of healing, she was still holding onto a supreme burden of sorrow. She had to continue to bear it all her own."

"Looking back, I do remember during those first tragic days after Father's death, she didn't cry at all. The in-laws mistakenly thought that this was a good sign. Her resilience was thought to show that she had the strength to face the daunting obligation she would shoulder of being solely responsible for the care of her children. In truth, it was a totally unhealthy response to her yet unexpressed mourning."

"Thus, her outburst of, 'Daddy's home!' was not in fact, a lie to us. It announced her breaking point. Some years later I would understand that those words marked the exact moment of her being overwhelmed. It was a plea to the remaining glimmer of Hope she still wanted to be true. But the answer to her Hope was that it would not be realized—not then or ever. In that moment, she found that Hope by itself was not enough on its own to change the reality. As we all looked out onto the drive, the reality held nothing more than a desolate winter afternoon and drifting snow."

"And Julie, *that* was the moment of witness for me. My Mother had reached the terrifying depth of despair. For her, in that instant, there might not be a moment to follow."

In the softest whisper, Julie repeated my analogy.

"The bottom of the exhale and the fear that there might not be a next breath."

I nodded. "It was at that moment, that it could only be the Almighty that interceded and drew from His unlimited well of strength to get to her the next moment, the next breath and the one after that."

"Then, for the first time since Father's death, she burst out in terrible sobs that were for *her* loss alone. Her children could be of no help to comfort her. We had no skills in knowing how to at our ages. There was no one else to say 'let me hold you up' except her God in that moment. In that moment, God replaced the H*ope* of her husband returning—which could not be, with His *Faith* and His *Strength*, as she clutched her apron and sank into the same upholstered chair as she had the day the *long black robes* had come to the house."

"But then, within her uncontrolled crying, she let the words escape, 'I wish Father were here.' Those words signaled that she understood that he was not home and would never be again. The last holdout of personal grief had finally visited her."

"For some time, she continued sobbing uncontrollably as it racked her body. But this inevitable reckoning of reality of the last few weeks, had also told her that there would be no father, husband or other men who would be there to help from now on. She should not expect it. Based on what she now accepted in her heart, the job would solely be hers. Aside from a few cursory offers of assistance from a few close relatives, no leaders of built-up institutions or insignificant community groups would be of help to her. They would offer only lip service to her plight. Just like it's written about in the Gospel of Mark. They *devour widows' houses, and for a pretense make long prayers*. Beyond that, there was no practical benefits coming from any of the men. She knew that now for her and from her knowledge of family history, that their nature was to be either absent, unreliable, drunks, abusive, dead or superficially ceremonial."

Tears welled up in my eyes at that point and my voice cracked, "To this date, Julie, I have never mentioned this to anyone before. I intended to take it to my grave."

Drying my eyes and clearing my throat, I finished the story. "So, my Mother continued to cry into her apron but only for a few more moments. It was certainly not enough time required for the enormity of the loss. After the worst of the sobbing subsided, she finally said the words again, but this time in a simple tear-filled whisper into her apron. 'I wish Father were here.' And then she added. 'But he's not going to be.' To my amazement, Julie, her sentence had started out in unimaginable grief, but had ended in a sense of acceptance and resolve. At the very depth of her sorrow, I had witnessed a transformation."

With that, Julie let out a long, shuddering breath, but then tenderly smiled.

"Well." I continued. "In a remarkably very few seconds, she regained most of her composure—with only a few sniffles remaining and resumed the routine of caring for her children. Miraculously, she rose from the chair, smoothed her apron, and with that, regrasped the responsibility of the days, months, and years of determined effort it would require to fulfill her sole obligation. She had drawn from the well of strength provided by her God, taken its refreshment and continued the family tradition of stoic determination."

I gripped Julie's hands tightly and looked into her eyes, "That was, without a doubt, the single saddest *and most wonderous* moment I have ever witnessed in my life."

Julie whispered—thick with tears "Oh, Michael, I am so sorry for you and her. That is beyond sad. I'm sorry you had to live through that. But it is also beyond inspirational."

"Now you know why I've never told anyone." I said, sniffing and wiping at my eyes and nose. "But I wanted to share it with you to let you know, you are not alone with *your* grief."

Julie's sobbing had now completely stopped. The look on her still flushed and tear streaked face softened. "Michael, thank you for sharing it with me."

"Thank you for listening, Julie, and for being so understanding about everything." I said. "I hope it helps you."

"Well." Julie took in a big breath. "Now I completely understand where you're coming from and why it is so important that your children—especially since they are girls, are not subjected to the same kind of second-class status as—well, so many have been. You want them to grow up strong with an ability to face any challenge. I know how much that hurt you to witness it with your own Mom and why you want to avoid it for your children. I apologize for thinking you had no real compelling motivation for your current thinking, beliefs, and actions, but I'm glad you thought enough of me to share your story. I promise it is locked in my heart and I will never tell anyone about it. It hurts my heart that I was not there to help your Mother when she needed it most."

Fortunately, there were no more tears for either of us to shed. Julie and I were emotionally drained. She calmly summarized. "I wish I had relied on Him in my last second of despair like your Mother did. I thought I was alone in what I perceived then to be an impossible moment of my life and had no other choice. I was wrong. I wish I had waited for my lost *Hope* to be replaced by *Faith*."

"Julie, neither one of us can go back to change those events." I told her. "But I am here for *you* now."

She put her warm hands around my neck, drew close and whispered in my ear. "And I am here for *you* now, Michael."

I moved even closer to Julie and tightly wrapped my arms around her. I felt somewhat guilty that I had to go to the extreme of retelling my forgotten stories to her in order to pull her from the depths of her despair. However, finally telling someone served to lift a weight off my conscience that I had maintained for over four decades. We sat in silence, melting into each other's embrace.

After several minutes, Julie pulled back and said. "Michael, about the situation at work. I'm sorry I didn't understand that the one true thing that drives you is *love*—love for your two girls. You *don't* compromise or abandon your children. I should have done the same—choose my child over everything else, no matter the consequences." The corners of her mouth drooped downward and her chin began to shake.

"No more crying, Julie! We'll get dehydrated!" I comically said to uplift her mood.

"Ok, ok. You're right." She said, quickly restoring her calm. "So, returning to the rift we had over the Bible. After reading for myself those things you highlighted in it and a lot more, as I said, I couldn't pretend that they don't exist. I saw, in all its stark truth, that I had been pushed into that same kind of second-class role and I accepted it—the one you steadfastly reject for your girls."

"You're right, we can't change the past, but, right now, Michael, I don't want to lose your friendship over the misunderstanding of how we differ in religious philosophy or how we think we should approach things at work. And I know it's selfish of me, but I don't want to lose those little girls from *my life* as their friend or big sister or whatever, just because I wasn't capable of recognizing what it is that creates and sustains true, dedicated and transformational love. I know I'm just a friend to you, but all three of you mean so much to me, in more ways than I can explain right now."

Julie's pace increased as she attempted to reconcile everything and laid out a series of aspirations that sounded like she was dancing around the issue of having a more serious relationship with me.

"Michael, I know you don't treat women in the way a lot of men do." She explained. "To you, in every way, they're equals. You've treated me that way! That's the kind of man I want in my life someday. I want someone who respects me and that I can respect in return. Maybe I'll find someone like that someday. I don't know when that will be, but I won't settle for less." She defiantly digressed and added, "I'm no one's second choice! I won't settle for that again. So, I'm sorry for initially thinking the way I did about you. But I won't anymore. I want to continue to be friends. You and I both need that. Being alone can be a lonely journey." She finished on a hopeful note. "But together—I mean as *friends*, I think we can make it less so for each other."

Taking all that in, I realized she had invested far more thought in the importance of our friendship than I had to date.

"Hon, you're a wonderful *friend*." I replied. And as I said it, I realized it didn't sound right. The word *friend* wasn't strong enough for how I was beginning to feel about Julie. But I also danced around that issue and then continued. "Look, I hated that our *friendship* had run into the same old brick wall that it always seems to do with me and some people. That same old topic of religion and my convictions about it was once again going to ruin something that was good. I'm so sorry it almost did."

We embraced again—rocking gently in each other's arms, knowing that we had reached a moment of clarity and purpose. We pulled back, still holding hands, looking into each other's eyes with caring smiles.

It had been difficult, but we had accomplished something here. We had built a bridge of Trust. With it, now we could put every problem we had experienced in our lives into perspective and effectively behind us. We could go forward to face any challenges that lay ahead. I felt compelled by the strength of our new bond—which was part friendship and part something more than that, to share myself with her in a way I had never done with anyone before. This kind of friendship was a whole new thing to me.

Still in our embrace, Julie said. "Michael, there's something else you should know. I have to be completely honest with you and it will most likely make you angry all over again."

"Ugh," I groaned.

"Just before all the commotion you had with Orrin in the Prep Lab." Julie tentatively said. "Well, I was processing a batch of specimen samples. There were two of them that you should know about—your children's."

"What?" I jumped from the couch and stood up rigidly. "My *children*—how?"

"And Lanie's too." Julie, added. "She must have been the one to submit the samples for them."

"Why didn't you tell me? I shouted.

"Well…" She dragged out her response. "I was going to. But before I had the chance, there was your big blow-up with Orrin, and then you lost your job, and he died, and they sent us home, and then our phone call—I didn't want to make things worse."

"*Worse!* How could it get any worse?" I bellowed.

"I don't know. I'm sorry!" She pleaded.

"That conniving bastard!" I growled. "He sent test kits to them and he was the one who invited them to the service. It was all him! I don't want my kid's DNA associated with Orrin and his company in any way. You're supposed to be 18 and give consent to be tested. It's just more of his frickin' leverage to make sure I went along with his plans. God, that bastard! It's never ending with him. Well, *now* it has!" I said, feeling somewhat vindicated by his death. "How am I gonna get those samples back? How do I reverse this nightmare?" I shouted. Neither Julie nor I had any ready answers. I slumped back onto the couch, my head in my hands, defeated.

I had never been through a roller-coaster of emotions like this before. Julie and I had spent every amount of our emotional capital in our revelations to each other.

It physically and mentally drained each of us to the same extent.

"I'm really sorry, Michael, but there's nothing we can do right now." She concluded.

I agreed with a "Hmm, true." We decided to call it a night. As Julie stepped toward the door to leave, she turned to me and rushed back into my arms. We embraced deeply. It was not a romantic one, but one of offering safety and comfort to each other in response to all the threatening events of the day, and a reassurance to each other after sharing what we had held captive in our hearts for so long.

We parted and planned to meet the next day after a full night's sleep to see if there was anything that could be done to retrieve my children's samples and expunge their mentions from the Genome 23 History systems. As Julie drove away, I again silently prayed for direction. It comforted me to know that she would be doing the same. I went straight to bed.

Chapter 38.

Written on the back of a business sized envelope from Union Central Life Insurance Company, Cincinnati, Ohio. Postmarked, December 1869. Archived in the book: The Great Galveston Disaster.

"Trust in the Lord with all thine heart; and lean not unto thine own understanding. In all thy ways acknowledge him, and he shall direct thy paths."

Proverbs 3:5-6 - King James Version

Written on a loose piece of lined notebook paper. It was included at the end of Helen's manuscript—the one tied with a pink ribbon.

Undated

One should pray for the Lord for Divine intervention and be confident of His eventual answer. But one can never be sure how His answer will come to you. Be mindful that it may come to you in the voice of a man or woman or even a child's voice.

Helen Laurinda Wilcox

Written with a fountain pen in black ink on the outside margin of page 58 of the book: The Eleventh Annual Report of the Secretary of the State Horticultural Society of Michigan – 1881. Not sure who wrote this but based on handwriting comparisons, I'm giving credit to Chloe Stevens. Although, I think I do remember my Grandmother Helen saying it before. And even if she didn't, it sounds like something she would.

"Bad is never good until worse happens."

Old Danish Proverb

A call came early the next morning. It was Julie. "I have a plan." She said forcefully. "I'll be there in 15 minutes."

On time and still as disheveled looking as when she had left a few hours earlier, Julie stepped inside. I made coffee and we sat at the kitchen table. Early morning light filtering in through the window curtains. The sun seemed to lighten the mood in the room and that was a welcome relief.

After a few sips of caffeine to clear our heads, she detailed her plan like a field general strategizing a battle. "We can go back into the building after everyone is gone and get those samples, order forms and any other trace results for the girls. I'm sure none of those results for the day have been shipped since we all went home early."

"You're forgetting I was fired." I interjected. "They'll never let me in the building."

"But I wasn't." she replied. "I have a key. I'm the fill-in Executive Secretary, remember? I can access pretty much everything except the Final Lab, but I'm sure there's a master key for it in Orrin's desk. I think in an hour or so of snooping, we can find everything and destroy it—including anything about them on the computer system in the Final Lab. I have all the passwords and all the pertinent customer data is only on one spread sheet program anyway. Orrin wanted it simple. I'll delete their names and entry numbers and it'll be like they never had a sample come into the building. Oh, and we'll shred any paperwork—like that fake letter of resignation regarding your firing. You didn't get an exit interview from Welch yet so that's still in process. But we'll have to do it soon. There won't be anyone around this weekend and even if they are, no one of any importance knows that you were fired anyway. And the one that did is dead. Dead men tell no tales."

"Now that wasn't necessary." I exclaimed. "I still feel guilty about it."

"Sorry, caught up in the moment." She apologized.

"Wait, what about *Mrs.* Orrin?" I said. "She was in the next room. I heard her close the door when Orrin got amped up and began his tirade on me. She would know I got fired."

"I don't think that will be a problem." Julie cut in. "I've been in her side office before when Orrin has gotten *amped up* as you say. When that happens, she shuts the door as her way of saying, '*I don't want to get involved. I know nothing.*' You think she hasn't heard him blowing off before and ignored it? They've been married half a century. She tunes him out all the time. He makes every decision. She just follows orders. Mrs. Orrin has never taken the lead on anything or has ever stepped up to him. I doubt she will even remember yesterday—outside of him dying. She'll be consumed with a funeral and out on bereavement for days. Odds are she'll never be in the building again. She's near 90."

"And what about Welch and the Shadow Brothers? Surely, they know." I continued to object.

"No, I don't think so." Julie assured me. "I don't think Welch knows you're fired. I'm fairly sure Orrin hadn't told him yet. That's where he was going next though, but he never made it. And besides if Welch somehow does know about your firing, he owes me a favor. If he tries to pursue it, I'll rat him out on his secret stash of vodka I found in the warehouse. He takes a lot of walk n' talks like we do—only his are *walk n' guzzles*. I caught him taking a nip one afternoon. That was before you got hired. I found out he also mixes his booze with the coffee in his thermos. He thinks no one notices it. I'm sure he drinks during the day just to cope with Orrin. And the Shadow Brothers were nowhere to be found during all the commotion with Orrin in the Prep Lab. I don't recall them even being in the building that day. Maybe they were and never heard it behind the closed doors of the Final Lab.

"If they were in the building, they'd have heard it. But the bunch in the Prep Lab?" I questioned. That was the last variable. "They saw everything."

"There are not gonna make any waves. What do they care if you work there or not? I bet they wish they could've been fired to put them out of their collective misery and then draw unemployment. Or, they would have liked to have the *cojones* to tell him off like you did. You're probably their hero!" Julie sarcastically joked. "Monday morning you'll show up, punch in and pretend nothing happened. If anyone else questions what went on, I'll set them straight. I'll say it was all a big misunderstanding—a big blow up for show. There'll be no documentation to contradict me after we get rid of it. We just need to plan on a night to get back in there when no one is around."

Then Julie's phone buzzed.

"Today?" She said astonished as she read the text.

"What?" I asked. Then a second later, I heard my phone buzz from the living room.

Julie said, "Its a group text from the H. R. manager, Welch. The memorial service for Orrin is *today at 2 pm*. That can't be right. He just died yesterday.

I retrieved my phone from the coffee table in the living room. Returning to the kitchen I informed Julie. "I got a text too. It does say *today*. So soon? Why today?"

"I don't know." She reasoned. "I guess Mrs. Orrin wants to get it over with. They had no children, friends, or other family that anyone knows of. Just work and the church was all they had in their life. But you're right, that's strange. However, it's a good sign you got the text too." Julie said optimistically. "Welch wouldn't invite you to the service if he suspected you were on the outs with Orrin."

I decided to jump in and help Julie with our ground plan. "So, we have to do this tonight or Sunday night before everyone gets back to work on Monday. We'll attend the memorial service together this afternoon to make it a good show. I doubt anyone else from the Prep Lab will be going with such late notice and since I'm guessing they could care less about Orrin. We'll have to roll the dice and hope the Church Council is still in the dark about me being let go. So, tonight or tomorrow?" I left the decision up to Julie.

"The sooner the better." She decided. "We better get this done tonight."

"I hope this works" I reluctantly agreed.

"Now, Michael." She hesitated and took a breath then continued. "I also have another thing to tell you. It goes along with my first confession about Orrin having your kid's DNA."

"More? Oh God! How much more complicated is this going to be?"

She began. "In the confusion in the Prep Lab when Orrin collapsed, no one noticed this."

She went back toward the door where her coat was draped over a chair. She reached into its pocket and pulled out a manila envelope. From that, she extracted one of the familiar green ledger pages we worked with every day, unfolded it, and revealed what was enclosed.

I recognized it immediately. It was the glass vial that went missing from my desk in a batch of customer orders a couple months ago. I remembered it was late on a Friday afternoon right before closing. It and all related paperwork for it was gone from my desk the next Monday morning.

Julie held it in her outstretched hand, saying nothing.

"That's the vial that went missing from my desk." I explained to her. "It was a couple months back. How did you come to get it?"

"You've seen this before?" Julie asked.

"Yes, it disappeared from a batch of samples. I had forgotten about it. But where did you get it?"

"In all the confusion, I guess no one saw it fall out of Mr. Orrin's coat." Julie said. "You say it was missing from your desk a couple months ago?"

"Yes. I thought I was gonna get fired for losing it, but nothing ever came of it. And you say it was in his coat?" I asked.

"It fell out of his pocket when he collapsed." Julie said. "I think it got kicked out of the way while they were doing CPR on him. It was on the floor just under your lab station desk. I don't know why, but I picked it up—I suppose to get it back to him at some point. But then they sent everyone home and I found I was still holding it along with my coat, keys, and purse when I got to my car. I was going to go back in and put it on his desk, but in all the confusion—the ambulances and the medical people, well, I just left with it. I was going to put it back in the office on Monday."

"Why was he carrying it in his coat?" I pleaded.

"Not sure." Julie replied. "But it had to be special to him for some reason for him to be toting it around in his coat packet."

I got curious and took a better look at what Julie held. The unforgettable vial had to be the same one I encountered. I checked the ledger. Yes, entry for sample #17-80043 listed it as from a P.O. Box in Bruges, Belgium. That was in my writing.

"Yeah, I remember writing this number down on my calendar blotter to ask someone about it. Then it was the end of the workday and that was the last I saw of both the vial and this ledger." I said.

"Michael, that entry has *two* yellow stars next to it." Julie said.

"Now, those were *not* on there before." I replied. "Only Orrin or the Shadow Brothers do the yellow stars thing after they've tested." I continued to theorize. "I handled this on a Friday. I'll bet Orrin grabbed it off my desk over that weekend for some reason. I do remember seeing his car in the parking lot when the girls and I drove by on that Saturday as we were going for breakfast. Maybe he held onto it because the sample was nothing like he'd ever seen before. I never have."

"It's more than that, Michael. I think this might be a clue to why its significant. Look at the bottom of the page."

I scanned further down the names and numbers—none of those meant anything to me. However, at the bottom, in Orrin's handwriting was the entry #17-80043*A*. with *two* yellow stars.

"43*A*?" I questioned. "We don't use *letters* to identify samples. So, is this the same person's sample vial I handled months ago? It looks like the same one from what I can remember, or is it a *second identical* sample of #43?" My head was swimming. "Who in the hell is this person. Julie?"

"Turn over the page Michael."

I did and a chill ran down my spine. To my horror, in pencil, were the names of my daughters, Elizabeth Jacobs and Mary Jacobs—each with one yellow star next to their names.

"None of this was on the ledger when I first saw it months ago, Julie. He added them later. That's Orrin's penmanship."

I now felt violated for my children. The thought of the Grim Reaper taking Orrin while my children's DNA results were in his creepy clutches sickened me. I collapsed into the kitchen chair. Julie slid her chair closer to mine, reached out and placed a hand on my knee. We both stared at the ledger and vial—examining it from every conceivable angle. We tried to peer through the cloudy glass of the vial to see its contents. Like before when I encountered it, it looked to contain a fragment of cloth—a linen with a dark brown stain on it. It had all the appearances of dried blood. The bottle was sealed with a string affixed to it with a yellowed and brittle wax seal. We couldn't guess it's age, but it was nothing made recently.

Questions swirled. Why were my children's names added to the back of the same ledger documenting the bizarre glass vial samples? Were they somehow similar? The girl's entries both had yellow stars next to their names. Sample #43 and #43A both had *two*! "What does that mean?" I pleaded.

"Search me!" Julie said. "But look here. At the top of the page. It's like a heading."

There, also in Orrin's scribble, were the bold capital letters, P. B.

"Hmm, now you can *search me*. That tells us nothing. But why was this in his coat?" I repeated. We kept coming back to the same questions. "If we have one sample, and there *is* a second sample, where is that one now?"

Julie said. "Well, since it was months ago, that first one has to have been processed in the Final Lab by now, you would think."

"No, not according to the ledger. The Shadow Brothers always put a *red* stamp on the ledger when they are done processing it. Red stamp means *done!* There isn't one for #43 or #43A. It's still in some sort of testing phase. Yellow means something else. I wonder if Orrin picked up sample #43A on his recent trip to Belgium?" Our questions were growing exponentially without any answers.

"I haven't the foggiest." Julie admitted.

"And finally," I said. "Why was this vial so important to him, that he never, and I mean *never* let it out of his sight or leave his person—only relinquishing it from his clutches upon death?"

Chapter 39.

Written on notebook paper. It was included in the book, The Compleat Housewife, or, Accomplish'd Gentlewoman's Companion. It is a lesson in the value of biting your tongue and restraining yourself from destructive behaviors that one might regret later and will only hurt you.

24 February 1938

This morning took me to spit feathers. The high and mighty King and his offspring put me in a conniption. The complaints: 'The oatmeal was too lumpy.' 'I thought you were going to make over-easy not scrambled.' Does anyone ever think of scraping their plates and stacking the dishes in the sink? The snippy comments: 'Where are my black pants? These are brown.' Yes, I can see that. The black ones are still in the dirty clothes because the wringer on our old washing machine is still broken and we don't have the money to call the repair man to come fix it till payday.

Last night was when it started, 'Soup again? We had that last night.' My stars and garters! I didn't have the gumption to break the news to him. It will be on the menu tonight as well. I'll bet a nickel that when Adam himself was served the forbidden fruit by Eve, he said, 'Needs more salt.' Roast beef on the shopping list comes after fixing the washing machine.

Only after they had all left the house for work and school, and I was alone, my anger and frustration boiled over. I took the wet dish rag I was using to wipe down the vinyl tablecloth and threw it with all my might at the door in the dining room. I picked it up and threw it again and again and again until I lost count of the number of times, I hurled it against its enameled surface and my arm ached. The tears flowed and after a bit I felt better but ashamed too so I picked up the dish cloth and wiped down the entire door with it so there would be no water stains on it.

There would also be no evidence of my brief rage for my family to discover when they came home that night or any hint in my demeanor that I had lost my temper because of them which made me throw the dish rag. That was the appropriate response to my rage. Tossing a wet rag at a door wouldn't damage anything, I reasoned. I would never dream to break one of my lamps or smash my good china over something like this or any of them. That wouldn't amount to cut ice with them. It would only hurt me. I've worked too hard to make a nice home to ruin any of my things over their boorishness.

They wouldn't understand my outburst anyway. I'm

not allowed to do what they do without so much as a thought. They don't comprehend that it might be helpful to me if they don't always complain about everything or be the least bit grateful for what they have, and they could pick up after themselves once in a while. My mind milled on those thoughts.

Then, almost as soon as it started, I breathed a deep sigh and my tears dried. Nothing was damaged and the door benefitted from a cleaning which was needed because someone had smudged their dirty fingerprints on the woodwork. What good is the doorknob if no one uses it?

No. No one but me and my Lord will ever know that I had lost my temper. I only need to apologize to Him.

    Helen Laurinda Wilcox-Phillips

The next day, the early hours of Saturday passed slowly. Finally, 2 pm arrived. At church, the shaky organist struggled with the selected pieces for Orrin's memorial service. Maybe one was *Amazing Grace*, but it was hard to tell. The melody sounded like all the others she attempted. I did my best to slouch in the pew to better blend in with the sparse turnout.

My worst imagined fear was that during the service someone might jump up from the congregation, turn to me, point a finger and shout, 'Murderer! Murderer! He's the one who killed him!' But there was none of that. The service was brief and without passion. The men in long black coats from the Church Council each got up and read a passage from Scripture. I struggled to make the connection of what they were reading and how any of it pertained to Orrin's passing. It was a disjointed presentation that seemed to focus more on their oratory performances, rather than offering a solemn eulogy for the deceased. Mrs. Orrin sat at the front—a noticeable distance from anyone else. She looked alone and abandoned and unimpressed—devoid of any outward emotion. I had witnessed that same kind of isolated widow's demeanor once before in my life at age three. All I could think of was that this scene was all very inappropriately sterile.

The short service over, we filed out of the church saying a brief sympathetic word or two to Mrs. Orrin. We then shook hands with some of the Council who made sure they were in the receiving line on the front steps of the church to get accolades for their part of the memorial service. And that was it. The plain, grey stone urn containing Orrin's cremated ashes were left on a table at the front of the church. No one bothered to grab them on the way out, so poor Mrs. Orrin hobbled back in and down the aisle to retrieve what was left of her married life. We left, but never saw her exit the building. Maybe she held back to say her own private goodbyes to her husband without anyone else making a pretentious spectacle of it.

With that chore done, and with no one outing me during the event, the ominous job we had to do that night was all I could think about. I had my doubts we could accomplish it without getting caught. Not only would I then *officially* lose my job, but Julie probably would too, and we might even be charged with breaking and entering. The odds seemed stacked against us that this would succeed.

The one thing we did have going for us to remain undetected was, true to his skin-flint nature, Orrin had never installed video surveillance of any kind in the building. With Orrin, he was not worried about theft. Anything he thought important, he kept close to the vest—literally *in* his vest. That fact alleviated some of my worry.

Finally, 9 pm came. That was when Julie and I would make our way to the building. We would park down the block and walk around to the back entrance to avoid detection. Before we exited the vehicle, I started to get cold feet and whispered my apprehensive thoughts to myself.

"I'll probably lose the girls, have to move far away for some other job. I'll lose contact with them and be like so many others. I'll be labeled a dead beat, absent Dad."

It was loud enough though for Julie to hear my trepidation. "Oh, no. None of that is going to happen." She said.

"I'm glad you're so sure, Julie"

Fumbling with the key ring, Julie unlocked the door and we entered but did not turn on any lights. We did not want to alert anyone to activity inside the building. Purposely wearing dark clothes and operating by flashlight, we were the epitome of thieves. This had every appearance of a criminal activity now.

Our plan was set. The only variable in this covert operation that we would need to negotiate on the fly, was the cellblock-like secured Final Lab—if we needed to access it. It had no windows and a massive lock on its impressively sturdy door. Julie was confident that most of my children's data and related materials would be in Orrin's office. But the actual plastic bottle samples and the slides that were made from them could be in the Final Lab. However, if we needed to access it, she was sure we could find a key to it in Orrin's set of master keys, which he kept in his top right desk drawer.

Ascending the stairs to the second floor, we stood before the glassed wooden door to Orrin's office. It was akin to something you would have seen in an office building of the 1940's. Also, it was in keeping with the style of Orrin's personality—battered and creaky. It was unlike any other door in the more modern building. Its faded, varnished oak frame even had an old-fashioned windowed transom above it. That was always kept slightly open to allow for airflow into the stuffy office. As you might expect, the old man detested '*that new-fangled, expensive air conditioning.*' We found the door locked as expected. Julie fished through her crowded key ring to search for an old-fashioned skeleton key, which would unlock the curio cabinet-like office door. I could only imagine that this kind of lock would have been a nostalgic treat for any cat burglars of the 1930's to pick open.

"Darn." She said. "I don't have one of those on the key ring that fits this door."

"Great!" I said more loudly than any criminal should in a situation like this. "Now what, break the window on the door?"

"No, keep your shirt on." Julie replied, "I'm pretty sure he kept another one above the door." She looked up. "Can you reach the top of it?"

Mr. O was consistent in his antiquated thinking about security. Just as Julie suspected, there *was* another skeleton key on top of the casing. We entered the office and tried to quietly close the door behind us— the squeaky hinges on it crying out our crime to the echoing metal walls of the warehouse.

Among the disarray on Orrin's desk, under a pile of papers and another three-inch stack of 99-dollar checks made out to Genome 23 History, was a blue binder. A piece of masking tape was stuck to the cover with the scribbled words: *P. B. Missions Minutes.* But that by itself did not explain much.

"*P. B*—just like the letters written on the ledger." Julie said. We opened the binder and began to read. It had all the earmarks of a detailed action plan. The somewhat disjointed cryptic notes were in bullet points in Orrin's handwriting. We scanned down the page.

- *Identify the final few of the 144,000.*

We now understood what that meant.

- *Secure additional sample from Bruges to allow testing and preserve original.*

That entry had a line drawn through it—confirming that Orrin had secured his needed duplicate sample—probably the one we had in our possession. The bullet points continued.

- *Continue R and D to identify yellow stars.*

R and D—we knew that meant—Research and Development.

"Identify yellow stars?" Julie questioned. "Again, the mention of *yellow* stars." The bullet points went on.

- *Continue development of innovations for sample testing. If proves successful canvas populations of Middle East, Istanbul/Constantinople, and southern Europe/France for P. B. descendants.*

- *If innovations unsuccessful, use fallback marketing strategy.*

"What is a *P.B descendant?*" I whispered to Julie, but she did not answer. There were still more bullet points.

- *Establish inquiry fee regardless of results.*

- *If innovation successful, establish a second substantial paid subscription fee to maintain one's status in the*

144,000.

The next entry also had a line drawn through it.

- *Secure an identifiable PR person to promote our missions*

"Oh, I guess I was to be that P R person." I gasped. "But by what means would I be *identifiable?"* The final bullet point was:

- *Prepare public relations releases and prepare for unveiling at general press conference at large Christian forum— to be determined, when we have identified minimum number of customer/believers for profitability.*

"Unveiling of what, Julie?" I asked perplexed. "His *innovation* in testing?" She just shrugged. "And a *customer/believer*—never heard those two words in a mash-up before." I said.

Overall, the document was as mysterious and vague as Orrin himself. At the bottom of the last page, it was signed in Orrin's unmistakable scrawl and three additional sets of signatures, which were unfortunately illegible. We surmised that those had to be from the Shadow Brothers. When we reached the end, Julie and I looked at each other in amazement. The creepiness of it had unnerved us.

"My God, this is a combination religious, cryptic manifesto and a 5-year business plan all rolled into one." I exclaimed.

"If I read this right," Julie said. "His *business* mission and his *church* mission are one in the same."

"And all of us employed at Genome 23 History have been working toward that." I informed Julie.

"So, providing a genealogy readout for customers is only a secondary business function of Genome 23. The main purpose is to create an "Armageddon data base" of what he and his three signatories think are the remaining chosen few of the 144,000—whatever the number is, by possibly some new scientific method he has the boys in the Final Lab developing. Am I getting anything wrong here?" Julie asked.

"And his business angle is to profit off it— *regardless!*" I said. "He'll try to make money, either with his Plan A—if all their testing goes successfully, or with a *fallback* plan." I said. "That's what it says. Not sure what they're testing for, but whatever it is, it sounds fishy. It's not worth the pay raise they are giving me to promote it. I'd just as soon go back to $16.85 an hour and lay low."

"$16.85 an hour?" Julie asked. "That's what you make now?"

"It was another unforced faux pas by me. "Well, I don't like to discuss wages." I sheepishly replied.

Julie glared at me and said, "Don't pee on my leg and tell me it's raining, Michael." She turned and marched to the locked file cabinet containing personnel records.

Seeing what she was up to I warned. "You know, you're not supposed to access another employee's files.

"Really!" She shot back. "I think you're forgetting again that I'm the fill-in Executive Secretary. I have legal access to it all!" She unlocked the drawer and retrieved my personnel file—clenching it in her fist. "So, you make 16-85 per hour?" She asked again.

"Yeah." I admitted. "Don't you?" Oh, if I had only stopped before asking her the follow up question.

Julie launched into a series of angry rhetorical questions and statements. "You make 16-85! I didn't know that! I only make 14-85! Mrs. Orrin must have processed your employment forms. If I had, I'd have noticed it. How are you worth two dollars more every hour than me? I do the same work as you with the added responsibility of backup Executive Secretary. How is that fair?"

I had no words *now*. The stereotypical Irish temper you would expect from anyone who looked like Julie, was now fully unleashed. She picked up Zephaniah's dog food dish and with a swift, drop-kick, punted it and its contents across the room—bouncing it off the Executive Secretary's door. The impact scattered the contents of dried kibble to all corners of the room— which blended in with all the other dog food and droppings already on the tacky blue/green shag carpeting.

Her outburst was not enough to completely vent her anger. Now, with my admission, Julie, had no need to violate employee privacy concerns by reading my file. So, she hurled that against the door too, while censuring herself in mid-outrage by substituting the *F-word* with the infrequently heard, but socially acceptable, "F-fffiddle-sticks!"

"Julie," I meekly said, "I had no idea."

Regaining some composure a few seconds later, she said, "I know. I know, but it dusts my draperies how they go about their two-class system in this place and how women like me are screwed!"

I thought better than to tell her how her outburst of colorful language reminded me of the prose I had recently read in my Grandmother's cookbooks. After a brief cool down period, we again tried to focus on the bullet points of Orrin's action plan.

"Well, there's nothing more revealing in the rest of this binder." I summarized.

Julie had one more question. "So, Mr. *Identifiable*—and you are the chosen candidate to be awarded that title, just how much more was Orrin gonna pay you to be his front man?"

I confessed straight away to it—not wanting to catch any more of her wrath. "Um, he said something approaching a…" I lowered my voice to just above a murmur. "…hundred-grand."

"Six figures?" She almost shouted as her *Irish* returned. Her arms went rigid and she balled her fists, but she restrained herself from throwing something else against the door. Then her calm quickly returned. "Oh, I'm sorry. I don't blame you, Michael. I'd have taken the raise too. Well, to your credit, he wasn't able to buy you off with money—albeit that's a lot of money."

I felt the need to continue to defend myself in the presence of her annoyance. "He knew I didn't want to participate, but that was just a formality." I pleaded. "He was coercing me with money and by holding my kid's DNA hostage as insurance leverage to get me to comply with his master plan. Evil personified!"

"Hmm, that's was why he was so angry when you refused to go along with it. His wheels were already in motion." Julie added.

I shivered noticeably. The thought sickened me. "C'mon, grab his key to the Final Lab and let's get my kids samples and any other related stuff about them and let's get outta here."

We looked in the desk drawer. "His key ring is gone." Julie said astonished. "They've always been kept in this drawer. Orrin was a creature of habit. Somebody must have them." She said in an ominous tone.

We searched every other drawer of the desk and in every cabinet and file drawer of the sparsely furnished office. They were nowhere to be found. We descended the stairs back down to the Final Lab. "There's no way we're going to be able to break into this" I exclaimed. The door was as solid as a bank vault.

"I'm sorry, Michael. I'll look again Monday. Maybe the keys will turn up by then. Let me put this vial and the ledger back on his desk so no one is suspicious."

"No, I'm keeping them." I said defiantly as I snatched the envelope from her. "I'm keeping it as insurance. If I can't get my kids DNA back, then they aren't getting this. It may be my only leverage."

Julie again protested. "Then that *is* theft!" If there are some other related materials locked in the lab, and they find out the vial and ledger are missing, they will probably suspect you, and then put two and two together. You'll be arrested and jailed. Then what will you do for your children? Did you think about that?" But she knew her argument was in vain.

"This is my ace in the hole, Julie. And I'll hold on to it until I must play it. If I don't get what I want, it'll get tossed in the river. I'm taking my chances. I've learned that things happen when you least expect it and in ways you could never imagine. I have faith they'll be *good things.* God, they just have to be. I'm clinging to that."

"Point taken." She conceded. "I guess *we* have no choice. Let's go before someone finds us here."

I took note that she emphasized the word *we.* I was thankful that besides God, I was not going this alone. However, I gave Julie one last chance to back out.

"You know, Julie, you have no obligation to be involved in this. I appreciate all you've done, but this is not your fight. You don't need to put your neck on the line for me and my kids."

"Yes, it is." She stated with determination. "It's my choice and I promised I would help. I don't break promises."

"Well, thank you then." I said with deep appreciation. Everything about this woman impressed me. Her generosity, kindness, and fortitude—even her recent display of temper left me awestruck. "Let's go back to my hideout in the woods and figure something out. ok?

"Hideout?" Julie quipped.

"Yep, we're now a full-fledged, second-story man *and woman*. I replied. "Might as well start using all the criminal jargon."

"Ok, but first go back up to Orrin's office with me and help clean up. There are some paper towels and spray cleaner in the Executive Secretary's office. I can't leave a mess like that and then have to walk back into it on Monday."

Chapter 40.

This note was written on the back of an opened envelope containing a letter dated, 15 August 1896. The letter was addressed to Chloe's daughter Alma Stevens from her cousin Mary. It was found in the book: The Great Galveston Disaster.

I fear my Alma has the eyes for a boy. I'm sure, based on this letter the postman delivered. It may have been wrong of me, but as a Mother entrusted with keeping morality in this household, I plead guilty to have opened it. I'll just keep it here in the kitchen drawer. Giving it to her can come to no good use for an unblemished young girl of her age. I'll give it to her when she's older.

Chloe Stevens

Written on letter stationary, it is undated. It is a story I heard my Grandmother tell a few times when I was a child. Based on the historical timeline, it would have been written sometime in the late 1920's. The entry was found at page 216 of the cookbook, The Compleat Housewife, or, Accomplish'd Gentlewoman's Companion. That page had the recipe: To make Elder Wine at Christmas.

I wanted to maintain my virtue before we were married. Your father was flirtatious. He always was trying to kiss me when we were courting. One time, as we were fond to go for a picnic lunch on the banks of the Reese Dam backwaters, we would fish for perch with crawlers from the shore. The ones we caught that weren't keepers, we would use as bait on a big hook under a bobber for Northern Pike fishing out on the water. I worried that once we were out in the rowboat, I couldn't get away from him advances unless I jumped in and I could not swim. Luckily, the rowboat was very tippy and we both had to remain very still, or we'd go over. As I always tell her, if the girls would behave, the boys would have to.

Helen Laurinda Wilcox-Phillips

There was no talking during the trip to the little cottage in the woods. We hadn't eaten anything all day and despite it being almost 11 pm, I made scrambled eggs and toast. Julie and I agreed we also needed a drink. There were two bottles of a local semi-dry Riesling in the refrigerator. We downed the first and were well into the second bottle before we knew it.

I lit a fire in the fireplace to take the chill out of the living room, and we relaxed a bit. Mesmerized by the dancing flames and comforted by the warmth, we both started to get drowsy. However, before we fell asleep or put it off, I suggested we force ourselves to do some more investigation into the vial and find out its significance. I sat down at the computer and Julie pulled up a chair to my right so we could both see the screen.

"Let's see if we can find out something about this curious vial. Let's call it *exhibit-A* as they would in court." I stated. "And make no mistake, that's what it will be called if they found out we stole it."

"Borrowed it! Please! I'm still not comfortable we

have this. It goes against my principals." She exasperated. "Imagine. Julie Douglas—miss goody two-shoes, now a common thief." She laughed.

"Not a *common* thief, my dear." I teased. "I'll bet you'll be the only one in the cellblock with naturally curly red hair. And if I'm not mistaken, I think prison jump suits in this county are orange. The question is, does a fashionable common—that is *uncommon* thief such as yourself—soon to be an inmate after a lengthy trial and conviction, wear orange with your native red hair?"

She started to giggle. "You're so stupid." Her statement made her burst out in gales of laughter. Then I started laughing at her silliness. It really wasn't all that funny, but it must have been a release from all the stress we had undergone, and I think the wine had something to do with it too. We shared a mild, gallows humor lubricated by 14 percent alcohol.

"You're right, you're right! We borrowed it." I said in a fake contrite way. "That's what we'll tell the Judge."

"Puh-leeze!" Julie protested and gulped more wine. "Ugh, it goes back Monday."

Our giddiness subsiding, I told her with a big sigh. "It's nice to be able to laugh. It's been too intense for the last couple days."

"Yeah." She agreed through the gentle smile of the inebriated. "That felt good." Julie settled in her chair and moved a little closer to me.

We redirected our attention back to the task as the computer had finally booted up. "Ya know, the internet is so full of crap. But one thing, it sure makes research a lot easier." I reasoned. "Can you imagine how much time and effort would have to go into this if we had to go to a library to find this stuff?"

Julie replied. "Most likely we would lose interest in the whole project." She paused then added. "Probably spend our time on more *interesting* things." She said coyly as she gently slipped her right hand over my right hand which was resting on my knee. We both froze for a second realizing what was happening between us.

I instantly comprehended how her hand on mine made me feel and it how it urged me to respond to her as a man. However, I was also sure that this was not the time for any of that. In our condition, it was difficult not to give in to an alcohol-fueled urge as I could feel her form slowly press into my side. Her softness and her intimate position were unexpected, but I had to admit, was very pleasing. The fragrance of her perfume or lotion was something I had never noticed before. It was floral and filled my senses as I breathed in steadily and deeply. I held it as long as I could—hoping to absorb it into me. Instinctively I turned the palm of my hand up to meet hers and we clumsily interlaced our fingers, even though I knew the message that was sending her.

Turning to her slowly, we met each other's gaze. I had never seen this side of Julie before. I had no idea she was interested in me—not in this way. In all the months we worked together, during the miles we logged in our walk n' talks, not even when she spent time with me and my girls, did she ever once show any *real* romantic curiosity. It was only friendly interactions with me. Prior to this moment, it was almost as if Julie was devoid of this kind of passion. Or, was it that I had never noticed before?

Thinking about that, I deliberated that maybe it was because she, like me, had sworn off relationships after the bad experiences of our last ones. Also, I had never really been completely alone with her before for us to explore any *intimate* opportunities. Or, maybe tonight it was the three—or was it now four glasses of wine that we had each consumed. Regardless, there was no mistaking her interest in the moment. Honestly, it aroused me and that startled me in this setting.

Prior to this moment, the sanctuary of my little cottage in the woods stood only as a citadel of safety for me and my children. This refuge was not a bachelor's pad for a swinging-single, and in it, my libido had no residence. It simply wasn't a part of my life anymore. I had been so self-absorbed in my own plight to ever contemplate romance or notice someone like Julie. Was it possible I failed to see her hand outstretched to me for more than friendship? It was highly probably that I was that dense. Then again, tonight it might just be the booze.

As quickly as it settled upon us, this brief couple seconds of passionate thought and feelings suddenly vanished with the results of our online search popping up on the computer screen. I had mixed feelings about that. Part of me didn't want the intimacy with Julie to end, but I was apprehensive of what emotions we might be opening between us. Besides, we had too much to do now to get distracted.

So, I did not succumb to any of the building passion. I took the correct choice for this moment—do nothing in response to her advances. I knew taking that kind of plunge might jeopardize our friendship, and we had just patched it up. However, my inaction was counter-intuitive to what would be a normal reaction for a man and woman in this situation—especially drunken ones. But there was to be no thinking below the belt. Not right now.

I needed time to sort out this new aspect of our relationship—if that was the direction it was going. So, I attempted to refocus on the task at hand. Maybe that would give me enough space for my emotions to regroup. In the interim, I hoped Julie would not take my lack of interest in her romantic overtures as an insult to her. I truly did care for her—just not sure at what level yet. She had been through a lot and I did too. So, we both needed to venture slowly in this new realm.

My hand holding hers—the right one, was my computer mouse hand. I needed it to click on the links. That need was what finally broke the intimate moment. I moved it back to the top of the desk and my vision refocused on the computer screen. Unfazed, Julie remained pressed up against me. I think after all the alcohol she consumed, she needed me as support to keep her from falling over.

"What do those letters, P. B. stand for on Orrin's ledger?" Julie asked unfazed. "Peanut Butter?"

"I highly doubt that, young lady." I said affectionately. She pressed into me tighter in response to my use of the endearing term. I had already typed the initials P. B. in the search engine bar along with the word, Belgium. Nothing on the first page of results seemed to be relatable—just websites where you could book a bed and breakfasts in that country.

"Redo the search with, P. B. Bruges, Belgium. B, r, u, g…" She started to spell.

"I know how to spell it, Julie!" We started laughing again.

"Well, that's what it said in Orrin's action plan. Type in: P. B. Bruges, Belgium." Julie repeated.

We were definitely in a state of stupefied drunk. I did as she said and hit search again. The top result was a page listing the top 10 tourist attractions in Bruges, Belgium. Hitting on that link, about halfway down the page appeared, Basilica of the Precious Blood, in Bruges, Belgium, and images of a relic.

"P. B. equals *Precious Blood*, Michael!" Julie gasped.

We read that the relic is called the *Precious Blood*. According to legend, it is a crystal bottle containing an encased fragment of blood-stained cloth that was used by Joseph of Arimathea to clean and prepare the body of Jesus after his crucifixion. There no mention of it in any of the Canonical Gospels, but it is referenced in one of the apocryphal gospels.

The article went on to say that the relic was probably included in a trove of them regarding the crucifixion and taken from a museum in Constantinople—modern day Istanbul during one of the Crusades. The Count of Flanders—Flanders would be in modern day Belgium, either pillaged it or it was awarded to him and brought back to Bruges around the year 1250 where it remains on display in that chapel.

"That relic in the picture doesn't look anything like this vial." Julie compared.

"No, that's just the outer capsule and gold ornamentation." I corrected her. "It's inside that glass case. That's what they're describing as the crystal bottle, or if you want to call it a flask or tube. The gold ends and connecting rods on the outside are just for embellishment and act as a protective enclosure and a place to connect a chain. The priests in their long vestments wear it around their neck and allow worshippers to come up to them in services and touch or kiss it."

"Hmm, to worship it!" Stated Julie.

I corrected her in a disgusted tone. "No, so *they* get worship by association with it. They could've just left it in its tabernacle or bring it out and put it on the front altar for worship. Adorning themselves with it is obviously in keeping with *men who desire to walk in long robes.*"

"Michael, maybe they were just worried about

someone walking off with it, so they keep it chained to them." Julie objected.

"Well, maybe." I agreed. I enlarged the image and we were stunned.

"Oh my!" said Julie. "The bottle inside the outer shell looks *exactly* like this one." She pointed to our vial laying randomly on top of the printer next to the computer.

What did we have in our midst? It dawned on us that this was not just ordinary stolen property or a common sample for the lab. Was this potentially one of the most cherished items in Christianity and human history? Our thoughts began to spin—not only because of all the wine we had consumed, but because we began to consider all the intrigue and possibilities.

"There are an awful lot of loose threads that need to be pulled to unravel some of this, Julie." I said.

Julie noticeably gulped. "So, start pulling." She said as she took another slug of wine.

"I'm not sure where to start." I struggled to say. "I'm just not sure. There are so many variables to consider."

Julie, now overly inebriated, started to comically slur her words and meaning. "Michael, if this is the real deal—the Blood of Jesus, we are handling it in such a cavalier fashion having it stuffed in our coat pockets tossed on a computer table. But then again, so did

Orrin—the vial in his pocket—not the table. But wait." Julie questioned. "If that's the real one in the *pic-shurrr* online, how can we have the real thing here?"

"Good point, but I don't see any articles that would confirm that we have *that* one—no thefts or mentions of it coming up missing." I said. "That would be big news if it had been recently stolen. So, we have to assume the real deal is still intact in the Basilica in Bruges."

"So, there's more than one of them. One, two, three!" Julie drunkenly counted. "There's the one we have now and the earlier one that the company has and the one in Bruges. We need to read more."

We did, but I'm not sure any of it was sinking in with Julie as she was way over the limit on wine. Scanning all the links regarding the Precious Blood, there was nothing else revealing to us—other than the continuing schedule of regular rituals and ceremonies of worship for it that had been going on for decades. I did note that there was somewhat of a checkered history regarding the Basilica's many renovations and its proximity to wars and conquering armies. With those, there could be some possible gaps in the relic's chain of custody over those times, but nothing recent. I was going to point that out to Julie, but her eyes were now closed, and she was snoozing on my shoulder. I elbowed her to wake her. "As I was saying, it appears the real one is still in Bruges." I said as I wiped at the spot of her drool on the sleeve of my shirt.

"Let's see if I have all the variables covered so far." I said. "Per Orrin's ledger, sample #43 is the one that went missing from my workstation. The one *we* have is most likely a second sample, #43A, that Orrin must have brought back with him from his recent trip to Belgium."

"Right." Julie agreed after another sip of wine.

"No more wine for you, Ms. Julie. I'll make some coffee in a minute. You'll have to be sober enough to drive home."

"Ho-kay!" Was her wistful response.

"Now—I can't believe I'm saying this" I posed the question. "Both samples, #43—which may or may not be in the Final Lab for testing, and #43A—which we have here, are actual samples of Jesus' blood?"

Julie didn't answer. Just like that, she had again fallen asleep against my shoulder. I smiled at her look of inebriated innocence, but quickly grabbed the glass of wine from her as it started to slip from her hand. She was out completely. I managed to scoop up her petite and limp body as easily as I would one of my daughters, and gently placed her on the couch. I made sure she was covered under Elizabeth's and Mary's snuggle blankets and I retreated to the rocking chair where I soon drifted off too.

Chapter 41.

Written on the margin of a clipped magazine ad, circa 1911, for Premier Vinolia Soap—promoting it as a shampoo for the new hairdo style, *Bobs*. Premier Vinolia Soap has notoriety and it was used in the first-class section of the RMS Titanic. It was found in the book: The Great Galveston Disaster.

"Her hair looks like she'd been drug through a knothole back-ards."

    Helen Laurinda Wilcox

Sunday morning. We both woke with hangovers, but after some coffee, we again took up where we had left off the night before.

"So, do you think they're fakes Michael? Julie questioned. "You think that our sample vial and the other one is a modern creation made to deceive and to look like the one in Belgium?" She pointed to the vial on the coffee table. "This thing could just be an old bottle, cork, string, and wax seal with some linen inside stained with some unknown, modern person's blood. Maybe they're all fakes."

"Possibly." I said. "Historically, there's always been a lot of that kind of relic fakery. Yeah, I'd say fake is a definite possibility."

Julie posed a question in wonder. "But *maybe* they're

all *real?*"

"Let's contemplate that idea." I answered. "If we can believe the apocryphal gospel stories, in all or any one of these vials in question, there is a piece of cloth used by Joseph of Arimathea to prepare Jesus' body for burial. From what we know of the historical account of the terribly bloody process of crucifixion, you would think that the cloth used would have to be more than the tiny fragments inside these tubes. To perform that task, it would need to be a much, much larger piece of cloth. Maybe more than one would be needed."

"So, what happened to the rest of it or them?" Julie asked.

"I'd speculate that they handled it like they did with some of the other supposed relics—like a so -called True Cross or Crown of Thorns." I answered. "Based on the nature of what it meant to believers, they all might like a small piece of it as a keepsake."

"So, you think they cut it up and distributed it?" Julie asked.

"That's logical." I replied. "Could be one or more of the Apostles or other early evangelists might have wanted a fragment of it to use as a kind of proof— like a visual aid to show folks while they spread the good news. They might cut it into hundreds of pieces for missionaries. They give it to a congregation, preserve it in a bottle, and it becomes a point of worship. Remember what we read online? A version of the legend says the relic in Belgium came from a group of antiquities surrounding the crucifixion that was originally housed in a museum in Constantinople."

"Of course, that brings us to the second possibility—they're fakes! We have to consider the potential of that outside of the religious slant to it." Julie countered. "In antiquities, there are numerous cases over the centuries of profiteers making a buck or two by building a fake meant to deceive."

"True Ms. Julie. This could be just another case of that with Orrin, his company, and/or his church. According to his blue binder, he was meticulously planning for either scenario—with one strategy to follow if his samples were positive for whatever they are testing for, and one as a fall back, if his tests are inconclusive. Regardless of either outcome, he'd stand to gain financially and religiously."

"For *both*? How so?" questioned Julie. "This is so complicated. Maybe my hangover is making it that way."

"I'm sorry. I should have stopped you from drinking so much." I said.

"I'm a big girl, Michael. No one to blame but myself. Go on. I'll try to keep up."

"Ok. Well, with Orrin's acquisition of this *second* sample, #43A, the one he guarded in his pocket and would keep in pristine condition, he would then be able to perform our DNA tests, and maybe another new and improved one on the now sacrificial *first* sample, #43.

"Some in the religious community might not forgive him for defiling and destroying the integrity of it." Julie countered.

"True. But I'm betting, and he was too, that most of them, and an overwhelming number of the faithful, would say it's ok because of what Orrin *says* they discovered. It would be too big an opportunity for him to pass up then. Though, Orrin's not gonna reveal the specifics of that to anyone." I said. "Then in the business angle of this, they take the readout from their *Precious Blood* and look for similarities of the DNA sequences in their growing select clientele database."

Through the hangover haze it became clear to me. "The *Yellow Stars*—that's the select clientele—the ones they have initially identified to potentially be in their 144,000." We said it together. "The ones who are a distant cousin of Jesus!"

Julie pondered the enormity of it. "That includes you and your children, Michael." She now understood Orrin's machinations completely. "It's true, he sent the tests to Lanie and the kids to leverage your compliance with his plans, but you also needed to be fully on his team—to be one of them. To be *Identifiable*. He's not going to have someone in his inner circle if they're not one of the 144,000. However, he's not going to come to you and say, 'In order for you to get this new position and pay increase, first you gotta take a DNA test.' He did it by testing a close relative—your children. Your children, in theory, have this same identifiable DNA markers inherited from your paternal DNA. That's the same technique they use to solve crimes now. They check DNA profiles of relatives of suspected killers to match blood evidence at a crime scene. The ledger shows that your girls received a yellow star for their samples. The indicator says you are undoubtedly in the mix to be one of his *remaining few* too. That's what that means. To Orrin, it was imperative that you passed his litmus test for you to be included in his circle of sycophants."

"I gotta say, that was summarized succinctly, Julie." I said admiring her analytical mind.

"Wow!" Julie exclaimed. Then in the most granular way she deliberated. "Imagine how valuable a new scientific, proprietary DNA sequencing method would be if you can successfully demonstrate that a person has significant shared DNA with the Messiah?"

"Of course!" I added sarcastically. "The principals of Supply and Demand! If you are a relative of the Messiah—as determined by Orrin, *and* willing to pay the substantial renewable subscription fee he mentioned in his blue binder, you would go to the front of the relatively short line. That would disproportionally be rich people looking to buy their redemption. It's the Salvation train to Paradise—if you are able to afford a ticket!"

"However, to do that, the Final Lab would have to have developed something more than we have now in the way of testing." She said.

"Agreed. But what?" I asked. "Currently, I'm only aware of the entire industry being able to trace people's DNA back to around the eighth century with something like our $99 test. Beyond that, the DNA is so fractional, and few other records of genealogy exist going back further in the general population, that it's not cost effective for the industry to go beyond that. Besides, most of our regular customers are satisfied if their DNA results go back a few generations or show if they're related to a famous person, like Charlemagne or Henry the VIII. They're content with that and a chart showing from what area of the world their ancestors originated."

"Unraveling all this is sobering." Julie said. "I wish it had been more sobering last night, Michael. I have such a headache. I'm never drinking again."

I refilled her coffee cup. "Acetaminophen or Nsaid?" I asked—holding out a bottle of each to her.

"I'll take this one. Thanks. You can continue while I nurse these down."

"Ok. My head is splitting too, Julie. I think I'll join you on the wagon after I take a couple."

Washing down the pills by draining my coffee cup, I continued. "Even if our Shadow Brothers are in the process of developing a more specific test to trace fractional DNA all the way back to the first century of the Christian era, it still wouldn't show a direct link to Jesus himself. In current theory, even a new and improved test on our samples would only show that a person's profile shares a high percentage of DNA markers with others from that general region of the middle east where Jesus and his relatives lived."

Julie gulped down her last pill and said, "Yeah, I guess that's true." She said dejectedly.

Julie looked off out the window onto the clearing at the edge of the woods where two does were pawing at the frozen turf to find browse to eat. She was either engrossed by the deer or waiting for the pain killers and caffeine to start working because she said nothing. A moment later she broke her silence and spoke a haunting soliloquy.

"There is something—*something* unique about the DNA sample in this vial, Michael. The *sine qua non*."

"Seen a *what*?" I asked. "You lost me. What's that French?"

"No, Latin. It means *essential*—a pre-condition, a necessity that Orrin must have to make his scheme come together. The *sine qua non* is what they are pursuing."

"What would possibly be unique about the DNA in this sample versus the rest of humanity? I said. "Same set of chromosomes, DNA chains of letters A, T, C, G."

"That's where religion comes in, Michael. Think about it. If we believe the Gospel accounts, Mary, a human, was Jesus' mother, and God, *not* a human, was his father."

I finished her thought. "And we know that a person

inherits roughly 50% of their DNA from their mother and 50% from their father."

"In normal cases Michael. But, if we were to expand the DNA profile of Jesus, what would it look like? Would there be some unusual aspect—an anomaly in it that would be like nothing the scientific community has ever seen before? For example, would Jesus' DNA only have 100% human mitochondrial DNA from his Mother and none from his Father, since they say it was an Immaculate Conception? Who knows if God even has DNA at all? Or, if God has regular DNA—they say we are created in His image, would science be able to isolate something in His paternal DNA that could be passed on to relatives? Would it be something *extra* and *singularly* different from the rest of humanity?

"I'm not much of a scientist, Julie, but I did learn a few things working at the International Genome Project. I think they call them the *nucleotide bases*. That's the string of letters, A, G, T, and C in a person's DNA. What if a portion of His sequence of those letters is unusual? Or, if there is a distinct and overly complex order to his letters? Or, they see an additional base—call it letter M? Or, maybe they've discovered a complete chromosome mutation? Julie, I read that a single letter out of place is what causes things like sickle cell anemia or cystic fibrosis."

"I agree. You're not much of a scientist, Michael." Julie humorously countered. "However, if we only go by what the Gospels say, only one person in history had the combination of both a physical and spiritual makeup like him. Theoretically, the Final Lab must be confident they can isolate whatever that is and see traces of that same unique marker in others who are now being tested in modern society. That's what they might have already discovered. That's why they're so secretive. The yellow star folks are the ones in whom they hope to find the *sine qua non*."

"Unscientific speculation aside, that makes sense." I agreed. "But if the Shadow Brothers continue to pursue their—*sin uh*, um, what you said, on sample #43, and it comes back inconclusive or indistinguishable from other genetic readouts, you would think they fail. But no, it wouldn't matter—not to Orrin. He wouldn't have to have that ultimate breakthrough where he finds his yellow star folks to achieve a *business* success and realize some of his religious aspirations."

"I think I know where you're going with this." Said Julie.

"Great! I'm not even sure I know where I'm going with this, but I think this is it." I replied. "Best case scenario, call it Plan A. Upon testing results, it shows something about this sample—Jesus' sample, that is unique and can also be identified in some of the current population. That would be sure to draw worldwide attention and he'd make millions from a select group of that population who are willing to pay a premium to see if they have "it." And, it would also achieve his ultimate religious goals of determining, by his standards, the remaining few of the 144,000— where he would be the highly paid gatekeeper. But a plan B—a *fallback*, would also be profitable."

"That is, if plan B is a fraudulent enterprise. They fake results." Said Julie.

"No, I don't think they'd get away with that, hon. There'd be too much risk and way too much scrutiny from the scientific and religious community to perpetrate a fraud. Besides, Orrin's religiosity wouldn't allow him to risk ruining the integrity of the artifact to even attempt to test it if they only had the one sample. C'mon, if they believed it to be the actual blood of Jesus in the first vial, they're not going to destroy it. Just like they don't experiment on the vial in Bruges, Belgium. But they definitely would with an identical backup—our sample right here, #43*A*. Then they'd be willing to sacrifice sample #43 in testing for the greater good."

"So, what you're saying, Michael, is that even if testing on the first sample, #43 is a bust *and* they bury those results, they would still be in possession and maintain the integrity of what many still believe is one of the most highly sought-after relics in Christianity."

"Yup. That's Plan B." I affirmed. "They still perpetuate the belief that the blood sample in #43A is genuine—like they do for the one in Belgium. It's the mere discovery of its existence and the promotion of this artifact that will make a buck—albeit not quite as much as Plan A, but it'll be all over the news. It will already have a built-in shroud of mystery and a backstory to add to its legend of authenticity—just like the one in Bruges. That alone would drive interest, prestige and the faithful to Orrin's expanding, now *mega* church. He could get out of that plain-Jane, VFW-like hall his church is in now. We both know, to someone like Mr. O, who is, *or was* the epitome of self-righteousness and money-grubbing capitalism, it would still be a win-win for him with either plan."

"There's nothing new under the sun in Plan B." I lamented to Julie. "Orrin's ambitions are no different than countless other preachers and religious institutions over the centuries. They all somehow get it in their head that they're brand of Christianity is better than the next guy's. They rely on perversions of, or emphasis on certain parts the Christian message in the Bible—coupled with their charisma to draw the faithful."

"Orrin certainly had his preferred view of Faith," Julie mildly agreed.

"However, he lacked the personal charisma, but he did have a couple relics." I summarized. "What makes his attempt different from preachers of old is that he had the possibility to add Science to the equation in his attempt to prove his brand." I said. "And, being the businessman that he was, *inclusion* into his brand, was gonna cost you some large coin!"

Julie was miffed at my snarky explanation. "Michael, Science and Faith have always been at odds with each other. They are not compatible."

I ignored her observation. "That conniving old man has found a way to potentially use Science to prove

Faith. Brilliant! But for his plan to go forward, they gotta have *both* samples. They can't make the biggest score without *both*! Unfortunately, for Mr. Wendell Francis Orrin, he died right before his financial-religious enterprise was about to be launched. That put a grinding halt to all the advertising blitzes, the press conferences, press releases and money flowing to the man who *desired to walk in long robes*. It all depended on this, Julie! This little glass vial."

Spellbound, we both stared at it.

Big questions remained. At what stage of testing are they at in the Final Lab? After the death of Orrin, do the Shadow Brothers still believe he or his widow is still in possession of the vital backup sample? Do they even know its missing? If they do, is there an active search by them to locate the sample we have?

"Michael," she sighed. "Unfortunately, all of these variables require far more time to investigate than we have right now."

Chapter 42.

Archived by Chloe Stevens. It was sewn onto page 290 in the cookbook, The Compleat Housewife, or, Accomplish'd Gentlewoman's Companion. That page had a recipe for: To prevent After-Pains.

"Now faith is the substance of things hoped for, the evidence of things not seen."

Hebrews 11:1 - King James Version

Written in pencil on an un-mailed postcard depicting the Belle Isle Bridge. Detroit, MI which was torn down in 1915. It was saved in the book: The Eleventh Annual Report of the Secretary of the State Horticultural Society of Michigan – 1881.

This is where Houdini jumped in and escaped from chains in '06. So, it is evidence that nothing is impossible.

Helen Laurinda Wilcox

After more coffee, breakfast, and a couple of hot showers, we retreated to the comfort of the living room.

There we sat. Julie was curled up in the recliner rocker under one of the girl's snuggle blankets and I slouched in the rocking chair. Both of us quietly stared aimlessly at the glowing coals and dancing flames of the wood fire through the creosote stained glass doors of the fireplace. It was late afternoon and I noticed a light snow had begun falling outside, which slowly dusted the ground. It gathered steadily on the branches of the towering white pines surrounding the yard and slowly bowed them toward the ground under the increasing weight.

We redirected our focus to the vial that Julie held in her hand. I could see she now lovingly held it with a reverence and care deserving of a relic of Christendom and humankind.

"Well?" I said to Julie without much emotion.

"Yeah." She responded after a few seconds, equally placid.

"Well, are you curious? Should we be the ones to break the seal and open it so it can be tested?"

"What?" Julie answered with astonishment.

"If this is a fraud made to deceive, don't we owe it to the world to expose this scheme?" I explained. "If the boys in the Final Lab are fixin' to test the other sample or already have, there's a great chance they will end up promoting it in some way to profit off it, whether it's fake or not—whether Orrin is alive or not. You read their action report. They all signed it. They're going to try to turn these mystery vials into big bucks. We owe it to the public to expose it."

Julie stared perplexed, trying to form a word, "Um."

"Look, if all goes well," I continued. "Monday we could open the vial, add all the liquid buffers and reagents to rehydrate the blood sample to extract a liquified DNA—at least give it a try. Then put it in our regular plastic tubes, dummy-up a name, get a P. O. Box and mail it to the company. It won't raise suspicions that way. It'll come in the mail just like a regular customer order. Then we prep it along with all the others for the Final Lab."

"If it comes back with one or two yellow stars on the ledger, it will tell us they have isolated their *sin a*—I don't know, I'm just gonna call it a *Heavenly DNA* marker in our sample." I theorized. "However, if there's no yellow star when it comes back to us for shipping out, it means it tested out to be just a regular, old, common mortal DNA and the relic is a fraud. We then expose their business and religious scheme as corrupt. I think we need to pursue this. It's so wrong for them to try to monetize this kind of thing."

"Maybe." Julie said. "But what if our sample 43A and its readout don't come back to us at all—like they kept the first #43 sample. Then we'll know it is extra special."

"Perhaps." I agreed. "Or, they somehow recognize it with their tests as an exact match to the other one. In that case, I guess we'll just have to see what happens and play it by ear. But if it's one they want to pursue—if they think its extraordinary, I'm sure at some point they'll reach out to our made-up P. O. Box person. We'll have to figure it out as we go."

"Yeah." She said in a drawn-out response. "It's intriguing."

We stared transfixed on the fire and then the vial.

"We could do it Monday." I repeated. "When we get back to work. I'm curious for the sake of science and to debunk some of their religious deceptions."

After a long minute, Julie sighed and said, "I'm not sure I want to be the one to do this."

"Oh, ok, I'll do it all. You don't have to get any more involved. I don't want to jeopardize your job any more than we already have." I assured her.

"No, I mean, I'm not sure we should be one to break the potentially two-thousand-year-old seal on this and destroy what this relic *represents*." Julie corrected me. "If we do, we start a process we cannot reverse, and it changes everything, Michael—*everything!* It will change Faith itself."

Now I was confused. "How so?"

Julie continued. "Michael, if we test and it shows this relic to be a fraud, in a scientific way, think of what that would mean to the billions of worshippers who have thought a certain way about this and the matching relic in Bruges for hundreds of years? We would be altering what they thought to be true."

"Yeah, that would be a good thing." I said.

"Not necessarily, Michael. Yes, a whole new group of people won't be hoodwinked this time into coughing up money to a profiteer like Orrin and his company, but what it will do is work to destroy two millennia of Faith. Think about it. Faith is the glue that attempts to hold a Christian society together. Take the original relic in Belgium. It illustrates my point."

"Michael, thousands each year make pilgrimages to it

to renew their Faith. That's the positive effects of it as an intact relic—regardless of how it has been monetized or props up a religious institution and those that oversee it. It's the preservation of relics like this one—whether they're genuine or faked, and the resulting strengthened Faith that comes from it that sustains lots of believers and gives them strength. Michael, that kind of Faith is what gave people like your Mother the strength to continue."

I felt as though I was being lectured by a Doctor of Theology from some great institution of higher learning. Julie had grasped far more of the implications and possibilities of the vial than I had.

"Don't you see?" Julie asked. "That relic—that drop of blood on a tiny fragment of linen in a glass bottle represents this: One special person was willing to sacrifice His own life to provide a way for us to achieve the transformational love he wanted us to have and to share, and the promise of the chance to be with Him. The resulting Faith from that is a confirmation of our Hope. All that is evidenced in this tiny preserved fragment of cloth with a blood stain. It has and still serves as the most compelling reason to go beyond just having a fragile Hope. If Hope vanishes—like we know it can, Faith is there to renew Hope—like for your Mom. It's the same kind of Faith that you draw upon for the sake of your children. Do you want to destroy something that facilitates giving you *direction*? The *direction* you say you pray for every night. The kind of *direction* I pray for. Do you see the parallels?"

I nodded. "I guess I see your point."

"I know what we've been through." She said. "And I mean *we*. But I can't be a part of something that seeks to tear down the Faith that countless previous generations rallied around in order to nurture a *direction* for them. I don't want to be the one, who tells my ancestors they were fools to believe in a relic and more importantly the idea behind it. That's not fair to them and their legacies. It's not fair to people we knew, respected, and loved. And it's not fair to so many more who will come after us—like your children and their children. If we scientifically test this, we set in motion the potential for destruction of Faith."

She held out the vial in her hand to me and summarized her thoughts in a kind of meditative chant. "Hope alone can run out. Hope ran out for your Mom but was immediately replaced by her Faith when her greatest Hope was not to be. Her Hope alone was not enough. Her Faith was. Hope by itself it's not enough for anyone. It wasn't enough for me when I needed it. I don't see how it's enough for me now." Julie lamented.

"So!" I wanted to clarify. "The question of real or fake for that thing is immaterial to you and an infinite number of others because you don't believe we can or should subject our Faith to cold, clinical scientific test results?" I asked.

"That's right Michael. The two are incompatible by that measure. I tried to tell you that earlier. Granted, I don't know everything. There may be a day in future years, decades or centuries from now where this sample or the other one or the one in Belgium might warrant cautious scientific testing for some yet unknown purpose—but not to destroy one for the other. Not to destroy it and to heck with collateral damage. Does that make any sense? I've talked too much."

The sobering conversation had made our hangovers from the night before, even more draining.

I exhaled deeply. "I never thought of it that way, Julie. Especially when you throw in my Mother's experience—and compare it to yours and mine. I only looked at the thing clinically and myopically. I never contemplated the repercussions of what it means to me and my children and to billions of ancestors and the billions who are yet to be born."

We sat there absorbing the implications.

After a while I said. "Ok, I guess I agree, but what *should* we do?"

"Nothing." She replied.

"Nothing?" I questioned. "I don't think so." I snatched the vial from her hands and wheeled in one motion hurling it into the fireplace shattering the vial. The hot coals and flames quickly consumed its wooden cork stopper, the wax seal, and the fragment of blood-stained linen. In a second, it was gone.

Julie reacted in horror and took a quick step toward the fire and lunged for the vial, shrieking, "Why did you do that? You asshole!"

I shouted back at her as I grabbed her wrist and held her arm away from the blistering fireplace. "Just repeat everything you said over the last five minutes. That vial—whether its real or a fake threatens Faith itself by its very existence. You said it yourself. Maybe we won't do it, but someday it might be subjected to some sort of verification. If it is, there's a chance it will be the upheaval of all we and countless others have believed—*if* it allowed to exist. But it does not exist anymore. It can't alter the existence of the relic in Belgium or the Faith derived from it. That one, still intact physically and what it stands for, remains the same. But *that* thing!" I waved my hand at the flames, "*That* thing and the other one—God knows where it is, can only alter that. We can't do anything about that one, but we can with the one in our possession. So, I just made it easier for everyone. Now it can't threaten anyone or upset their Faith. And more importantly for us, it won't be like a millstone around our neck constantly weighing us down to investigate it—consuming our thoughts. Pragmatically, *that* thing, could never do anything to change your core beliefs or mine. It could only serve as an agent to destroy them for others. You don't want that. I don't really want that either. It's better that it's gone from our lives. It's as if it never existed."

I released the hold I still had on Julie's wrist. She relaxed as she absorbed what I said, and I could tell she knew I was right. She slumped back into the chair and stared into the fire. I eased back into my chair and did the same. We sat for the longest time to absorb the unexpected calm that overcame us as a result of destroying the vial.

"Well," Julie took a large breath. She began to summarize our thoughts in logical bursts. "You're right. That makes sense. If it exists, there's the issue of what it may destroy. If we were to keep it, it will haunt us for the rest of our lives. If we give it back to the company, it'll be compromised and used for misguided financial and religious purposes. Every scenario would degrade our Faith and our direction. We're better off without it." Julie exhaled again. "I'm sorry I called you an A-hole. It's just that I was so shocked."

"That's alright. It's not the first time I've been labeled that." I laughed. "I didn't think you used that kind of language."

Julie's cheeks and neck flushed red—obviously embarrassed. So, I stopped teasing. "Hon, you and I are just not set up to grapple with the scientific and religious implications for all of humankind. That's above our pay scale." I said but immediately realized only one of us was on schedule for a *larger* pay scale.

That fact did not go unnoticed by Julie. "Righhhhht! *Pay scale!*" She sarcastically added.

Now I was the one who could feel my face flushing red. I quickly breezed past it. "We weren't planning on giving it back anyway—not without the return of my children's DNA samples, and who knows where they are? The chances of ever getting them back is minimal. So, that's a moot issue."

"So, we put it all behind us?" Julie tentatively asked.

Answering her question with a question, I asked. "We forget it?"

Julie wryly replied. "Forget what, Michael?"

"Exactly!" I exhaled deeply, confirming we had made the right decision.

Chapter 43.

Undated. Written in ink using a fountain pen on a blank piece of letter stationery that was found in the book: The Great Galveston Disaster. Upon first inspection, the handwriting appears to be that of Chloe Stevens, but it could also be attributed to Helen, as her penmanship began to progressively look more like her Grandmother's over the course of her life. Versions of this same thought appear two other times in the cookbooks.

"The past cannot be revisited or it's story changed. Be assured visiting is for the future, where it's story will be written then."

It was Monday morning—Christmas Eve. Sadly, it was just a regular workday for Genome 23 History.

At least I would get tomorrow off and spend the day with my children. Lanie had them tonight.

Any misgivings I had about my earlier decision to keep the vial and then destroy it, rather than return it to the company, vanished when I rolled into the parking lot to continue work like nothing had happened.

At the employee entrance of the building, a crowd had gathered. Julie was in the middle of it. The door was padlocked, and all were reading a notice taped to it. It read:

> *ATTENTION EMPLOYEES*
>
> *GENOME 23 HISTORY HAS CEASED OPERATION UNTIL FURTHER NOTICE. PLEASE INQUIRE FOR FURTHER EMPLOYMENT INFORMATION AT THE LOCAL UNEMPLOYMENT BENEFITS OFFICE, 325 WEST THIRD AVE.*
>
> *SIGNED,*
>
> *MANAGEMENT, GENOME 23 HISTORY*

You could hear a few of the workers grumble to each other about the notice and then they shuffled back to their vehicles. That left just Julie and I alone in the rapidly emptying parking lot.

"Well?" She asked bewildered.

"Come to the little cottage and see if we can figure out our options—if there are any." I replied dejectedly. There seemed to be few.

Chapter 44.

Saved in one of the cookbooks. It was written on a card, which was placed in an envelope addressed to Chloe Bishop on her wedding day in 1865.

Dearest Niece,

You have been blessed with a partner to share all things. Good advice is to never end the day with anger between you. Uncountable poor choices are made, and many hard feelings are fortified without a good night's rest.

Love, Aunt Margaret, and Uncle Vincent

Returning to my home, we rehashed the events of the last few days. Mr. Orrin's death, our discovery of the vial, and our late-night visit to the building provided nothing. We again covered our research, reasoning, and conclusions of what, who and why. Nothing became any clearer.

Morning turned to late afternoon. We stared silently

for long periods at the dancing flames in the fireplace. Neither of us had any appetite for food or the taste for any more wine. Instead we sipped hot chocolate and Julie cuddled in the recliner under Liz's and Mary's snuggle blankets. The day after Christmas we would both have to start the process of finding new jobs. However, right now we hoped the security and warmth of the little cottage and our shared company would lighten our mood and numb our anxiety.

As dusk began to settle in the woods, I looked out the window onto the chilled and quiet scene. The clear sky above began to reveal an abundance of stars only visible from this location away from any city lights. For the last several hours, snow had continued to accumulate on the white pine boughs encircling the yard. It weighed some of them down to touching the ground. It created a scene like a glistening, idyllic, Christmas card.

My thoughts turned from the vial to Julie.

This woman before me—this incredible woman had reconciled our differences, came to an enlightened viewpoint, but not changed at her core. However, I had changed—enlightened as well, and the lens through which I viewed her had become crystal clear. When given the opportunity to experience her incredible depth and beliefs, I found that she was not so different from me.

By comparison, previously, I had viewed the entirety of all religious doctrine that had been compiled centuries before—the ones that had been enforced upon societies with dubious institutional authority, and I had dismissed the entirety of religion itself because of it. I had reasoned that those in power had abused the *original* message and so I wanted no part of it. Whereas, Julie had viewed the entirety of the religious doctrine in which she had been raised and fully accepted it without question. But, prompted by our disagreement, discussions, and introspection, she found that some of the doctrine, beyond the core tenets, could not survive the scrutiny of today's modern realities.

In turn, I explained that I had witnessed Faith in action during the most painful experience in my life, and she was able to contrast it to the lack of it in her own. Then with incredible depth, she was able to articulate the overall importance of the role of Faith to her and billions of others before us—while artfully drawing a parallel to my experiences. We had aimlessly and independently revolved around the same issues all our lives without a satisfactory conclusion. But it took the two of us—*together,* to find solace.

In our new understanding, we found ourselves at the initial steps of rejecting the ideas and institutions that stood for the unsustainable parts of our Faith—the add-ons, opinions and outdated conventional wisdoms that we deemed were without merit—albeit ones still embedded in Scripture. And when we did that, we recognized the true genius of the guiding principles set forth for us in the life of Jesus. We then found it easy to disregard the chaff of what our religious institutional bureaucracies and those who would coerce it spewed forth. They were the ones who *desired to walk in long robes.*

Considering the enormity of all that, I was now convinced that what Julie and I had was the beginning of a transformational kind of love that I had never experienced before. But that was not entirely true. It was not foreign to me at all. On the contrary, I found that it was the exact kind of love that I had witnessed in my Mother and had read about it in the accounts of my Grandmother and Great-Great Grandmother. It had always been there for me, but I failed to see it until now.

From that moment on, Julie and I would share a common purpose directed toward that kind of love for each other and for my children. We felt the love triumph over us, but we had not yet verbally pledged it to each other. I found that this heady stuff of enlightenment was still sinking in for me, and the transformation going on in my heart was an in-progress restoration, which was impossible to sort out in the moment.

Julie sat mesmerized by the flames in the fireplace. She was unaware that I was completely in awe of her. I marveled that she was unlike any other person I had ever met who had been indoctrinated into the culture that the Bible was incontrovertible truth. Unlike the countless, dutiful followers, apologists and institutionalists who had been forced to memorize and recite a system of beliefs without thinking of its consequences, Julie walked the walk, not just talked the talk. She was considerate of other's interpretations—even the somewhat belligerent ones she heard me espouse earlier. She took the time to research the points I had attempted to make to her about the inconsistencies of Scripture. She truly considered my nuanced viewpoints about the need for an evolving Gospel which had the potential of transforming our society in ways no one from the leaders of institutional Christianity had ever seriously undertaken. She focused on what really did matter, the Message. And she was filled with the consequences of accepting that Message, Love! I saw that she embraced every aspect of the plain directives that were contained in the Beatitudes. I realized she got it. And I was impressed by her depth of understanding.

And most importantly, I had come to the ultimate realization that to live the life we were supposed to, the Message was the ultimate *sine qua non.* This was the moment my heart opened and regained the ability to trust again.

Thus, I sat not moving or saying a word—purely admiring the *entire* person of Julie Douglas. I liked and loved what I saw and was feeling. This required *something,* but what?

Chapter 45.

Handwritten on the margin of a picture of a tiered wedding cake that was clipped from a magazine. It was cellophane taped to page 147 in the cookbook,

The Compleat Housewife, or, Accomplish'd Gentlewoman's Companion. That page had the recipe: To ice a great Cake. There was a penciled-in note next to it saying, "Good for Wedding!"

Undated.

Love can happen when one least expects it. And in a way one could never predict.

Helen Laurinda Wilcox

I sat for the longest time just watching Julie. She was unaware of my gaze. Suddenly I reached over, took Julie's hand, and said, "Come with me." Getting up from the rocker, I pulled her up from the recliner and grabbed our coats.

"What are you doing." She asked.

"Come with me." I encouraged. "Bundle up. I want you to experience something that I get to see far more often than anyone else on the planet on a night like this."

Julie's eyes widened with curiosity.

"Have you ever seen the northern lights? I quizzed. "They're supposed to be out tonight. If the sky is clear, we might be able to catch a glimpse of them."

"I'd love that." Julie exclaimed. "Do you really think

we can? Being a city girl most of my life, I've never seen them."

I led her to the middle of my front yard—a small area carved out of the trees of the forest. A barely perceptible wind circled us through the woods. It rattled the remaining brown and dry leaves which had refused to fall from the stands of beach brush, causing them to make a sound like far away applause from some distant concert venue. The sound would rise and fall to silence with each refreshed breeze.

I had stood alone in this setting before. In times past, I looked up and was in awe of the vastness of the universe, and humbled by the insignificance of my awe—as it had to be the same as trillions of others over the millennia, who had also looked up to the heavens and pondered the same feelings.

This time, the setting and my renewed perspective unraveled the twisted emotional jail that had held me. I could now see in a renewed light what had freed me from it. It was Julie.

For the first time, I looked deeply at her in a physical way, and appreciated the delicate curve of the outline of her lips that formed the smile she perpetually wore. Her smile was the outward expression of what was contained within the depths of her soul. It was genuine, heartfelt, and revealed the blessed goodness that was in her every thought and deed.

The fog which had initially clouded my opinion of her had lifted. I thought to myself, so this is what a virtuous woman is like on the inside, and that it shows on the outside of one too—if you are looking for it! With this new perspective, I now noticed her freckles and natural blush of her cheeks. How did I miss the refined quality of them before? Suddenly, the intricate and varied colors and curl of her tresses now were not viewed in a comical way—as they were on the job when they bushed out of the headband of her face shield. Now I saw how delicately they feathered and danced with each faint breeze of the frigid night air. I swear I saw the emerald luster of her eyes catch the reflection of the intermittent glow of the northern lights as they randomly pulsed overhead in the infinite darkness. Was that ability always there before and I'm just now seeing it?

Julie, equally sensitive to what was going on in my head, recognized the transformation that our relationship was undergoing.

She turned to face me, reached up and placed her delicate hands into my coat pockets— sliding them over the top of my wrists and joining my hands. Her hands were surprisingly warm. With purpose, her delicate fingers settled into my palms. I squeezed them gently. With the leverage she had now gained, she pulled me closer to her.

I drew in toward her too. I breathed deeply and was filled with her chemistry and exhilarated by the essence of her spirit and passion. I held that breath in as long as I could, then reluctantly released it. Then, for the first time since I could remember, there was no apprehension accompanying the bottom of the exhale—with its uncertainty of whether there would be a *next* breath. This time, the apprehension was replaced with a noticeable anticipation and joy. It was a joy unlike any I had ever felt before. It was the delight of the redemption of my soul. And it was the feeling of exultation that sweeps over you the moment you realize you have fallen in love.

At that moment, a light and silent snow began falling. It landed on the fluttering wisps of Julie's hair. It instantly melted into tiny droplets on her wire rimmed glasses—partially veiling her sparkling eyes.

Looking up at me, she removed her glasses, put them in her pocket and returned her hands inside my coat pockets. This time she intertwined her fingers with mine. It was my turn to draw her closer. Without speaking, we dwelled a few more moments in our blissful surroundings and the intense atmosphere of our new love. My thoughts turned to the spiritual nature of what was happening between us and all the unknown, challenging, but wonderful possibilities unfolding before us.

"Julie," I whispered, trying to form a coherent sentence. "I'm uh, I'm not sure where all of this is going yet. But, uh…I don't think this is the end."

Julie nodded slightly and knowingly whispered softly. "I'd like to think it's the *beginning.*"

It struck me that Julie had said those same words to me when we first met. In full understanding and agreement for what this moment meant for us now, I replied. "Julie, I'd like to think that too."

As we continued to look deeply into each other's eyes, in the calm following this shared profession of our desire, it was obvious we were being healed, and a nurturing peace had replaced the hurt in our previously troubled hearts. We were filled with a mutual contentment and overcome by the unstoppable chemistry found in our discovery of love. Another breeze circled the woods creating a new round of applause from the leaves of beech brush—as if to approve of our performance in this romantic scene.

Julie and I pulled even closer to each other—to within a fraction of an inch. Her voice dropped an octave and she barely breathed, "Merry Christmas, Michael." And in the same intensity, I responded, "Merry Christmas, Julie." We melted into a gentle but passionate kiss.

At the utterance of my last syllable, I did something I have rarely been able to do in my life. I stopped my impulsive mouth from what I was about to say next. They were the words: I Love You. I wanted to say them. I felt them. But it was all going so fast. After taking in everything we had just witnessed and discussed and would still have to deal with in the coming days, I could not bring myself to say those words.

In times past, I would have not been able to restrain myself and would speak impulsively. Always before, without thoroughly thinking things through first, my words would spill out indiscriminately. Invariably, they would end up being words I would regret in some way. So, this time, I held back. I couldn't ruin this. This time, I held in check those three special words out of caution and to allow myself the time to fully appreciate what those words meant to me and what they would mean to Julie.

The lesson learned from all my previous mistakes was: *Do not be impulsive.* And with that, I felt a shroud of sadness fall upon me because I wanted so desperately to say those words to her. They were so tantalizingly close. However, my sadness was tempered because I knew I *would* have that moment soon, where I would say those words and have full confidence that I would hear them in return. At that time, Julie and I would profess our transformational love and commitment to each other and seal our partnership by sharing every aspect of passion and begin our new journey together.

Romantic interests aside, I forced myself to think in practical terms. It was already late on Christmas Eve. Tomorrow was Christmas Day, and I had already planned for the girls to be dropped off by Lanie early the next morning to open presents with me, as was our tradition. Just the three of us would share that joy together as a family and rightfully focus on the true meaning of the day. I didn't want to insert Julie at the last minute into what the girls were expecting. That wouldn't be fair to them or her. But I would ask her to join us later in the day after the girls had opened their gifts. We could then all spend the rest of the day together—while the two of us quietly explored our newly found feelings in a preview of what would be our family. With my fresh perspective on the merits of thinking things through first, I determined *that* was the appropriate thing to do.

Chapter 46.

Written on 8-1/2x11 notebook paper. It was stapled onto the end flyleaf page of the cookbook, The Compleat Housewife, or, Accomplish'd Gentlewoman's Companion.

19 February 1962

We had long established the pattern. The children and friends brought me scraps of material from their sewing projects or old clothing beyond repair and no longer wearable. I could rip them into strips sew them together on the treadle and hook crochet them into rugs. They would in return receive those rugs which were filled with memories of a favorite outfit weaved into the piece that you would be able to see every time you walked on it. The rugs and memories would last for years and the only cost was that of the thread which was often included with the donation of cloth. It was a perfectly fair arrangement. I always felt crocheting these inexpensive items was an inherited repurposing I owed to the memory of my Grandmother who taught me how to do it.

I remember lazy summer afternoons swinging on the glider in her screened in porch where I would watch her care-worn hands work her magic with a hand-

carved hickory crochet hook while we chatted and I played the game of counting blue automobiles.

Crochet now gives me plenty to do over the long winter months and at the summer cottage. It also gives me joy to give my work to family, friends and donate some to the Ladies Auxiliary as fundraisers and to the Community Chest for the Poor. Those countless hours of work were worth every second. I'm glad for those hours I spent with Grandma and I have no regrets for not saying and showing how much she meant to me and how much all my family has. I still have that crochet hook and have used it for over half a century. It's a bit worn but will be good for another generation I suspect.

More these days, when I'm working the fabric, I'm struck by how much my hands look like Grandma Chloe's.

Helen Laurinda Wilcox-Phillips

For the first time in my life, I took the time to fully consider the repercussions of something I wanted to say. I had considered all the variables and outcomes. So, even after another full day to think about it, my mind was even more sure. I would tell Julie I loved her, but with the luxury of extra time to consider all the possibilities for that event, I wanted to make it even more special. So, I also decided that I would ask her to marry me at that time, and that would require the purchase of an engagement ring to make it right. I made plans to do both on the upcoming Friday evening. Well, I still had *some* impulsiveness in me.

Despite the spontaneity of my plan, I never really considered the possibility that Julie might say no to my proposal. It was a calculated leap of faith on my part based on how overjoyed the girls were when Julie arrived later Christmas Day, and the wonderful time we all spent together. In my mind, she couldn't possibly balk at saying those three little words in reply to me. Maybe that was overconfident on my part, but I was especially sure when Julie and I kissed at the end of the evening. Sometimes you just know.

So, as planned, on that Friday evening, Julie and I were again were drawn to the clearing outside the little cottage in the woods. The northern lights were still spanning the sky with a spectacular light show befitting the occasion. The breeze again generated applause from the beech brush to approve our pledges of love to each other and again when she said yes!

Our journey together as a family could now begin because we were both determined that our marriage would not just be between two people, it would be a marriage of a family. It would be a marriage that would heal my life and enrich my children's. And from everything I had learned about Julie, our bond would complete her deepest desires to attain a committed relationship and to be a parent. I knew my daughters would be thrilled to have Julie as a combination big sister, best friend and stepmom added to their lives.

The next day, Julie and I shared the joyful news with them. We became a family reclaimed from our aimless individual and unachieved previous hopes. Julie would put her whole heart into the joyous task of being a parent. The girls reciprocated by fully accepting her—even calling her Mom.

Happily, too, after her troubles with the law, my Ex, Lanie would eventually turn her life around for the sake of her children. She attended recovery meetings and excised alcohol and questionable people from her life and found some spiritualism herself. She began taking her responsibilities as a parent with renewed enthusiasm and invested herself in her children to her fullest.

As an ex-couple with a shared interest in the children we created, over the coming months, we began to communicate better. It became easier to bury the old problems and we were able to renegotiate custody to an every-other week arrangement. The girls benefitted from having a fully engaged mother in their life, and Julie and I benefitted with extended times to focus on our new relationship.

Economically, with the sudden demise of Genome 23 History, Julie and I needed to find new jobs. Rather quickly though, I landed a job with a marketing agency and she took her secretarial skills to a small, local law firm. We did ok but we would never be considered rich or even well-off. That didn't matter. Our interest was not in material things. We lived a simple life and enjoyed the natural beauty of the northern woods and waters. We gardened, hunted for spring Morels and were fond of taking long walks where we could discuss our relationship with God, each other, and plan for things we could do to make a difference in our community. We decided that those were the true core elements of our Faith that we would pursue.

After a while, we rarely thought about our time at Genome 23 History and knew it had little bearing on our lives. Our promises to someday research and delve into the mystery of the vial of the *Precious Blood*, Orrin's plans and the padlocked company were never undertaken. We never heard about Genome 23 History again. There was never an explanation of what happened to it or the mysterious Shadow Brothers. They were never heard from again that we knew of. For me, the whereabouts of my daughter's DNA samples did reserve a place in the back of my mind, and was an occasional worry, but there was never an answer to what happened to them.

The building that once housed Genome 23 History sat empty for years. And one day another manufacturing company bought the vacant building and put in a medical parts warehouse.

Orrin's church was also vacated and padlocked the same day the company was shut down. The homemade sign out front of the Church of the *Six-Liv*—as Julie had once mistakenly called it, had been removed. That building also would sit empty for decades and was later suspected of being used by homeless people for shelter. One cold winter night it accidentally burned to the ground. The local Fire Marshall suspected it was due to an open fire set inside to create some warmth. The rubble was bulldozed and is now an empty, brush-filled lot.

Over the next few months, Julie and I found ourselves in a pleasant whirlwind of activity. Our plan was for a June wedding. It would again happen in what had become our place—the front yard of the little cottage in the woods. For the ceremony, the girls would wear matching white summer dresses and carry bouquets of Shasta Daisies and Black-eyed Susan's. Those grew wild on the property and were gathered from the surrounding meadows. The setting matched our love. Both were perfect.

I think the perfection served as notice to us and to all, that our recent chaos had ended, and we could begin a pleasant and somewhat normal existence. That revelation reminded me of the progression of thoughts I had read about in my Grandmother's cookbooks. At a certain point during her life, I suspect a similar thing had happened.

As all our relatives lived out of state, our wedding would be a simple ceremony with only a few close friends attending. Those that could not make the event sent cards with well wishes and some sent gifts. Those continued to arrive in the mail for the next couple weeks.

"Oh, it's from my Great Aunt Elenore in Billings." Julie said. "She's 92 this year." She then pulled a colorful handmade crocheted rag rug from the large box. "It's one of her beautiful rugs! She's made these all her life from scraps of material. Everyone in the family always gave her boxes of it. It was her hobby. She would rip it into strips and sew them together and crochet them. Then she gave every one of them away to family, friends and to charity. It's so pretty. I hate to use it."

"Well, I don't think that's an option" I said, "Her card says; *This is not a museum piece. I want you to walk on it and see the memories in it everyday*"

"What a loving heart. Such a sweet and practical woman." Julie whispered. "Oh my." She pointed to different parts of the rug. "I remember this. It's material from the curtains that used to hang in my bedroom in our first house." Then Julie's eyes welled with tears and she lovingly traced her finger over a piece of material woven into the pattern. "And this one is from one of my Mother's favorite dresses. I remember the Easter Sunday she wore it to church services. It's hard to see, but the pattern in the cloth is a Peony flower. It was her favorite."

"Open this one next Daddy." Elizabeth said as she handed me a small package wrapped in plain brown paper. I handed it to Julie as I read the unsigned antique-looking card that came with it. It said: *Congratulations on your marriage. This is something you will need someday.*

As Julie folded back the layers of tissue paper in the box, all the color drained from her face. She reached into the box and lifted out another vial of *Precious Blood.*

CONCLUSION

Written on a blank recipe card. It was attached with a straight pin in the book: The Eleventh Annual Report of the Secretary of the State Horticultural Society of Michigan – 1881.

17 June 1929

"And if I have the gift of prophecy and know all mysteries and all knowledge; and if I have all faith, so as to remove mountains, but have not love, I am nothing."

> *1 Corinthians 13:2 - American Standard Version*

Prior to our marriage, Julie and I had made a commitment to each other to forget our troubled pasts, the vial, Orrin, his company and church and the stress filled experience that was probably the most difficult of our lives. But on the positive side, it *had* worked to bring us together. Never-the-less, we pledged to only concentrate on the future. We decided that pursuit of anything to do with Genome 23 History should fall to someone else and for them to take up the investigation if they chose.

We had tried to distance ourselves from the mystery and we failed. Apparently, someone determined that the burden of custody for it should be in our possession. Though, we had no idea of how to proceed beyond that. So, we became passive caretakers of the vial and its secrets. It remained untouched or considered for months. Then months turned into years—turned into decades.

After all that time, Julie and I instinctively knew our time to engage in the story of the vial of the Precious Blood had passed. Our lofty goals during the height of the drama to someday investigate the vial, were set aside. Hmm, *lofty goals*! I had read about lofty goals in my Grandmother's cookbooks. We did not pursue ours because those were difficult tasks, and our newly found love was the easier choice. Perhaps that was the same choice my Grandmother had made in her time.

Julie and I never again discussed the strange wedding gift. It was sealed back in the box and put in a locked trunk of memorabilia in the attic. Inevitably, it will be rediscovered by a future generation when we are gone. When they do come upon it and understand the enormity of possibilities and intrigue associated with it, it will probably take their breath away. My hope is that when they reach the bottom of *that* exhale, their next breath will be filled with wonder, determination, and purpose to pursue the deep mystery surrounding the most consequential person in the history of Western Civilization. It would also be nice if they too found their own transformational love on that journey.

EPILOGUE

According to the date, this is one of the last compositions included in any of the three inherited cookbooks. It was written on letter stationery with very shaky penmanship. It was included at the end of Helen's manuscript-essay which was tied together with a pink ribbon.

17 December 1971

I don't cook much anymore. I hadn't taken the time to crack the cover of Grandmas cookbooks in years. The only reason I am now is that at Thanksgiving dinner, I had been admonished for not making my rolled-out molasses cookies in recent memory. Daughters Donna and Janelle had mentioned how much they always liked them, and that my grandchildren had never had them. I found that hard to believe but they insisted it was true. So, I decided to try to find the recipe and see if I could still make them the way they fondly remembered.

In the kitchen drawer next to the sink, there was my favorite well-worn wooden mixing spoon, nested aluminum measuring cups, biscuit cutter and toward the back were Grandma Chloe's cookbooks--right where they had rested since the last time I had opened them. When was the last time I did that?

Leafing through the pages, my fingers touched food stains of long-ago prepared recipes by me, my Mother and Grandmother. The stains of vanilla extract, butter, chocolate, and others of an unknown kind all provided a family culinary history.

Midway through the first cookbook, after reading Bible verses that someone—probably Grandma, had thought to be worthy of reciting, as they were delicately hand sewed onto the pages with needle and thread, I stopped. There, nestled between the pages was my trove of essays bundled together with a ribbon. I had forgotten these were in here. I see it had been almost a decade since my last entry in this journal of my life.

It made me remember.

After father had died, I had been surrounded by my children, grandchildren and great grandchildren which filled the void. The concerns of my life seemed less important now in the grand scheme of things and older memories had begun to fade along with an increasing number of recent ones which was worry-some to me. I flipped through the writings as if reading them for the first time. But I knew that logically that couldn't be possible. The early ones filled with uppity youthful exuberance gave me a nostalgic smile. As I advanced through the decades of essays and observations, they progressed from thoughts of an idealistic young girl and were gradually replaced with the middle-age trials of raising a family and contending with the predestinations for me as determined by those who did those sorts of things. Now, all these years later, my more pointed observations and remedies seem insignificant when taken over the course of a long life.

I do have to admit, in rereading my prose, I was

surprised and proud of myself. I was quite the eloquent writer in the day. I thought back to my dreams in the early days when I first started writing, but I also remember the day I decided to leave the lofty ideals of youth behind for the more practical ones for my life's path.

In the earlier years of the essays, I could see I still had a desire to continue writing about things that mattered. But there was never enough time. Often, I had to dismiss any thoughts of adding to the writing or rereading some of the more prolific ones for personal inspiration in trying times. Someone always had more urgent issues presenting themselves to me for my attention. Those could be difficult days.

My routine was that Father would be home soon. He would expect dinner to be on the table 'by 530pm sharp!' He would be arriving home shortly and in a harried mood from what he considered his stressful day of handshakes and accolades. His business practices of weighing the merits of salespeople who sought his acceptance for their product or services was 'a tough day at the office—one a housewife would'nt understand.' He would breeze through the kitchen in his overcoat at workday's end, pay a cursory hello to me and toss his long robe onto a dining room table chair. Then he would settle into his recliner and there he would remain with the daily news until that evening's meal was ready for him. It was the meal which was expected by him as due respect for all his hard efforts. But they were also meals that were made for him because of his hard efforts. Both were part of the covenant and by accepting it, the conventional ways would continue.

All in all, it was not a bad life. Like others, we had our ups and downs and challenges. We were blessed with children and grandchildren. And although they did bring countless joys to an adult, I must admit those kinds of joys are not the ones that would ever meet the expectations of a young girl's desires. But as I grew, I knew my time adding to this storehouse of ideas and ideals would be increasingly limited.

To persevere that kind of sustained effort it would require time and commitment which was not available to someone like me, living in my time. To be involved in a suffragette movement or on a speaker circuit was unreachable in my social circles. To continue to push the issues of championing equality and break through the norms of the established institutions of society, religions and even domestic homelife was just too hard. Thus, the choice was an inevitable one made years before by those more powerful than me, where I would be groomed to be included in the larger group, to be liked, protected, and seek some happiness. Because the opposite— loneliness, being ostracized and marginalized, was a much harder existence, and was an untenable choice in the reality of my surroundings.

Rather than fight the current, I decided to leave my aspirations in these cookbooks with the knowledge that someday a future generation would inherit these recipes, rediscover them and reconsider the clippings, thoughts and essays I had penned or ones saved I found significant. My Faith gives me Hope that whoever it is, they find my works an honorable cause to take up again. But now, there were no more challenges of that scale for me. There are only these reflections.

My brief reminiscence is over. I suspect this will be my last entry here. I will refold this final note and slip it in near the bottom of the collection and retie the ribbon around them where they'll be preserved. It is time to turn the page.

Ahh, there is Grandma Chloe's recipe. I suspect making these molasses cookies will be more than a mere treat, I will be creating a memory for my precious grandchildren. That is of far greater importance now.

Helen Laurinda Wilcox-Phillips

A note written on a blank 3x5 inch recipe card. It was attached with a thumb tack onto the front hard cover of the book: The Eleventh Annual Report of the Secretary of the State Horticultural Society of Michigan – 1881

Give these to Helen someday.

Grandma Chloe

Fortunately for me, at a most critical time in my life, I

had met a genuinely good woman in Julie Douglas. Without knowing it at the time, she had given me the choice between continuing what I thought was my nature to defy, lash out verbally and rail against the same injustices that had been around for generations, or to settle for a middle, less confrontational path where we could surround ourselves with good people and practice our beliefs based on fairness. We agreed to reject the social and religious institutional bureaucracies with their enforced rules of inclusion. With that, we would go forth to share a transformational love which grew from that decision. By doing so, it strengthened our bond and would ensure that our children would not be indoctrinated into those outdated conventions either.

Additionally, what we did learn from this experience was that we would never allow any person, group or religious institution—no matter how long their legacy, to dictate to us how to live our lives in a manner that we knew was contrary to the core tenets of Christianity. We determined that we didn't need to be a part of those types of institutions with their self-righteous *scribes* in long robes.

To be clear, that decision and this story is not a condemnation of the Bible *in its entirety*, but only serves as an admonishment to some who cling to some of the ideas expressed in it that are not reflective of the realities of modern men and especially women. Rather, I think my story is intended to emphasize the elements in that compiled document that is the Bible, that clearly express what our Almighty expects of us, as exemplified in the life of whom, we as Christians, accept as our Savior and our *direction*.

So, again I will pose the question as it was framed in Helen's essay at the beginning of my story and here in the Epilogue. Where do we find ourselves today? Surprisingly, and unfortunately, not far removed from where we had been two thousand years ago. Apart from a few of the more enlightened people, cultures and scattered groups that have emerged since then, there are still far too many that continue to act in the same manner for which we were admonished by our most revered individual in Christianity.

Despite clearly expressed direction, there are still the institutions where the traditional leaders demand respect, make long speeches and steal from widow's houses. There are still those who scheme to promote their brand of Faith above others and some by devious means to acquire fame and fortune by their methods. Sadly, the *scribes who desire to walk in long robes* will most likely always exist and they will await their punishments as proscribed by our Highest Authority as forewarned in Mark. For far too many of them, it is as if the message He brought fell on deaf ears, and His act of supreme love has been diminished by them. We have all heard the words, but many have not listened to their meanings. For those who fail to heed the direction and continue in their shallow practices of making long pretentious prayers, their Hope on its own will eventually run out. However, for those who heed the words, *and act upon them*, there is ample evidence that their Faith will be there to sustain them in their time of need.

With that belief, Julie, and I—along with my daughters have chosen to reject the ambiguities in *some* of the Christian tradition. I see there are signs that even Lanie has made that same choice. We have preferred instead to seek out the transformational love promised to us, through a better nature traced to that single, celebrated life from two thousand years ago. It is the one life that was historically remarkable and ended tragically in an unparalleled act of love. And most importantly, we are satisfied and completely comfortable with that choice.

And finally, at the time of this writing, many questions regarding the mysterious vial remain unanswered. My generation has chosen not to focus on those hard questions, but to accept His easier answers. Thus, this is not the *complete* end to this story as secrets remain. But for now, for us, for the foreseeable future, it is the end of our portion of it. Grandma Helen's impactful essay follows.

Helen's Essay – Circa 1920

Where do we find ourselves today?

By Helen Laurinda Wilcox

Where do we find ourselves today? I would like to start with a verse from Scripture from the fairly recent translation of the Bible—the American Revision of 1901. It is from Mark, Chapter 12, verses

38 to 40.

"And in his teaching he said, Beware of the scribes, who desire to walk in long robes, and to have salutations in the marketplaces, and chief seats in the synagogues, and chief places at feasts: they that devour widows' houses, and for a pretence make long prayers; these shall receive greater condemnation."

How many of us knows somebody that fits that description? No one needs to raise your hand. It is a rhetorical question.

First and foremost, in our present western society—a Christian society of now the 20th Century, we continue to exist in the evolving aftermath of a single, celebrated life—the one who uttered the warnings in the verse in year 1 of the Christian era. We believe that life was historically remarkable and ended tragically on this earth on a cross. Most of our society believes that the celebrated life, and most critically, the death of that individual on a cross, to be an unparalleled act of love—which was intended for His contemporaries and the society in which he lived and for every future generation including ours.

According to our Christian beliefs, that act of love was freely offered to transform humankind by providing forgiveness for its sinfulness that had developed from the time of our beginnings by the choices of our free will—along with the aid of Satan. Although I personally believe he may have made the seven deadly sins more available to us, but we should not pass all the blame onto him. I'm of a mind that we should hold claim to the lions-share of our own bad behaviors.

None the less, the prevalent belief in our Christian Faith also encompasses the conviction, that with the completion of that act of love, it would provide a way for us to rejoin our God upon death. In the interim, the act of love was to inspire us to live a transformative life of love and to share it with everyone. Sadly, for far too many, this has seldom been the outcome as most have ignored its simple directive and a few have used it as a way to gain power and benefit themselves—mostly at the expense of women.

Over the span of two millennia, much of the above orthodoxy of the Christian belief—which has been continually cultivated and re-enforced in our religious institutions, tended to perpetuate a blind adherence to it, while offering no way for Christian culture to question, modify or refute any of it—that is, if they had a mind to continue to be fully a part of the Faith. To question, modify or refute would find you on the outside looking in through the stained-glass windows.

With little or no checks on the leadership scribes and their institutions, and with human nature being what it is to get over on folks for their own benefit, there arose documented examples of prideful and sometimes dishonest interpretations—what you might call add-ons to their preaching of the Gospel and its original tenets. The subsequent applications of those misguided views by the leadership have always fell on each of us in discouraging ways.

An example of that was the practice of granting Indulgences way back when for the remission of sin to achieve salvation through the payment of money to Church authority. That is about as convoluted as it gets. Somebody in the church took the basic Christian rule of doing good deeds for your fellow man, in order to better a person's chances of getting to heaven and turned it into a fruitful enterprise for the Church hierarchy. Thus, with this covenant, the rich—who could afford to pay to compensate for their earthly transgressions, got in line in front of poor folk who were stuck with their sins. On account of the church wasn't accepting I. O. U.'s on a sinner's debt, the poor were left with the choice of either purchasing a ticket to Heaven or pay the mortgage with their take home pay.

Another ugly manifestation of veering away from edicts of doctrine was the acceptable practices and methods used by leadership during the Inquisition. Do you remember reading about the Inquisition in school? The torturing and killing anyone who does not accept a uniform idea of Christ's Divinity was subject to be roasted over a fire or drawn and quartered by a team of oxen.

Eventually, and thankfully for us, those misguided application and interpretation of doctrine and some others like it were deemed to have strayed too far from the pure message embodied in the celebrated life and death at the core of our belief. Those most egregious transgressions and perversions of the Faith eventually and rightfully fell out of practice with the onset of the Protestant Reformation for the former and the emergence of the Renaissance for the latter. It seems in the former, folks preferred to read the Gospel in their own languages instead of Latin so they could see for themselves that shelling out pay for Indulgences was not mentioned in the Gospels. And for the latter, they preferred fleshy paintings and statues by Michelangelo as inspired artworks over exercising prudishness. And from what I have read, there has never been a record of the Church issuing a refund to those who paid Indulgences or ever issued an apology to the families of those who were roasted.

Other diversions from the clear instructions in the Gospels have come about by leadership largely ignoring them—in particular, the ones expressed in the Beatitudes in some form or another. No matter whether it was the ones in the Sermon on the Mount or the ones in the Sermon on the Plains taken from Matthew and Luke, respectively.

Examples? Alright, let us go through them. Despite the guide of the Beatitudes, to this day—right up through the recent Great War, a fair quantity of the scribes refuses to bless the peacemakers. In a convoluted way of thinking, they continue to engage in and support wars and violence as an erroneous way of achieving peace. Such folly! Some in this room have lost our sons under the guise of this way of thinking and for that I am sorry. War is wholly contrary to the edict to Love Thy Enemy expressly mentioned in the Gospel of Matthew.

The scribes revere pride over meekness with their displays of arrogance in their preaching and self-righteousness and their choice of long colorful gowns and vestments. I dare say none of us would have the gall to dress in that fashion or be self-assured in their ways.

Also, there is continued admiration of wealth by many Christian scribes—and many of us, which widely differs from what is said in the Bible that condemns these. The miserly give relatively little from their coffers to the poor—lest they cut into their budget to buy long clothes for their public prayers. Some equate their value in the accumulation of wealth as a byproduct of fervent belief and worship.

I should mention that if your spouse works at the bank as a teller, I am not speaking of you. Your spouse only handles other people's money and has no real amounts of it himself. On the contrary, a bank president might search his soul and contemplate repenting.

Additionally, there are other examples in Scripture—including the references to and the dynamics of slavery and servitude and the assigned roles of women which are contrary to the norms of equality for most but not all in our modern free society. Almost 60-some years ago we freed the slaves—to a point, but they still struggle for equality with Jim Crow. And it is the same in regards to the subject of women, their limited roles, lack of the Right to Vote—which we hope will be amended to the Constitution in the coming year throughout the Union, and the continuing struggles we have in our gender that are all caused by the behaviors of scribes—as highlighted in the above verse from Mark.

In total, the many ambiguities found in the words we hold dear, the ones we recite in church, the ones we are told to follow, and how some have interpreted what we adhere to or choose to ignore in Scripture, amounts to a widespread contradiction. There is a huge disconnect from what is said versus what is done on many counts. It is downright hypocritical. The results of this disconnect is that it completely ignores the sacrifice of that single, celebrated life.

So, where do we find ourselves today? How has this evolving mindset and erroneous spiritual direction been allowed to progress to now and been maintained in our religious institutions? Simply, power and control—and that has been all in the realm of men.

Because the established orthodoxy of these religious institutions—the powerful, the leadership— historically, men, insulated themselves from criticism or calls for change with their persistent tradition. They insisted to their congregations that the words contained within the Bible—their code of mandates, are not to be questioned by the unlettered. And they kept the number of them down by restricting education unless you were favored or royalty or well-off. They decreed their infallibility based on their attained authority and with an added leap of logic to claim that the directives in Scripture were either penned by God himself—through His inspiration to humans, or labeling them collectively as the Word of God based on their own governance and fiat resultant from their line of Apostolic succession. I think some allow their congregations to think that the Lord published the book himself with a Guttenberg printing press and then handed it down through the clouds.

In reality, the compiled writings in the Bible are a collection of individually written manuscripts which were deemed to be inspirational by the leaders of the early Christian movement over the first few centuries of the Christian era and then compiled into the Canon of law for the Church, in order to maintain a consistent message and to maintain control of it. At least initially.

Other movements—albeit ones that were also Christian, like the Gnostics—who came along in the first and second century, used some additional and later labeled apocryphal manuscripts in their doctrine for worship, but they were eventually culled from the orthodox church. Their sect of Christianity faded, and their books were destroyed as the eventual winners of a struggle often do. We know the Gnostics existed at some point though, because early Church leaders like Irenaeus of Gaul said they did and didn't like them. He advocated for their manuscripts and ideas to be destroyed. I heard the Gnostics let women participate in their church ceremonies. I sure wish their Gospels were still available to read as I would like to see them for myself.

Factually, there is no established proof that the adopted religious manuscripts that made the grade for the Orthodox and the resulting practices permissible under their authority are all equally

inspirationally written or directly reflective of Jesus'
overall message. The conventional wisdom
maintained is that it is so, due to the leadership's say-
so, which is based on previous leadership's say-so
and so on. That is tantamount to the schoolhouse
game of one student whispering a simple story in the
ear of another. And that student whispers it in
another's ear and so on down the row till it gets to
the end. After many retellings of the story, it is never
the same as when it started out. Imagine a story being
retold for 19 hundred years. That is what we have
with the Gospels. Along the way some things and
writers and ideas got added to the original account.
Some things got left out. And some along the way only
listened to and took heed of some of the story.

The result after generations of leadership succession,
is that many of our current religious leaders are
hard-pressed to even name a couple of the original
decision makers in the early Christian movement. I
gave you one in Irenaeus of Gaul. They have no
contextual knowledge of what was chosen to be
included in the doctrine and Bible and what was
considered spurious or by whom. They, in fact, are
ignorant as to what measures or historical reference
was employed to determine the choices. They just
never consider those questions and they only know
what they have been told to believe.

What they have been told to believe comes from a
succession of traditionalist bureaucratic
institutionalist scribes—filled with self-importance
and attained status. Those are the ones who vie on
wearing long robes. It is problematic that the scribes

have drawn their expertise, not from study or research, but from opinion—some decades and even centuries removed from the origins of the movement, with scant historical evidence to shed light on those opinions and how they were shaped by the norms of the times.

It is important to note, the continued efforts on the part of the leadership to control the message in this way was tremendously aided in the early years by the Roman Empire's conversion to Christianity as the state religion and their subsequent governing and enforcement of it upon the populace. This resulted in making the Canon a compilation of indisputable dogma. It was orchestrated by the royalty, the educated, clerics and government and used as a tool to govern the mostly illiterate masses—who had no choice but to bend to its enforcements in order to be included in the Christian societal movement at best and avoid persecution at worst.

Again, where do we find ourselves today? The place where our society find itself now as opposed where it was intended to be by the celebrated life and death, is at least in part, because of the above cited human responses to it.

After all that, today we are left with some troubling conventions of the Christian tradition that are unsettlingly explained in the circular logically way: It is the way it is, because that is the way it has always been. Oh, and do not so much as question it, because of the tradition of forbidding that too.

You may ask yourself, what is it about us humans—

and especially male humans—who are the ones who mostly had their finger in the above kettle of soup, got the rest of us to where we are today?

I think there are two underlying forces embedded deeply in humankind from the origins of our existence that were there at the start and remain with us today. This is not an advocacy for Evolution but if you hear me out, I believe you will agree with the logic. Those two forces have contributed greatly toward how our religious and other institutions operate.

Those two principal forces are found at the foundation of our ability to survive as a species. They were not deleted by the potentially transformative life, death, and example of Jesus. Thus, through our untouched free will they remain with us, and many times they are at odds with the intended purpose and directives of His—let's call it, course correction.

The two principal forces are:

- *The **human nature** to desire inclusion, to be accepted and protected.*

- *The **dominant nature** of some to seek to control the inclusion processes.*

The resulting hierarchy in family groups and organizations established from those shared traits are observable in both humans and animals—where it can be seen in the attributes of pack mentality. For both man and animal, it is embedded in the universal principal of: Survival of the Fittest.

To explain, in ancient man, survival of the fittest was evident in the hierarchical development of human tribes. Our desire to be included, to share, to be protected and to provide protection was essential for the species to survive. With those basic human traits, the natural development in the group was to have the physically strongest lead and the weaker follow for the group to endure. This logical social structure emerging in the earliest societies was shaped by our immediate needs to deal with challenges and dangers posed in our environment. Those practices were passed down to succeeding generations as essential. In humans, they could be capable of developing respect and admiration for the revered leadership, but they have also shown to be practices that can and have generated forced compliance, fear, abuses and domination over the followers and the weaker members.

Today those practices remain with us despite reduced environmental dangers and the lessening of the need for raw survival skills. Thus, many of the conventions used to govern those earlier societies simply do not make sense in present ones.

In modern times, our tribes have become family groups and business, social and religious organizations, and others that we create and sustain. They are less a requirement for basic survival but are still created and exist, in part, to address our enduring desire to be needed, to be included, protected, and provide protection and opportunity. Therein lies the same ageless prospects for some individuals and institutions to work to control the above. It is an inescapable characteristic of humanity for most to be vulnerable to exploitation by the few who seek leadership, power, money, and prestige. For them, this enduring ugly attribute of humankind is used as a tool in their arsenal to control the inclusion processes at the expense of the weaker/followers. I might add, none of the above I describe would recognize themselves as a scribe, but that's exactly who they are.

For the vast majority of the rest who are the followers, the pressures to conform to the whims of the scribes come in many methods. Some are subtle. Some are overt. Efforts to coerce conformity can make us change our looks, alter our actions, and often bend our beliefs in order to remain in a state of favor, so we can continue to be included in our modern groups and relationships. The pressures to conform are systemic and incremental. They all lead to fatality of our individualism.

Under these pressures, we both consciously and unconsciously abandon our principals—which promote self-reliance, to make it easier for us to fit in. If we do not compromise, we are then often ostracized by members on the inside, who have already chosen to abandon their independent desires to attain member status. Those who choose to remain steadfast in their beliefs, rather than comply with the majority's accepted ones, risk isolation and loneliness.

And now this brings us to how all of the above historical background and perspective regarding human nature, the celebrated life and death of Jesus and the verse of Mark applies to the dynamics of men versus women—which is the focus of the transformational love aspect of this essay.

To address that, consider additional subsets that derive from the above human behaviors at our core.

Going back to our beginnings, there has always been an inherent unfairness in that men—the ones who were biologically the strongest and thus more likely to become leaders, have historically ascended to be the controllers and decision makers—with little input from women. Women have had to accept their roles of subservience due to many reasons. The most easily identifiable are the basic facts of size difference, physical strength, and functions of their bodies. Their unique abilities to both grow and nurture future generations came with that as their primary responsibilities. Men got a biological pass on that one.

Historically, with men assuming leadership roles and women confined to their organic secondary significance, restrictions were also placed on them in social, legal, and political settings to prevent them from equal participation with their male counterparts. Centuries of limitations curbed their access to educational opportunities and constrained their civil rights to impede or altogether stop their paths to any sort of leadership positions. Some societies—both Christian and non- Christian, still employ these practices. Look around the world and you'll see it everywhere.

Possibly the most egregious arena of unfairness toward women remains in the systemic enforcement of the status quo of men over women in many of our religious institutions. In Christianity, some men steadfastly point to archaic Biblical opinion of women in their canon of texts—which go back to the portrayal of Eve, as justification for their second-class status. They cite this as reasons and an undeniable proof that the social order as it was established then, is how it should be forever—as authorized by the Almighty in the pages of the unquestioned book of tenets they use to support their authority.

However, times have changed since those traditions were established. The historic recent ascension to leadership roles by women in modern society, and general logical agreement on their equal intellectual abilities compared to men, has leveled some of the playing field of men versus women—but not all. There remains some resistance by certain men in institutions and domestically to relinquish their domination over women. But we are working on it as evidenced by the number of you who are here tonight.

In terms of Christianity, for most men in leadership roles of their denominations these days, they know enough to skim over those portions of text in the canon of their archaic manuscripts that do not stand up to today's scrutiny. Dwelling on them would surely cause many female members who strive for equality to be driven away. I know it would make me feel that way if I were to hear some of it at Sunday service.

Some of those examples of text in the Bible are in Paul and Timothy. I suggest you read those for yourself. Let me warn you. You will have questions and probably are not going to be happy after you do.

It is in the best interest of those men in their leadership powers and for the survival of their institutions, to turn a blind eye to the passages in the Bible that diminish women and to gloss over any plain directives and/or opinions of certain authors in it that serve to oppress them. Some though, in some denominations, defy the fair-mindedness of modern times and the accomplished equalities for women to adhere to the verbatim of those troubling passages in Scripture. They continue to argue for them in public and to their congregations. They do so to perpetuate the status quo in their church, and I might add in their own homes, because they are emboldened by their own hubris and attained status as a religious scribe—despite modern societal realities.

However, many that do not come right out and advocate for the continued old ways of oppressive behavior toward women, still quietly cling to those beliefs and work behind the scenes to preserve them. In addition to their inability to view the ambiguities in their doctrine and their outdated view of women, they also harbor their hidden convictions that treats the entirety of womanhood as but a second-class citizen. Female subservience ensures that their lofty status remains intact. Again, refer to the verse from Mark.

I'm not sure who if anyone believes in Darwin's Evolution. And we'll save that discussion for another

*talk. But regardless of your belief, if it does exist, I
don't see that cave men have evolved much at all in
how they have treated us womenfolk."*

*In summary when one looks at our religion, our
beliefs, and our leaders*

* * *

That is where Helen's essay-manuscript ends. The
final portion—perhaps several pages, are missing.
Some that were still in the bundle near the bottom
have sustained water damage, which has caused the
ink to blur and make it illegible. For the reader, it is
safe to assume that the summary would not vary
much from the themes already expressed in the body
of the composition.

Also, one should note that there is no evidence to
confirm that the above essay/speech was ever
presented to anyone—as it seems to have been written
for an audience. There is no reference in any
documents I've come across as to a time or date or
possible gathering that would coincide with its
writing to make one believe it had been. Due to its
controversial nature, if it had been delivered to a
group as written, it would have been viewed as
scandalous. There would certainly have been a
backlash generated in the community and
domestically. Most likely, family folklore, local
newspaper coverage or even a commentary about that
would have been included and preserved in one of
those precious cookbooks. They did a lot of that kind
of thing. However, there is nothing in them that I
have seen to confirm any of that.

So, I end with this. It is written in a graceful, calligraphy style in black ink with a fountain pen—in the same style as our Premise of the story, on the last flyleaf page of the book: The Eleventh Annual Report of the Secretary of the State Horticultural Society of Michigan – 1881.

The past cannot be revisited, or its story changed. Be assured visiting is for the future, where it's story will be written then.

Chloe Stevens

Another version of that same thought is written just under it on the same page with a modern ball point pen.

18 June 1977

The past cannot be revisited, or its story changed. Be assured visiting is for the future, where it's story will be written then. Yes, it will.

Helen

The End.